# SANDY JOHNSON

## Delacorte Press/Eleanor Friede

FOR GERRY AND BUDD
AND FOR MARK, BILLY AND ANTHONY

# ACKNOWLEDGMENTS

Although this is a work of fiction, it was inspired by an actual case; a CUPPI that appeared on the books of the Third Homicide Zone in October '77. I relied on the generous cooperation of the NYPD, who allowed me to play detective in order to research this story. For their willingness to let me tag along with them in the field and see how it really works, they have my deepest gratitude.

I want to thank Jerry Cummins, Chairman of the New York State Thruway Authority, who paved the way (pun intended) by introducing me to my favorite cop, Lieutenant Richard J. Gallagher of the Third Homicide Zone, who became guide and taskmaster.

I would also like to thank the many experts who took the time to talk to me: Reverend Bruce Ritter, Executive Director of the Covenant House; New York City Police Department Commissioner of Public Information Ellen Fleysher, who gave me clearance; Frank Rodgers, Commissioner of Criminal Services of New York State; John F. Keenan, Deputy Attorney General, Special State Prosecutor, State of New York, and Senior Investigators James V. LoCurto and Louis DiPasquale of that office; Lieutenant Frederick H. Stein of the Fifth Homicide Zone; Detective Peter Mangicavallo of the Third Homicide Zone (along with all the other men of that Squad); Midtown North Precinct personnel: Inspector James Maher, Deputy Inspector Eugene S. Brozio, Sergeant Peter T. Briong of the Task Force (the Posse), and Detective John J. Tumelty, Community Affairs Specialist; Manhattan South Public Morals Captain John Ridge; and Lieutenant Frank Damiano of the Pimp Squad.

Dr. Michael M. Baden, Chief Medical Examiner for New York City, and Detective Robert F. Willis, Liaison Officer to that office; Doctors Milton R. Sapirstein and Milton I. Levine; medical student Cecelia Martin . . . and the real experts, the children of the street who had the courage to tell me their stories.

My thanks to my friends who encouraged and helped me, some of whom even took my midnight calls with grudging good grace: Budd Schulberg, Ann Bayer, Paul N., Carmen, Sally Johnvi

son, Joe Siegel, Jon Goldstein, Bernard Hellring, Nancy Martin, Dickie Cummins, Margery Nelson, Bill Link, Norma and Howard Rodman, Nick T., and finally my friend and editor, Eleanor Friede, who made it all happen.

S.J.

OFFICE OF CHIEF MEDICAL EXAMINER
520 First Ave. New York, N.Y.

NAME OF
DECEASED

PLACE OF        Manhattan
DEATH           220 West 48th Street (in street)        SEX         AGE
                                                        Female      12

DATE OF         May 13, 1977                        14 May 77
DEATH           2120                        xxx
DATE OF POST MORTEM        xxxxxxxxxxxxxxxxxxxxxxxxxxxxxxxxxxxxxxxxxxxxxxxxxx

CAUSE OF DEATH        MULTIPLE FRACTURES AND INTERNAL INJURIES,
                     INCLUDING DEPRESSED FRACTURE OF SKULL, LEGS,
                     AND ARMS. CONTUSIONS OF BRAIN. INTERMENINGEAL
                     HEMORRHAGE. LACERATIONS OF LUNG, LIVER, AORTA,
                     HEART, AND SPLEEN. FALL FROM HEIGHT.
M.E. CASE #.6195     CIRCUMSTANCES UNDETERMINED PENDING POLICE
                     INVESTIGATION.
                                        IRWIN AUSLANDER
DATE ADMITTED TO HOSPITAL        xxxxxxxxxxxxxxxxxxxxxxxxxxxxxxxx        xxxxxxxxxxxx
FROM

PRECINCT        MTN
U.F. 61#        44791

DETECTIVE ASSIGNED        Halsey                REPORT OF CAUSE OF DEATH
                         3rd Homicide          OFFICE OF CHIEF MEDICAL
WITH                                           EXAMINER
                                               520 FIRST AVENUE
WITHOUT                                        NEW YORK, N.Y. 10016

She ran wildly through the crowded International lobby. Pushing the revolving door as hard as she could, she rushed out to search the street. There was no sign of them. The Sixth Avenue entrance was lined with people waiting for cabs; she tripped over a suitcase, knocking it over, and someone said, "Watch it, girlie." But she was already running down Sixth to Forty-eighth, and then west, darting between cars. Her ears began to pound, and she was gasping for air. Her chest felt ready to explode as she fought the scream rising inside her.

She came to a theater. It was intermission time, and a throng of playgoers was standing around on the sidewalk, smoking and drinking. She pushed past them, hardly slowing, mumbling "sorry." Her eyes blurred with tears. She arrived at the newsstand. The old man was there. "Alice. Where's Alice?" she gasped.

He jerked his head in the direction of the coffee shop down the street.

Alice was sitting at the counter, her large behind cushioning her comfortably on the hard stool. She was sipping coffee from a lipstick-stained cup and smoking a cigarette through a holder. She blinked and her enormous false eyelashes fluttered as she looked up.

"Alice, they've got Winter! She was supposed to follow me to the ladies' room. I waited but she didn't come. When I finally went back to look for her, she wasn't anywhere. They took her! Please, you've got to help me find her."

"I told you kids; you go around rippin' off johns, you're going to get yourselves in trouble." Her voice was flat, matter-of-fact. "They probably took her next door. He's had that room for a couple of weeks—"

"What room?"

"Fourteen-oh-six. But you can't go up there, the desk clerk won't let you."

She ran out then and darted into the shabby single-room-occupancy hotel. She hid behind a partition from where she could watch the clerk. *Go to the bathroom, you old creep. Goddamn you.*

He picked up the phone and, turning his back to the entrance, began to talk. She calculated the distance between her and the stairs. She'd never make it. She closed her eyes, concentrating her thoughts on Winter, willing her to be safe. PLEASE GOD, DON'T LET THEM HURT HER.

The clerk put the phone down and reached under the desk. He pulled out a brown paper bag and headed for the bathroom.

The moment she heard the sound of the door closing, she shot across the deserted lobby to the stairs. It was dark. Groping her way, she found the door to the second floor and ran down the hall to the elevator. She pushed the button again and again. She waited. Another new wave of panic swept over her. The elevator clanged to a stop and the doors groaned open. She pressed "fourteen" with her thumb and held it there until the doors closed.

At the fourteenth floor she got out and looked in both directions for number six. It was then that she heard the scream. It came from the left. She ran toward the sound, feeling as much as hearing it, and banged on the door with her fists. "Winter!" she cried out, kicking the door, pummeling it. "Let me in!"

Silence.

Suddenly the door was yanked open.

# PART 1

HOMER WOOD DROVE up Third Avenue to Seventy-seventh and circled the block looking for a parking space. After one more try he left it in a bus stop, flipping down the sun visor that said "Press" in large official-looking letters, and hoped for the best.

The bicycle shop was crowded. He looked around, wondering how to tell the salespeople from the customers. Four days straight of dazzling sunshine with the temperature in the high sixties were enough to convince even hardened New Yorkers that it was spring.

"And I thought everyone was jogging this year," he said aloud.

"Hi. Can I help you?" said a young man with an impressive blond beard.

"Yes. Thanks. I want a bike for my daughter."

"Ten speed? Five speed?"

"No, just a bike."

"Does she want it for touring?"

"No, riding. Something with pedals and handlebars—a couple of wheels. She's only twelve."

"Oh, you probably want just a three speed then. What price range?"

He thought a moment. He hadn't been prepared for anything quite this complicated. "Look, can we start over? I'd like to buy a bike, a red one. For a girl. You tell me how much it costs, I'll pay you, then we'll put the bike in my car—it's right outside—"

"We have a Panasonic for a hundred and twenty dollars. It's red."

"I don't want a radio, I want a bike." Wood looked at the salesman. His expression, which was normally that of someone slightly baffled, was now, as he regarded this boy with an old man's beard, downright stumped. Out of habit he put on his glasses, as much to understand as to see. Framed in tortoiseshell, the glasses gave his conventionally handsome features definition. "Don't you have a Schwinn or a Raleigh?"

This quizzical way he had of observing his surroundings was expressed in his work. One critic said of a recent exhibit of his: "Homer Wood has, in his photographs, caught the city with its pants down." New York was his fascination; its landscape of steel and glass was such a contrast to the lakes and gentle rolling hills of Wisconsin where he grew up. He had come to New York after working two years as a war correspondent in Vietnam. Since then he had free-lanced as a photojournalist for newspapers and magazines while collecting his own photographic study of violence in a civilized city.

His press card, issued by the NYPD, confirmed his ordinariness: Height, 6'0". Weight, 175 lbs. Eyes, hzl. Hair, bln. Birthdate, 11/18/34. (Missing statistics: Ethnic background, German/English. Education, M.A., Journalism, U. of Wisc. Marital status, divorced, one daughter. Religion, lapsed Presb. Notable human frailties, none.)

He spotted a bike leaning against the wall at the back of the store, covered with dust. It looked as if it might be red. He asked about it.

"Yeah, that one's on sale. You can have it for eighty dollars."

"Sold."

"I knew it." A voice boomed from behind him. "I knew it was your car. I've never seen anything like it; you think every goddamned bus stop in the city has the name 'Homer Wood' engraved on it!"

Sergeant Jack Danahy of the Third Homicide Zone had a build to match his voice. It was his eyes that gave him away. Soft baby blues that he had to keep hidden behind dark glasses.

"Next time I'm going to let them tow it."

"Thanks, Jack. You're just in time to help me load a bike into the car."

"Yeah? It's time you traded in that old crate."

Wood laughed. "It's for Donnie. For graduation." His 1964 Volvo was a long-standing joke among his friends in the Department. Bought in '69 when he got back from overseas for twenty-five hundred dollars, it had long since lost whatever color it once had. Now it just blended in with the rusted dents he'd never had repaired.

The sergeant looked around. "Maybe that's not a bad idea. Charlene said something about a bike for Jacky." It was warm in the store. He unbuttoned his suit jacket but didn't take it off. He never did in public, as he was self-conscious about the gun at his waist. "I must be getting old, but I don't remember getting a present for graduating elementary school, do you?"

"Hell, no."

Wood and Danahy were carrying the bike out to the car. Gus Halsey, a young black detective who worked as Danahy's partner, got out of the unmarked squad car to help. They had both rear doors open and were maneuvering in the bike when a beeper went off.

"Whose is that?" Halsey asked.

They listened. "Not mine," Danahy said.

"It's mine," Wood said. "Hold on a second, will you? There's a phone booth—I'll be right back."

Halsey looked at Danahy over the roof of the car. "What's he doin' with a beeper?"

"Don't you know about 'Deep-er Throat'?"

Halsey frowned, shook his head.

"Better you don't," Danahy said and shoved the rear wheel of the bike into the back seat. Halsey turned the handlebars around and they closed the doors as Wood came running out of the phone booth.

"There's a shooting down at Fourth and University—in front of a movie theater." He opened the trunk and got out his camera. "C'mon," he said, checking it for film.

"No, thanks," Danahy said, "it's not our station. We're going in." He took the ticket off Wood's windshield. "Here—for your collection."

"Thanks," Wood said as he jumped into his car and started it up. "And thanks for the help with the bike." Then he pulled out into traffic, sending a taxi swerving in front of a bus, and disappeared down Lexington Avenue, leaving a chorus of angry horns in his wake.

Danahy and Halsey got into the squad car and turned up the radio. Danahy unhooked the mike. "Car four-one-four to Central K."

"Go ahead, four-one-four."

"Got anything down in the First? Vicinity of Twelfth and University?"

"Negative—wait—stand by, four-one-four, something's coming in now—"

Danahy replaced the mike and looked at Halsey. "Let's go home," he said.

Wood heard the shots a block and a half away. He turned down Twelfth the wrong way and almost collided with a patrol car. He pulled up behind it, one wheel on the sidewalk, and, grabbing his camera, leaped from his car. Then, ignoring the shouts and commands from the officers ordering bystanders away, he set about photographing the old man slumped against the side of a car, lifeless eyes still open, staring into the lens of Homer Wood's camera.

Wood was preparing for an evening's work. Although he still paid rent on a darkroom that he shared with two other photographers, he found that more and more he preferred the solitude and familiarity of his own apartment; a fourth-floor walk-up in a badly renovated brownstone. It was peculiarly arranged; in order to get to the kitchen, one had to go through the bathroom, and after that was the bedroom. He had chosen the kitchen to double as a darkroom, using a dark cloth to block out the light from the one window and dish towels to snuff out the light from the cracks at the bottom of the doors.

He selected a record, Vivaldi's *Four Seasons,* and put it on the record player; then, whistling softly to the music, he set out his equipment, developing fluid in one tray, fixative in the other. He worked on, in total concentration, developing the pictures he'd taken that afternoon.

The first to come up was that of the old man. He knew as he watched it take form that it was a powerful picture. The old man's head was resting on his hollow chest, thin mouth hanging open, slackened. Except for the eyes he might have been asleep. The bullet had gotten him just under the breastbone, and the whole front of his shirt came up black on film.

All the other pictures were of bystanders. A frowzy woman, heavily made-up; a drinker, judging from the puffiness around her eyes. She was holding a shopping bag, about to drop it, and her mouth was open in a scream. Next to her was a young man in his twenties with long stringy hair. He looked as though he were about to be sick. Two waiters were rushing out of a restaurant, and in the background, in the upper-left-hand corner of the last picture he'd taken, was the movie theater. A man was standing, his back to the camera, in front of the box office buying a ticket. Had he noticed the man at the time? Probably not. He was, he remembered now, thinking what a great old movie was playing there: *It Happened One Night*.

He hung the photographs up to dry on a clothesline strung across the length of the kitchen. Then he got a beer out of the refrigerator and took it into the living room.

It was a ridiculous room, but completely comfortable. A daybed for Donnie, his twelve-year-old daughter; an old captain's desk that faced the window, so he could look out on the street as he worked; and a sagging, green velvet Victorian couch; he'd found it all at yard sales. The woman who sold him the couch said that it had a certain threadbare charm and she really hated to let it go. She did, though, for forty-five dollars, throwing in the little fringed pillows to hide the places where her cat had clawed the velvet into strings.

And there were his "impulse" buys—odds and ends Donnie referred to as UFO's, or Unidentified Far-Outs: a park bench; an old-fashioned sewing machine with a foot pedal, which when closed could double as a desk; and three feet of fence, ornately carved and painted white.

His own photographs covered the walls, except for the crime pictures, which he kept in the bedroom away from Donnie. Not that his daughter was in any way squeamish; on the contrary. "Did the bullet go all the way through him, Dad? Pshoo-om—right out his back? How big was the hole?"

His favorite picture was one he'd taken of Donnie and blown up to hang over the fireplace. She was perched on top of the huge statue of Alice in Wonderland in Central Park feeding a pigeon out of her hand. Her long, straight blond hair, tucked behind her ears, was pale and silken, shining in the sunlight; her rounded nose, not yet completely formed, was a reminder of her babyhood.

Just under the blowup, on the mantelpiece, was a small, framed photograph that Donnie had taken of him that same day. It was a terrible picture. It had taken her forever to get up the courage to snap the shutter, moving it a fraction this way and that, until Wood's face had frozen into a tight smile. The wind had blown his strawlike hair across his forehead and he'd forgotten to remove his glasses. They magnified his eyes in the picture, giving him an owlish look. Donnie loved it and insisted on having it framed, claiming it made him look exactly like Robert Redford in *All the President's Men*.

He looked at his watch, remembering he was supposed to call her.

Donnie answered on the first ring, saying, "Hi, Dad!"

He laughed. "That's very good."

"I always know when it's you. Listen, we're having a graduation party tomorrow night over at Stevie's, and Mom said she can't come to pick me up, so I can come home alone, can't I—it's only one bus."

"A graduation party? You're not graduating for another month."

"I know. There're lots of them. It's a big thing to finally be getting out of elementary school, isn't it?"

"Damn right."

"Well, can I come home alone? Everyone else is."

"Absolutely not. You can't go alone, either."

"Dad!"

"Let me talk to your mother, Donnie."

He could hear her complaining to her mother as she went to get her.

"Hello, Homer, how are you?" Barbara sounded faintly exasperated.

"Hello, Barbara. Don't you think Donnie's a little young to start going to parties?"

"Of course I do, but what am I supposed to do—tell her she can't go? I'm the one who has to live with her."

"Hang on a second, will you?" He put the phone down to give himself a moment—to let the anger go. It was Barbara playing tough, that's all. He didn't have to play. "Excuse me—coffee boiling over. You're taking her to Stevie's, aren't you?"

"Yes, but I won't be able to pick her up. Do you want to, or shall I call and see who's coming back this way?"

"No, I'd like to. I might get some nice pictures."

"Fine—Donna, what are you doing with my nail polish?—I don't believe it! Homer, you talk to her, I'm sick of being the heavy all the time."

"Dad, what's wrong with wearing nail polish, for Pete's sake?"

"Twelve-year-old girls don't wear nail polish, that's what's wrong."

"They do too!"

"Well, this one doesn't. I'll pick you up at nine. At Stevie's."

"At *nine?*"

"Bye, honey, see you tomorrow." He hung up quickly, shaking his head.

He went back to look at the pictures. They were dry. He took down the one with the theater in the background and saw that there was a reflection of the man's face in the box-office window. And there was something about the way he was standing, the angle of the shoulders or the tilt of the head, that interested Wood. He decided to enlarge just that section and to try to improve the contrast, which he did by darkening the next print a little, holding back the light areas with his fingers until the image cleared. Then he looked at it for a long time.

"Sergeant Danahy there? That's okay, I'll wait. Homer Wood calling."

Wood put the phone down to shut off the record player. When he came back, he heard Danahy's voice growling at him on the other end of the line.

"Yeah, Wood, what is it? Make it fast. Gus and I have to go downtown to some goddamned meeting."

"Jack, I've got something I want to show you. That shooting this afternoon—of the old man in front of the movie theater. There's something in one of my pictures."

"Forget it, Wood. They got her. They found the gun hidden in her shopping bag."

"I know how it got there. She didn't do it."

The sergeant sighed. "Wood, sometimes I wish you'd just take pictures of movie stars and politicians and let us do our job. The broad's a junkie. The old guy was passing her bad stuff. He burned her, she burned him. They hauled her in and booked her for murder one."

"During which time the man who killed the old guy was seeing a terrific movie. After he dumped the gun in the shopping bag."

There was a silence. Then, "Is that in your head or on film?"

"Both."

"Shit. We'll stop at your place on our way downtown and have a look."

"Why don't we meet at Red's? I was going to go get something to eat anyway."

Danahy and Halsey were waiting at the pub when Wood got there.

Red's was a favorite cops' hangout. The waitresses were friendly; some were ex-hookers who Red Kullers, an ex-cop, had rescued off the streets; the food was reasonably good, and the beer came out of a keg instead of a can.

Wood stopped to say hello to Red at the bar, then went to the last booth, where Danahy and Halsey were sitting.

"Okay," Danahy said, "let's see what you've got."

Wood took the two pictures out of the envelope and passed them across the table. One was the enlargement of the man at the box office, the other, a longer shot, included the woman with the shopping bag. Danahy studied the enlargement for several minutes, then passed it to Halsey.

"Okay," Danahy said. "I like him. So what?"

"D'you see the way his face, even his body, is turned to avoid the camera?" Wood asked.

"C'mon, he's buying a ticket to the movie. Where should he be facing?"

"Look at his eyes, though. The way he's watching the action going on behind him—in the reflection of the window. At the same time, if you look at the tenseness in his body, he's in an awful hurry to get in to see a movie that was already half over. By the way, remember how warm it was this afternoon?"

"Yeah."

"I took my jacket off and worked in my shirt-sleeves."

Halsey pointed to the man in the picture. He was wearing a raincoat, buttoned to the neck, his collar turned up.

Wood nodded. "How do you read the whole expression in his face and eyes? I mean forget that it's a picture. What would your reaction be if he were standing right here, looking exactly like that, immediately after someone'd been shot?"

"All right," Danahy said finally, "he looks good to me. What about you, Gus?"

"I think it's worth getting a make on him. There's two uniform guys at the counter waiting for take-outs. They may be from the First—want me to find out?"

"Yeah," Danahy said. "See if they'll run these down for us." Then to Wood he said, "Can you imagine me going to the DA with those pictures and your story? I'd get laughed right the hell out of the office."

Halsey gave the pictures to the men. As he sat down, Danahy said to Wood, "Interesting what you picked up. Right or wrong, it's interesting. Almost spooky."

"Nothing spooky about it," Wood said. "It's all right there."

"For one thing, he ain't even the right color, man." Halsey held out his hand. "See, to be a spook, you gotta be brown on one side and"—he turned his palm up—"pink on the other."

"And for another," Wood imitated Gus's speech, "you gotta talk with a lot more hip."

They laughed. "Hey, come on, let's order," Danahy said. "Those meetings never start on time. Have I eaten today?" he asked Halsey.

"Not if you don't count the two Blimpies you had for lunch, you didn't."

"Jesus, my wife would kill me—oh, before I forget—Charlene asked me to invite you and Donnie to dinner Saturday—if you're not doing anything."

"Great, Jack. We'd like to."

"Yeah, well, nothing fancy or anything. Just us and Jacky—and I think Charlene's asked someone . . . else." The sergeant moved uncomfortably in his seat.

Halsey and Wood exchanged glances. "What's Charlene cooking?" Halsey asked. "That terrific pot roast she made for me last week?"

"No, as a matter of fact I think she said something about doing a roast beef."

Halsey winked at Wood. "Roast beef on a cop's pay? I wouldn't go near it if I were you, Wood."

"C'mon, you guys. I don't do this for a living, you know. I've just been hired to deliver the message."

"Who is she?" Wood asked. "Have you seen her at least?"

Danahy shook his head. "Someone Charlene met at Jacky's school the other night. She gave a talk."

"On what?"

"How the hell do I know? Survival of wildlife in South America, probably. Charlene said she was a very pretty lady, that's all I know."

They smiled, enjoying watching the sergeant squirm.

"Hey! Look at the gorilla!" someone called out. They turned

to see four kids dressed up in costume making a noisy entrance into the bar.

"Have I missed something?" Halsey said. "I thought this was May."

The kids took a booth and ordered a round of beer. The waitress looked over in Danahy's direction. "Sorry, I can't serve you," she said.

The gorilla got up. "Then we'll serve ourselves."

"No you won't. There're police officers sitting over there," she said.

"Marie Antoinette looks about fourteen," Halsey said.

"Oh, fuck," announced Little Bo Peep. "Why'd you have to bring us here—the place's crawling with fuzz."

"Hey, look at them. They're guzzling beer on taxpayer's time. I think we should report them," said the gorilla from behind his papier-mâché mask.

Marie Antoinette giggled. "How come they're not in costume, oink-oink."

"'Cause they're *undercover men*," whispered the harlequin clown, loudly.

The three men looked at each other. "We could bust their asses, Sarge. They've probably got weed growing out of their ears."

"What for, Gus? We'd spend an hour on paper work, and they'd get to spend the night in the can with the pimps and prossies—what for?"

Red came out then from behind the bar. "Okay, kids," he said in his gravelly voice, "beat it."

They stood up. "Yeah, let's get out of this pigsty."

Wood watched them as they danced their way out, reciting, "This little piggie went to market . . ." He glanced at Halsey and Danahy, who were finishing their beer silently.

Danahy looked at his watch. "Almost eight—we gotta go." He gestured to the waitress to bring the check.

Red came over, shaking his head in anger at the kids. "Do you believe it?" he said and waved the waitress away. "This one's on me. Christ."

The beeper in Wood's jacket pocket went off. He got up to use the phone.

Halsey looked at Danahy. "Again?"

Danahy shook his head and with a brisk motion of his hand absolved himself of all responsibility.

"C'mon," he said, "let's get out of here."

Wood was speaking into the phone. "Yeah, Andy, what've you got?"

"A ten-thirty in progress. Liquor store, Ninety-fourth and Second."

"What's a . . . ?"

The phone went dead.

Danahy and Halsey were gone. Red was behind the bar drying glasses.

"Hey, Red, what's a 'ten-thirty'?"

"Armed robbery. Why?"

"Thanks, Red—see ya!"

It was all over by the time Wood got to the scene. The boys, described as teen-age Hispanics, had run when they saw the patrol car, leaving their gun on the floor of the liquor store. It was a toy. The owner was outside, screaming obscenities down the street.

Since it was still too early to pick up Donnie, he decided to drive over to the West Side as far as Broadway and take a walk. He loved the streets, loved to study the faces as they passed, inventing lives for them, and homes. This woman, he thought, looks pleased; she's just gotten an unexpected compliment, perhaps from the owner of that store she just came out of, and sees herself a little differently now. She's getting into a cab; the driver'll get a nice tip. Where's she going? Home, he decided, she's got packages with her. Her apartment, judging from her clothes, will be neat, modern, and uncluttered.

Men weren't as easy to read, Wood noticed, unless they were extreme looking. Otherwise they wore similar masks that said, "I'm late for a meeting" or "That stock isn't worth buying now, I'll wait till it drops to thirty"—even when what they're thinking might be, "How can I make her love me again?" Some hid behind beards or moustaches, others behind a clean-shaven blandness.

But the ones he really looked at and wondered about were the old people, moving gingerly, one foot in front of the other so carefully, their eyes clouded with memories. Where did they live? When they've bought the eggs and milk for the morning, where do they go? Will they fall asleep watching television, or will they sit near the phone hoping someone will think to call and share his or her life with them?

The job of an artist is to tell the truth as he perceives it. Wood was content to earn his living working for newspapers and magazines, but his art was his own. The camera was his paintbrush and his pen; these people, these streets, were his story.

Wood checked in his phone book for Stevie's address and headed across town on Ninety-sixth Street, his camera loaded and ready.

He was greeted by Stevie's mother, Joyce, who looked strained; the level of hilarity in the background had reached well past the decibels of sound the human ear is capable of handling. She led him directly to the kitchen and closed the door.

"God, I'm glad you're here. I was just about to make myself an emergency drink. Join me?"

"Sure. Where's George?"

"Next door, watching a baseball game, the fink."

The door burst open. "Hey, Mom, there's no more punch—hi, Mr. Wood—hey, Donnie—" he yelled out, "your dad's here!"

"Stevie, *please!*" Joyce begged, her hands flying to her ears.

"You gonna take pictures of us?" he asked, straightening his tie and buttoning his blazer.

At that moment Donnie rushed in, breathless and flushed, looking absurdly grown up in her blue silk party dress and curled hair. He leaned to kiss her, but she was already whispering something in Stevie's ear.

"We have a joke," she announced. "You start, Stevie."

"Wait," he said and whispered a question to Donnie. She nodded.

"Okay. I'm a little Indian kid and she's my mother," he explained, pointing to Donnie. "Ready?" He waited for the grown-ups' full attention, then he began. "Mommy, why is my brother named Rushing River?"

"Because," Donnie said on cue, "your father and I made love by a rushing river."

"I don't believe this!" Joyce said.

"Ssh, Mom, you'll spoil it," Stevie scolded. He went on. "Well, why is my sister named Weeping Willow?"

"Because your father and I made love underneath a weeping

willow tree," Donnie said. Then, sneaking a look at Wood, she said to Stevie, "Why, *Broken Rubber?* Why do you ask?"

Wood and Joyce looked at each other in silence. Joyce turned and opened the refrigerator, taking out another bowl of red punch. "Here," she said, handing it to Stevie. "Don't spill it."

"I don't think they got it," Donnie said to Stevie as she followed him out.

"Where's that drink you offered?" Wood asked.

Joyce handed it to him. "I don't think I knew what a rubber was at twelve, did you?" He shook his head. "Unless they were the things my older brother kept in the drawer next to the dirty postcards. I took them to school one day, to decorate the classroom for my teacher's birthday. They make great balloons. We filled them with water afterward and threw them at each other."

She sat down. "You're awfully quiet, Homer. I hope that dumb joke didn't bother you . . . ?"

"I was thinking how I'd love to move out of New York—if I could take Donnie with me."

"What do you think the kids are doing in the suburbs tonight? They're sitting around getting stoned while their parents are guzzling martinis and swapping mates with their next-door neighbors."

"Not where I come from, they don't," Wood said. "How many kids here do you suppose live with both their natural parents?"

"Two—maybe three."

"And have you noticed on the class list how many kids live with their fathers instead of their mothers?"

"Forget it, Homer. Barbara would cut your heart out for even suggesting it. She's doing a good job. It's an impossible age—and an impossible time they picked to grow up in."

"No, it's this goddamned city that's impossible. Where I grew up, there was a structure. The family, the church, the community. The rules were passed down from one generation to the next—my grandparents lived a half a mile away from us. My grandfather was my physics professor my freshman year."

"And you don't think it's changed out there now?"

"Oh, sure. I was even thankful my grandfather didn't have to live to see the day the students took over his science building. Although, you know, when I went out there to cover the story, my first thought was—it couldn't happen if he were around." He sipped his drink, stared thoughtfully into the glass. "Who's going to replace those people, Joyce? I don't think we're growing them like that anymore."

She was watching him. He frowned, suddenly embarrassed.

"Don't be embarrassed, it's just growing pains. We all have them when our kids start growing up. My oldest just turned sixteen, Wood. I saw her taking a pill with her orange juice last week. And guess what? It wasn't a vitamin."

He winced. "Well," he said, checking his watch, "it's already twenty after nine. If I'm going to get some pictures, I better get started."

A gust of air hit them as they opened the kitchen door. The racket had mysteriously stopped.

"Hey, who opened the window so wide? Stevie, that's dangerous, somebody could fall out!" Joyce said. Then she looked at Stevie suspiciously. "What's going on?" she said quietly, not wanting Wood to hear.

"Oh, Mom, it's nothing. Someone lit a cigarette—just for fun—"

"What kind of cigarette?"

"A cigarette, cigarette! What d'you think, we're smoking dope?"

"Okay, everybody, Mr. Wood wants to take some pictures."

"Joyce, don't tell them that. They'll get self-conscious," Wood said, getting ready to shoot.

"A little self-consciousness wouldn't hurt," she said and closed the window.

The kids hammed it up for the camera. Wood circled them, shooting away, but not getting what he wanted. "What's the matter?" he said. "Did you run out of jokes?"

Immediately they began, each outdoing the other, and forgot the camera.

"Hey, is there a doctor around here?" a young boy asked. He had just come out of the kitchen.

"You're supposed to say, 'Is there a doctor *in the* house,'" Joyce corrected. "What's the punch line?"

"No," the boy said. "Someone left a jacket in the kitchen, and there's a beeper in it—goin' off like crazy."

"That's mine," Wood said. "I'll get it. Thanks."

"There's a phone in the kitchen, Homer, if you need it."

He groped in his jacket pocket for a pencil as he dialed.

"Andy? Wood. Do me a favor, don't give it to me in numbers—"

"There are no numbers for this one. A young girl just took a dive out of a pimp palace. Forty-eighth between Eighth and Ninth."

"Jesus. Suicide?"

"Don't know. Could've been airmailed. It just came in. Your pal Danahy's there, but so's the lieutenant. Watch your step."

The phone went dead. Wood put on his jacket and went to find Joyce.

"Do you think George could possibly drive Donnie home? I've got to go downtown."

"Sure."

"Thanks. Tell Donnie, will you, I had to go," he said, running to the elevator.

Patrol cars had choked the street, their red and white lights spinning insanely; an ambulance screamed in the distance, growing closer. Wood put his car in a bus stop on Eighth Avenue and rummaged through the glove compartment for his press badge, pinning it on as he hurried past the uniformed cops who had the area roped off. He looked for Danahy. The ambulance was just turning into the street; Wood got his camera ready quickly. If she wasn't dead, they'd take her away before he had a chance to get his pictures. He pushed past some more uniforms, noting how few bystanders there were. People around here make themselves very scarce when they see all this blue, he thought, as he knelt to frame his shot.

Then he saw her. She was facedown; her long, straight, blond hair was spread around her, caked with blood. Her body was twisted and broken, so small it was, so helpless, lying there on the pavement, her skirt cruelly tangled up around her waist. His eyes went to her face. The side that was turned up was undamaged. It was a smooth, pink, baby face, with a rounded nose. Donnie's face.

He rocked back on his heels. A sudden, violent wave of nausea hit him in the gut. Someone grabbed his shoulder. "Get your pictures, Wood." It was Danahy's voice.

He choked. "Can't you cover her up?"

"If you want your pictures, get them now," Danahy said tightly. "I've sent one of the men to get a blanket from a radio car."

Wood brought the camera in front of his face and began

shooting. He circled the body, taking one picture after another, rapid-fire, trying to shut out the scream inside his head.

The ambulance attendant knelt to examine her.

"Wait a minute," Wood shouted to him. "Wait a goddamned minute, can't you!"

"Danahy! Get him out of here!"

Wood looked up, jolted, and saw the lieutenant standing there, his face set, hard. Icy gray eyes glared at him.

"I said get this guy the hell out of here. Now."

Wood backed away. The ambulance attendant pocketed his stethoscope. "DOA," he said. "You can call the ME." He started back for the ambulance. "My name's Rodriguez," he called over his shoulder.

One of the officers started to draw a chalk outline around the body. Another was waiting with a blanket.

"Lieutenant Gallagher? We're with Forensic. Where do we go?"

"Fourteen-oh-six. Danahy, I want you upstairs with me. Where's Halsey?"

"In the lobby, Lieutenant, talking to the desk clerk."

"Good. When he's finished, have him come up." He walked over to a young detective. "What's your name?"

"Connelly, sir. I'm new in your squad."

"Fine. You want to stay in it?"

"Y-yes, sir."

He shot Wood a look. "Then see that no one gets into that hotel. Let's go, Danahy."

Wood leaned against a car, his camera hanging loosely from its strap on his shoulder. He saw Halsey come out of the hotel and head toward him.

"Danahy told me you were here. Rough, isn't it?"

"Got to get my story," Wood said, his jaw clenched. "Can you get me into the lobby?"

"Sure, Wood." They started into the hotel. "Cute number, this clerk. Got a solid, thriving business, with as many satisfied customers as Ma Bell on Mother's Day."

A uniformed officer held the door open for them. Halsey nodded to him. "Rents every room, every twenty minutes, every day around the clock. No reduced rates on Sundays and holidays either."

Wood understood that the steady flow of shop talk was for

him, to help get him over the shock and get to work. He appreciated it, silently thanked him. It was over now. There must be a thousand girls who look like Donnie; she wasn't that unusual looking. She probably didn't look all that much like her, anyway. Just the coloring, and the long hair, that's what got to him.

". . . just came on duty fifteen minutes before it happened, and he's got all the people we want to swear to it, isn't that right, Mr. Pergola?"

Pergola shrugged indifferently. An unhealthy-looking sort, whose eyes, skin, and hair were all of the same grayish-yellow pallor. He looked like someone who'd spent the last twenty years of his life in a windowless room . . . or a cell.

"Come take a look at this register, Wood. All his guests must be related. Look, Mr. John Smith, Mr. William Smith, Mr. and Mrs. George Smith, and Miss Mary Smith." Halsey slammed the register shut. "Nice piece of work, wouldn't you say? Internal Revenue people been around lately?"

"Go shove it. I don't have to take any of your crap," Pergola said.

"No, you don't; you're absolutely right. You can take the lieutenant's crap instead. Detective Connelly!" he called out.

The young detective had just come into the lobby and was watching Wood nervously.

"My orders were not to let anyone in, sir," he explained to Halsey, still eyeing Wood.

"That's fine, Connelly. I want you to take this creep over to the precinct and keep him there until the lieutenant comes back. You can give him some of those girlie magazines you keep in your locker—to help him while away the hours."

Connelly opened his mouth to protest, then blushed. Halsey winked at Wood. The young detective looked suddenly puzzled; he hesitated, fidgeting with the buttons on his jacket.

"What's the matter, Connelly?" Halsey asked.

"Uh—nothing, sir." He strode over to Wood and took him by the arm. "Come with me," he said loudly.

"Not him! *Him!*" Halsey yelled, pointing to the desk clerk.

Connelly's mouth flew open. He looked from one to the other, abashed.

It took perhaps two or three seconds before Halsey's face broke into a grin. He looked over at Wood and began to laugh.

Wood went suddenly limp, emitting gasps of laughter that were almost sobs.

Halsey grabbed the confused Connelly, then, and hugged him. "Thanks, kid, you don't know how much we needed that! Now," he said, pointing to the desk clerk, "that one is yours. This one's mine." Still grinning, he picked up the register and said to Wood, "I have to take this up to the lieutenant. If you want to come up, just wait till you see him leave." He walked to the elevator, turning and winking to Wood as he got in.

The lobby was empty now, and Wood let his gaze wander over the dismal walls, the torn furniture, soiled with grease stains, the bare light bulbs dangling from sockets by strands of frayed wire. He picked out a figure partly hidden in the shadows. It was an old woman who, when she stepped out into the light, looked pathetically ordinary, someone's grandmother who'd been discarded.

He walked toward her. She peered at him with suspicious, street-sharp eyes, and he knew she must have been living in this place a long time.

"You a cop?" she asked.

"No."

"I heard her name," she said. "She called herself Freddie. They all make up names, you know."

"Who—all?"

"The girls. The prostitutes."

"Prostitute? That little girl couldn't have been more than twelve years old!"

"Neighborhood's full of them. They start at twelve, sometimes eleven. Boys, too." She nodded to herself. "I'll be glad to get out of here. And when I come back, believe me, it won't be in this century—I liked the seventeenth century much better. I hope her little friend's all right . . . beat her up. Bad."

Wood was trying to follow her ramblings. "What friend?"

"I need some pills. Do you have any?" she asked.

"Pills?"

"The kids get me Quaaludes sometimes. I have lovely dreams . . ."

Wood shook his head, smiling ruefully. "How about an antihistamine?"

"How about a pint of scotch?" she asked, pleased to have thought of it.

"Deal." He went to the liquor store two doors down. She was waiting, standing a little closer to the door when he got back.

She took it and thanked him. "This doesn't give me as nice dreams, but it helps me to sleep. I heard her scream—and I heard her hit the ground. Strange, even if you've never heard a person hit the ground like that, you know the sound, it doesn't sound like anything else. I hope she doesn't come back in this century either."

"You were telling me about her friend."

"Winter," she said.

He thought he'd lost her again. "What was her friend's name?" he repeated.

"*Winter*. She was—what do you call it when they're halfway between colored and white? There they are," she said, suddenly looking over his shoulder to the street outside. He turned quickly, but all he saw was a drunk sleeping on the steps of a deserted store, two teen-aged boys in tight-fitting jeans and leather jackets, and an elderly woman in baggy trousers. At that moment a tall thin black man got into a silver Buick Electra and drove away before Wood could get a look at his face. He read the license plate and wrote it down quickly. "Who do you mean?" he asked, but when he turned back to the old lady, she'd gone. The lobby was empty again.

He saw the elevator doors open and the lieutenant rush out, followed by Danahy. Wood stepped back behind a pillar, feeling foolish, but not yet ready for another confrontation with Gallagher. "When the Forensic people are finished up there," he heard him say to Danahy as he went out the door, "have Halsey seal the room off. I'll be in my office."

As Danahy turned, he saw Wood. "For Christ's sake, what the hell are you doing hiding behind pillars?"

"I didn't want Gallagher to see me—and get Halsey in trouble."

"If Gallagher didn't see you, it's because he didn't want to see you. Want to come up?"

In the elevator Wood described his conversation with the old lady and handed Danahy the slip of paper with the number of the license plate. "What d'you think? A pimp?"

Danahy nodded. "I think I know the guy. This is his territory."

"Funny," Wood said. "I thought it was yours."

Danahy looked at him. "That was years ago, before the upstanding citizens of our city decided we were the bad guys and took it away from us."

They got out at fourteen and walked to the end of the hall. "This is their Presidential Suite," Danahy said.

It was a shambles: half-opened suitcases, clothes strewn about everywhere, a rickety old floor lamp with a scorched paper shade that had been knocked over. The carpet was filthy. It was peppered with cigarette burns, stained and ripped in several places.

"Watch your step," Danahy said, pointing to a corner of the rug, "that can be dangerous."

There were two windows; one was open, all the way. The faded curtains had been tucked back so the men could dust the sill for prints.

"What time she go out?" one of the men asked.

"Put down twenty-one twenty."

Wood went to the window and looked down. He turned away quickly, his face white.

Halsey came out of the bedroom. "The men are finished in here, Wood. Why don't you start with the bedroom. There's still pieces of glass on the floor of the bathroom, so don't take your shoes off. Hey, Joe—where's the ashtray that was on the dresser?"

"I don't know. It was clean, anyway. We already processed it."

"Yeah, but who moved it?"

Danahy signaled Halsey to keep quiet, then gestured to him out of earshot of the others.

"The boss took it," he whispered.

"What for?" Halsey asked.

"I don't know. His locker's full of junk like that. He'll keep that ashtray on his desk until the case is closed. Then it'll go into his locker." Danahy shrugged. "Don't write that, Wood."

Wood was busy taking pictures. "You guys are really very messy, you know that? All I'm getting is a bunch of pictures of what a crime scene looks like when the cops get through with it."

"Don't worry about it," Halsey said. "The maid comes in on Tuesdays."

"Come on, Joe, tell your men to wrap it up. I'm starved," Danahy said. "Go ahead, Wood, get the 'living room' and let's get the hell out of here."

\* \* \*

"How do you tell the difference between male and female pancakes?"

"I give up."

"You look to see which ones are stacked."

"Gee, that's terrific, Donnie."

"Get it?"

Wood shot her a look as they turned off the Long Island Expressway at the Glendale exit. "Yes," he assured her. "I got it."

"I have another one."

He handed her a folded piece of paper. "Hold the jokes and read the directions, okay? They've put in a new road since I was here last . . ."

She unfolded the paper and read them.

"Out loud!"

"Oh. Why didn't you say so?"

He reached across the seat and poked her in the ribs.

"Okay, okay!" she giggled.

Wood slowed down to read the street numbers. Jack and Charlene lived at the end of a row of houses which, as Donnie pointed out, looked like the caboose of a train. Charlene had done her best, with limited money, to give it some character of its own. But if money were limited, nothing else in that household was; not the caring or the energy or the feeling of connectedness Wood felt from the first time he'd come there. And its source was Charlene. Barbara had said, after their first dinner there, that she was afraid she'd go into "sugar shock" from all the sweetness and goodness. And that the only person more self-righteous than a cop was a cop's wife. After that, he visited the Danahys' alone, even before he and Barbara were divorced, or with Donnie, who adored them.

Charlene greeted them at the door, wrapping her plump arms around them both, hugging them to her. She was tall and large boned and carried her extra pounds well. Her carrot-colored hair was pinned, as always, on top of her head, and brushing back the strays and tucking them in was a gesture so quintessential to Charlene that it was hard to imagine what she'd do with her hands if she wore her hair any other way.

She was doing that now as she told Donnie to go find Jacky upstairs. "And tell him to turn the television off. What would you like to drink?" she asked Wood. "Jack's gone to the train to pick up Shawna, he'll be back in a minute. Are you losing weight, Wood? Bachelors never eat, I think."

They were in the den, Jack's study, really. The bar was set into a shelf in the bookcase; Wood poured himself a drink, scanning the titles. There was a noticeable absence of crime or mystery novels but many classics.

"That's an interesting name—Shawna. Almost sounds Indian," he said, knowing she was dying to tell him about her.

"It is. Her grandmother was either Cherokee or Navajo, I'm not sure. Jacky will know."

"Where does Shawna live?"

"In New York. East Eighties, she told me."

"Really? Why didn't you tell me? I could've picked her up."

"Oh, well, I didn't want to push it," she said, fixing her hair again.

Wood's face broke into a grin. "Of course."

"Anyway, I think she was coming directly from the hospital."

"Oh? Is she a nurse?"

"She's an intern. Psychiatric." A car door slammed outside. "There they are!"

"A—what?"

Charlene was already at the door. Danahy was making his usual noisy entrance. "Can you believe it! He left that old crate right in the driveway! How the hell am I supposed to put my car in the garage?"

"Shawna, I'm so glad to see you. Oh, Jack, stop making all that noise and take Shawna's jacket. How was the train?"

"Fine. I had a lovely nap."

"Good! This is Homer Wood. Wood, Shawna McKinley. Jack, I already put out the ice," she called. "Go on into the den and have a drink," she said to Wood and Shawna. "I'll join you in a minute."

Wood was standing motionless, staring helplessly into the most miraculous face he'd ever seen. Dark blue eyes looked back at him, very dark, the color of a lake at midnight, glistening in the moonlight. Slender brows, high, fine forehead, strong cheekbones, yes—Indian. Her hair was dark, almost black, and hung straight to just below her shoulders. Skin the color of pale marble, tinged with pink.

She was looking at him quizzically. He realized he still had her hand. He flushed, embarrassed, and released it with a small laugh. "Nice to meet you," he said awkwardly.

She walked ahead of him into the den; long, sure steps. She was wearing straight black trousers and a champagne-colored silk shirt tucked in loosely at the waist. Her walk gave her the appearance of being quite tall. Actually she stood about five six, Wood guessed. He looked up to catch Danahy watching him with amusement. Jack quickly turned his attention to the drinks, avoiding Wood's eye.

"Scotch for you, Wood?"

"I have one, thanks."

"Shawna?"

"Do you have any wine open?" she asked in a voice as soft and cool as the spring breeze. Wood felt a small shiver of something he hadn't felt in such a long time that it unnerved him. He couldn't decide where to sit.

Shawna was examining the photographs and trophies. "What's this?" she asked Jack. She was looking at a framed citation signed by the police commissioner.

"We call that an 'atta-boy' in the trade," he told her. "Almost as good as a promotion."

"How many 'atta-boys' make a promotion?" she asked.

"Good question," Jack laughed.

"Charlene tells me you live in the East Eighties." Wood's voice sounded peculiar to him.

"Eighty-fourth, between Second and Third."

"You're right near my daughter."

Danahy brought the drinks to the coffee table and sat in a well-worn leather chair that was clearly his. Shawna sat in a corner of the sofa, her legs curved underneath her. Wood continued to stand. They heard a pounding on the stairs, and a moment later Jacky and Donnie swung into the room.

"Hi, Dad." Jacky was a husky twelve-year-old, a smaller version of his father. "Hi, Miss McKinley. I remember you came out to school last week."

Danahy reached out for Donnie. "Hello there, little one. Got a kiss for an old cop?"

Donnie kissed him, her eyes all the while on Shawna, looking at her with curiosity.

Wood made the introduction and Shawna extended her hand to Donnie. "Please call me Shawna," she said.

"Okay," Donnie said, giving her a brief handshake, then going over to stand close to her father.

Wood placed his hand on the side of her head and stroked her hair once or twice as Donnie, with an assessing squint in her eye, leaned her head against Wood. Shawna was listening to Jacky's account of the *Star Trek* episode they'd watched, when Charlene called them all in to dinner.

The dinner table was carefully set with Charlene's best china, fresh white linen, and cut flowers. Donnie, who sat across from Shawna, never took her eyes off of her.

"How come you were at Jacky's school?" she finally asked.

"I was invited to come give a talk. On adolescent sexuality."

"Far out," Donnie said, grinning at Jacky.

Wood glanced briefly at Danahy, who sat on his left at the head of the table. Danahy didn't look up.

"I must say," Charlene put in quickly, "I was a bit shocked at the idea. But after I went and heard the talk, I walked right up to Shawna and introduced myself. I had to tell her she really made me think about a few things. We can't have closed minds, just because we send our children to a parochial school, can we?"

The men were silent. The phone rang, as if in answer to a prayer, and Danahy got up to get it.

"Shawna's a psychiatric intern," Charlene said, making another attempt.

"You mean a shrink?" Donnie asked.

Shawna smiled. "Sort of."

"A kid in my class goes to one," she said. "He lies to her. Makes up all kinds of crazy dreams and stuff."

"What's wrong with him?" Jacky asked. "Why does he go?"

"Nothing. He's just nuts." Jacky and Donnie laughed.

Danahy came back and sat down. "That was the lieutenant," he said to Wood. "He called to say he got the ME's report today. That thing over at the Rockmoor Hotel the other night? We got a CUPPI out of it."

"What's a cuppy?" Shawna asked.

Danahy didn't answer right away. Charlene, noticing the children had finished eating, suggested they go upstairs.

"But no more television," she warned.

"I'm going to finish my helicopter model," Jacky said. "Then Donnie can paint it."

"Fine, we'll call you down when we're ready for dessert."

Danahy waited until the children had left the room, then turned to Shawna.

"CUPPI. It stands for Circumstances Undetermined Pending Police Investigation. It's a classification the medical examiner makes on the cause of death when the circumstances are uncertain. In other words, unless the medical examiner decides that a death is a homicide, it isn't one, officially."

Charlene started to clear the table. "No, no, Shawna. Stay put. I'll yell if I need help."

"The lab guys didn't turn up anything?" Wood asked.

"Zilch."

Shawna was puzzled. "So then if it isn't a homicide, what is it?"

Danahy shrugged. "Suicide, accident—we don't know."

"How does anyone ever find out?" she asked.

"A detective is assigned to the case. If he doesn't turn up anything, he's told to close the file with a report to the ME. Known homicides take priority, and we've got plenty of those to solve."

"So then there must be a lot of unsolved cases," Shawna said.

"Last year our zone—there're five homicide zones in Manhattan—had a seventy-five percent clearance. That means we cleared—*solved*—seventy-five percent of all the homicides we had."

"Does that include CUPPI's?"

"CUPPI's are not homicides. They're CUPPI's."

"Oh."

Wood had been watching Danahy, trying to decide whether the irritation in his voice was Danahy being defensive, or if it were really directed at Shawna. It couldn't be directed at her; Danahy loved the attention of pretty women. He always got a kick out of playing to their romantic notions about homicide cops. It must be this case. He knows damned well he's going to follow up on it himself—on his own time. He's too good a cop not to. Too good a man.

Shawna excused herself to go into the kitchen to help Charlene with the coffee.

Wood and Danahy were in the den.

Danahy got out glasses for brandy and poured them each one, shaking his head. "Adolescent sexuality. Do you believe it? Someone ought to show her what adolescent sexuality looks like

—splattered all over a city pavement. Jesus. Why the hell d'you suppose a beautiful girl like that would want to be a psychiatrist? Just what the world needs, right? At least if she were ugly, maybe no one would listen to her. And what the hell's gotten into my wife, talking like that? The whole fucking world's gone bananas!" He sank down heavily into his chair. "By the way, I know it's none of my business, but I'll say it anyway and I'll only say it once."

Wood held up his hand, stopping him. "Shawna? Forget it, you already said it. Message received and acknowledged. Now tell me about the collar they made. The old-guy killing—I heard I was right."

"You were more than right! Thing turned out to be a gold mine. His name was Angel Fornetti, a creep we've never been able to get right. The ID was made from your enlargement, and they got a make on him right away. Went down like clockwork, the whole thing—put out an alarm and had him within the hour. Turns out he was in trouble with the mob and was looking to make a deal with us. Beautiful piece of work. We really owe you for that, Wood."

"You're welcome—and I'm collecting. Now."

Danahy laughed. "Favor or contract?"

"Contract."

"Shoot."

Wood took a sip of brandy. "I want to go along on the CUPPI investigation with you."

"Why?"

"Because while our kids are upstairs playing with helicopters, there are kids the same age out on the street earning money for pimps with their bodies. Their *bodies*, Jack!"

"Yeah? And what do you want to do about it?"

"What do I want to *do* about it? I want to break every goddamn one of those miserable bastards, that's what I want to do about it!"

Danahy got up and closed the door. Then he turned and looked at Wood. "No deal."

"What?"

"I said no deal. I don't like your reason. If you told me you wanted to write a story, okay. That's professional. You tell me it's about those kids of ours upstairs, that's emotional. I don't like to work with amateurs. They get involved with their emotions and they fuck up. That's dangerous for everyone."

They stood looking at each other. Danahy lowered his voice. "I like you, Wood. I knew you when you first came back from covering the war in Nam. An angry kid with a lot of dumb ideas. I saved your ass a couple of times, didn't I? Pulled some strings, opened some doors—it paid off. You got to be a good, tough professional. The best.

"But I want to tell you something, Wood, I saw you lose it the other night, when you saw that kid."

"For Christ's sake, Jack!"

"Wait a minute," he shouted. "There's nothing wrong with losing it once in a while, that's human. But you still haven't gotten it back! That's why I don't want you near this one. You can't handle it!"

There was a knock at the door. "Coffee," Shawna's voice called.

Wood looked in the direction of the door. "That's two in one night, Sarge. Two that you don't think I can handle. The other one's at the door, trying to bring us some coffee."

Donnie was asleep in the back of the car. Wood and Shawna had said very little during the ride into town, each nonetheless acutely aware of the other's presence, and both somewhat discomfited. They seemed to sense that exchanging small talk was not the way they were going to get to know each other. It was the first time since his divorce he'd met anyone he really wanted to get to know. He wondered about Shawna, if there was someone in her life. How could there not be?

"You're awfully quiet," she said.

"I was thinking about you."

"Oh?" She paused a moment and said, "Funny, I was wondering if you were."

"Are you free?"

"When?"

He laughed. "I meant—in general."

"Oh. Yes."

"Dinner then—Sunday?"

"I'd like that."

He pulled up in front of the brownstone where she lived just as Donnie woke up.

"I'll just see Shawna to the door," Wood said to her.

"Okay," Donnie said, sleepily. "G'night, Shawna."

"See you soon, I hope." Shawna patted her. "Good night."

They were standing at the entrance. "Got your key?" he asked.

"Right here." She showed it to him.

"Sunday, then?"

She nodded and let herself in. Wood got back in the car and found Donnie sitting up front next to him.

"You like her, don't you?" Donnie said.

He looked at her. "She seems very nice—but I hardly know her."

"That's not what I mean."

"What do you mean?"

"Never mind," she said, and leaned her head against the seat, closing her eyes.

Lieutenant Gallagher came on duty at four o'clock in a lousy mood. He'd played a bad game of golf and had heartburn from the hamburger he had at lunch. He headed straight for his office with barely a nod at his men, who knew instantly to leave him alone. He opened his locker, took out a package of Di-Gel, and chewed two tablets. His private phone rang four times before he answered it.

"Lieutenant Gallagher," he mumbled into the receiver.

"Ray? Charley Miller here."

"Yeah, Charley, what can I do for you?" Lieutenant Charles Miller of the First Homicide Division was a royal pain in the ass. He had one of the lowest clearance records in the city for three years straight, and the son of a bitch was still arrogant.

"Listen, old man. I just wanted to thank you."

"Thank me for what?"

"For helping me with that drug shooting last week. I'd have come off looking pretty bad if one of your men hadn't tipped me off."

Gallagher paused. "Yeah—"

"Good man, that Danahy. Appreciate it. Thanks again, Ray—hope I can help you out sometime—"

"Right, Charley." Gallagher banged the phone down. *"Dan-ahy!"* he shouted loudly. "Sergeant Danahy!"

Danahy appeared at Gallagher's door and stopped. "Lieutenant?"

"What the hell's going on around here? I just got a call from the First—thanking me for something I didn't know I'd done—and passing along an 'atta-boy' for Sergeant Danahy. What gives?"

"Sorry, Lieutenant. It didn't seem all that important at the time. Wood got some pictures of the shooting down at Fourth and University last week. He spotted Angel Fornetti in the background so he enlarged the picture and showed it to me. I sent it down to headquarters—"

"Wait a minute, you lost me. How did Wood know Fornetti?"

"He didn't. He just thought the guy looked—suspicious."

Gallagher dropped his head in his hands, ran his fingers over his thinning hair. "I'm going to ignore that, Sergeant. I don't need civilians telling me—or anyone in my squad—what's suspicious. What's he got anyway—a camera or a crystal ball? If he's got information useful to the Department, let him go report it to the officer in charge like anyone else. Jesus."

Danahy waited, his face a mask. Gallagher looked at him a moment. "Hey, I'm a team player, Jack. I'll help anyone I can. Anytime. I just don't like mysteries, you know? If there's one thing I hate, it's a goddamned mystery."

Danahy nodded, started to get up.

"I hear you want to follow up on the CUPPI. Is that right?"

"On my own time, of course."

"Good. Keep me posted." Gallagher put on his glasses and picked up a sheaf of papers, signaling Danahy the meeting was over. But as he reached the door, Gallagher looked up. "I guess I had Fornetti figured wrong."

"How's that?"

"Well, I just figure any creep I can't nail must have some brains."

Danahy waited.

"How come he was dumb enough to hang around the scene long enough for Wood to get him in his picture?" He took his glasses off and leaned on his desk, looking at Danahy. "Like I said, I hate mysteries. Solve that one for me, will you, Sergeant?"

\* \* \*

Wood dropped Donnie off before he picked up Shawna. They went to a small Italian restaurant in a neighborhood that neither of them knew. It was outrageously romantic: candles and fresh flowers on pink tablecloths, Italian love songs playing softly in the background on a tape machine. They both agreed they loved the corniness of it. They sat at a table in the corner, their knees touching from time to time, accidentally, and ordered a bottle of the recommended red wine.

He was gazing at her, fascinated by the candlelight that was casting flickering shadows on her face, accentuating the contours of her extraordinary cheekbones. There were a million tiny lights dancing in her eyes.

"If you don't stop that, I'm going to get self-conscious," she said.

"I'm sorry. I think I was photographing you, mentally."

"You must do that all the time. What did you and Donnie do today? It was beautiful, wasn't it?"

He shook his head. "Not down where I live, it wasn't. A cold front moved in suddenly last night and it pretty much stayed that way all day."

"What?"

"Donnie. Does 'Oedipal' apply to girls?"

"No, that's 'Electra.' She loved her father."

"Right. Agamemnon. She had him killed, which is how the problem is solved in Greek tragedies. In real life, modern-day society, it's more subtle; the guilty parent is just ignored to death."

"Were you able to find out what it was about?"

"It was about you."

"About me? It can't have been the first time she's seen you around a woman—"

"It is."

"How long have you been divorced?"

"A little over a year. There just wasn't anyone I felt I wanted to introduce her to."

"Because you were afraid of this kind of reaction? Who were you protecting—her or you?"

He sipped his wine quietly. Then he put it down and looked at her. "Shawna, I'm very attracted to you. Half in love with you even. But whatever it is you do with the insides of people's heads, don't practice on me."

"I'm going to try not to take that personally."

"Good. It's not meant personally."

"I mean I'm twenty-seven years old and I stopped playing doctor when I was Donnie's age." Her cheeks were growing pink with anger.

"You just took it personally."

"If you're 'half in love with me,' how are you planning to get to know me, if when we talk, you suspect me of playing doctor?"

"I don't know. Maybe we'll have to find another way of getting to know each other."

"Oh. I get it." She poured some wine into both their glasses and took a long sip. "You like the way I look and you'd like to go to bed with me. 'Tais-toi et sois belle.'"

"What does that mean?"

"It's French for 'shut up and be beautiful.' Chauvin, you see, was a Frenchman. That's where the word chauvinism comes from." Her anger was mounting. "Originally the word was only used to describe patriotism; now it has a sexual meaning." She paused a moment. "I appreciate your showing me the scenario, and I admire your candor. I also have to tell you I'm not right for the part."

She picked up the menu. "Now, let's see. I bet they have a good spaghetti and white clam sauce—do you like that?"

"I don't know," he said. "How does it go with Crow?"

"Great! And for dessert—"

"I think I'll have the Humble Pie."

During dinner he talked about photography, she about the hospital, its politics and infighting. Then they walked to her apartment. The night was warm and gentle, lovers' weather, it seemed, judging by the number of couples walking slowly, their arms around each other. They passed a couple standing in the shadows, locked in a passionate embrace, and pretended not to notice.

At the door of her building he turned to her. She looked at him, her eyes friendly enough, but the contact was limited. He searched her face.

"I don't want to go," he said finally and moved closer to her. "Couldn't we renegotiate?"

"Not if you kiss me. It'll cloud the issues."

"I've forgotten what they were," and his arms were around her, pulling her to him. He kissed her with an overwhelming hunger and a desire that was nearly dizzying. He wanted her beyond reason.

She pulled away angrily, her eyes flashing. "Oh, no you don't. You're not going to get me to fall in love with you—and have it be *my* problem." She shoved the key in the lock roughly, trying to get it to catch.

"Shawna, I don't even know what problem you're talking about."

She got the door to open. "Of course not! No one can think with an erection. You don't have to be a doctor to know that!" He heard her footsteps on the stairs inside and waited until they were gone.

An hour later he was standing in his living room at the window, looking down at the street below. He'd played the conversation again and again in his mind; now he was beginning to rewrite it. Finally he went to the phone and called her. She answered right away, sounding wide awake. He was relieved.

"Dr. McKinley, this is Homer Wood. I'm a free-lance writer, and I was wondering if you could tell me something about the New Woman?"

There was a brief pause, then, "I don't know that I'm qualified, but I'll try."

"Oh, don't worry about being qualified. I just have a couple of questions: I realize the New Woman is self-supporting; marriage and children are obsolete, and sex is strictly for recreation, as opposed to procreation. Your slogan for the seventies is, Make Choices, Not Babies."

"Where'd you get that, off some bumper sticker?"

"No. I read it off a box of Girl Scout cookies. My question is— why is the New Woman offended when a man wants to make love to her? By the way, I can think clearly now. All my—uh, vital organs are functioning normally."

She laughed. "I apologize for the tantrum. As to your question —you want a quote, right? Okay, the thing about the New Woman is—she's stopped listening to love songs on the radio. She doesn't want your promises anymore, or your Arpège. And she's willing to do without your love if she has to pay for it with her soul. If you want her body, you're going to have to find a way to deal with her intelligence, because she won't talk baby talk to you anymore."

"That's great, Dr. McKinley, my readers will really eat that up. So one could say, then, that the New Woman has thrown down the gauntlet."

"Yes, that's good."

"Which is what you were doing tonight at dinner. Except you know what you did? You threw it down, then turned around and ran for cover without waiting to see if I picked it up. You lose ten points—for cowardice."

"Oh, yeah?" she said, doing a fair imitation of John Wayne. "Well, nobody calls me a coward and gets away with it."

"I am. What're you going to do about it?"

She paused and for several moments there was nothing between them but dead air. Finally, in her normal voice, but with an edge to it, she said, "Dinner tomorrow night. Here. Except we'll have to order something in, I can't cook."

The next day he called her several times, each time getting the same recording. He'd always hated those machines, but the sound of her voice pleased him and he grinned as he listened. They hadn't set a time last night and he didn't know how late she worked—or which hospital. He realized he didn't know anything about her. Only that she had a short fuse (was McKinley Irish?) and she didn't know how to cook. The chip on her shoulder had some very sharp edges. If he weren't careful, it was going to fall right on him.

At seven o'clock he went to her apartment anyway and she buzzed the outside door open. He ran up the stairs, pausing at each floor to look at the unmarked, closed doors. "Up here," she called from the top floor.

She was standing in the doorway, back lit from the lights in her apartment, making it difficult to see her expression. She was wearing something long and flared at the bottom, a robe of some sort, and her hair was pinned on top of her head. When he got to a few feet away, he could see her eyes and, not knowing what to expect, relaxed when he saw she was smiling. There was a fresh scent of lavender soap and her face was shining and pink, just out of the bath.

She turned and walked into the living room. He followed, keeping his eyes on her, barely noticing the room, and watched her as she bent over a small table and poured him a glass of wine.

"I'm sorry, I don't have anything else."

"That's all right. That's fine."

It was a robe she was wearing, navy blue, exactly the color of her eyes. Made of a silk that defined her body without clinging to it. Her feet bare and, he noticed without surprise, large. The New Woman, after all, would look ludicrous with tiny, delicate feet.

She handed him the glass of wine. "You're being your usual quiet self again," she said.

"It's hard to talk with that gauntlet lying there on the floor."

"Let's get rid of it then." She lifted a foot and with one swift movement, like a pendulum, she kicked the bothersome, imaginary thing across the room. "There," she said.

There was only one chair, a wood and canvas folding director's chair. Waiting until she settled herself on top of a stack of cushions on the floor, he sat in the chair. A fire engine screamed by; a dog barked in a steady staccato; a buzzer rang downstairs in another apartment. She picked at a thread on her robe.

"How do you—"

"What did you—"

They laughed self-consciously and she stood up. "Oh, for God's sake, let's go to bed," she said, and without waiting for an answer, walked to the hall leading to the bedroom.

He started to put down his wine, then decided instead to take it and followed her, feeling strangely disoriented and outside of time somehow; desire and anticipation gone. He stopped a moment, almost turning back. She called to him.

She was standing naked in the bedroom, facing him, taking the pins out of her hair. It fell, damp and heavy, to her shoulders. The windows must have looked west; there was a dark mauve glow in the room, the aftermath of the sunset. The colors and shadows played about her body, diffusing its shape; long and straight one minute, soft and curving the next. It crossed his mind then, that at this particular moment he'd rather photograph her than make love to her.

She turned on the radio to a classical-music station and came toward him and began to undress him, removing his jacket first, then unbuttoning his shirt. He stopped her, taking her hands in his and holding them firmly at her side. He looked hard into her eyes. She waited, looking at him questioningly. He shook his head slowly from side to side.

"I don't know what your directive has to say about the act of sex, but I know this much. There is no way you can make love from a point of view." Her eyes flickered, but she didn't look away. "Shawna?"

She looked down then, like a child, more exposed than naked, and grimaced. "I'm sorry," she whispered.

He covered her with his arms and held her; her skin had grown chilled. "Shawna," he said gently, "you can't fight a war if you don't know who the enemy is."

"I'm cold," she said. "Put me under the blankets and hold me, okay?"

They lay side by side, she wrapped in a blanket, he, in his clothes.

"I do want you," she said finally.

He turned to her and kissed her, small tender kisses on her face, her hair, his hands reaching under the blanket to touch her body. He undressed then. Shawna watched him from the snowy pillow, studied his body in the dimming light, then reached over and touched his back. He placed his body against hers; skin against skin, his lips pressed to her forehead. She raised her head, looking for his mouth. They kissed, tasting, opening to each other. His tongue filled the whole of her mouth, feeling the texture of it. She tasted clean, so clean. He ran his hands along her smooth, sleek skin, outlining its gentle curves, and pressed against her, his hardness between them. She reached for it and held it as he moved his hand down over her stomach, brushing against the soft, curled hair below. When she felt the fingers opening her and probing inside, she began to move—giving herself, giving, giving.

He was over her and inside her, his eyes watching her face intently. She looked up at him with an expression of bewilderment, like a child seeing something incomprehensible for the first time. He was moving slowly, deliberately, never taking his eyes away.

"Harder," she said. "I want you to do it harder." He kept on, not changing his rhythm.

"*Harder*," she repeated, and threw her head to the side, her hair whipping his face.

He slipped his hand under her head, and holding her by the hair, forced her face around to his, and covered her mouth with his. She pulled her face away and looked at him.

Her glistening eyes darkened. She thrust her pelvis against him again and again, each time with a force, faster and harder, using all of her weight to move up at him.

Then suddenly she slipped out from under him and, putting her hands on his shoulders, pushed him onto his back and mounted him. He grabbed her hips and held tightly at first, trying to control her as she began to move at her own pace.

He gasped, trying to keep his eyes focused on her magnificent wild face as she tightened around him, refusing to stop until at last a great moan came from somewhere deep in his center, taking hold of him, overpowering him. She had won.

Now she closed her eyes, and using his throbbing penis, she climbed to orgasm, shuddered, then collapsed, letting her face fall onto his chest, resting her cheek on the soft, damp hairs.

Something stirred near his feet, and he felt tiny prickles around his ankles. A low, steady rumbling was coming from somewhere in the distance, like a motor humming. He was lying on his stomach. By turning slightly, he could, without lifting his head, look down at his feet where the sound seemed to be coming from.

He opened his eyes. A light from another room shone across the bottom of the bed. There, sitting on top of his feet, was a cat, a large, fat one; black, with one white spot on top of his head. It was watching him intently and purring loudly.

"Who are you?" he said, sleepily.

"Did you think I turned into a cat?" Shawna was standing in the doorway, in the center of the light. She was wearing a long, white robe, tied at the waist; her hair was up on top of her head.

"I've just had a shower. Do you know how long you've been sleeping?"

"Who's that?" he asked, pointing to the cat.

"That's Houdini."

"How long has he been there?"

"You never know—he goes in and out through closed doors."

He reached out his arms as she came toward the bed and pulled her head to nestle in his chest. Houdini started to inch his way up.

"Go away," she said. "He's allergic."

Wood looked at her, amazed. "How'd you know that?"

"Because he never goes near anyone who isn't."

He laughed and hugged her. "Hungry?"

"Starved," she said. "Let's go out instead of ordering something in, okay?"

"Okay, we'll walk somewhere and hold hands."

It was almost midnight by the time they walked and found someplace open.

Afterward they walked a few blocks more before going back to Shawna's, where he spent the night.

He woke up early and slipped out of bed quietly. He searched in the kitchen for a coffeepot, but all he could find was a tea kettle. In fact, a tea kettle was all there was. No frying pan, nothing to cook with, and as he searched for some instant coffee, he discovered that the instant decaffeinated coffee and some bags of herbal teas completed the larder. The refrigerator was no improvement; one container of milk, a jar of peanut butter, a half-eaten container of yogurt, and a bottle of apple juice. There were six cans of cat food, though, stacked on top of the refrigerator. Houdini was rubbing against his legs, complaining loudly.

"I guess you're the only one who eats at home," he said and opened one of the cans. Then he put the water on to boil and walked into the living room.

It was a large, sunny room, with a high, old-fashioned ceiling and tall casement windows. She had dozens of plants, but very little in the way of furniture. Apparently everyone sat on pillows around here. They were strewn around the floor, huge, brightly colored ones, piled on top of a large American Indian rug that covered most of the floor.

He stopped. He looked around. Odd, he thought, there are no books, no photographs, not even a desk. He went into the bathroom, remembering the impression he had last night when he took a shower. He opened the medicine cabinet. A stick of deodorant, a small tin of aspirin, a toothbrush, and a small tube of toothpaste. There was a bar of soap in the shower and two towels hanging on a hook. And that was all. She'd said she'd been living here for almost two years. It didn't take much of a detective to see that she didn't live here at all. He heard the tea kettle whistling and went to turn it off. Then he dressed quickly, pausing once to look at her sleeping face. All right, he thought, the good news is, I found you. The bad news is, I don't have a clue who the hell you are.

By the time he got to his own apartment, he'd put the whole thing out of his mind, blaming Danahy for spooking him about

Shawna. She was obviously not a person whose life was about things, that's all. And she worked long hours at the hospital, had an office there. Why wouldn't her books and papers be where she worked?

He was still cursing Danahy when he heard the phone ringing as he got out of the shower. He ran for it, dripping water all over the rug, and it stopped ringing just as he got to it. He soaped his face, ready to shave, and the beeper went off. "*Shit!*" He decided to ignore it until he'd finished shaving. He cut himself when he heard the phone start to ring again, and threw the razor into the sink.

"*Yeah?*" he shouted into the phone.

"Wood? It's Andy. We got a problem."

"That's terrible, Andy, but would you tell me about it later. I'm standing here bleeding to death."

"What?"

"No—I cut myself shaving—what's the problem?"

"Sergeant Danahy came down here last night—"

"Danahy? What for? Hey, speak up. I can't hear you."

"I have to talk quietly, there's people around. He was asking a lot of questions. He said if he ever finds out who's doing it, he'll bust their ass."

"Oh, for Christ's sake. Do you have a location for him?"

"He's over at the Rockmoor."

"Do me a favor, have someone raise him over there and tell him to wait for me—I'm on my way. And don't worry."

Halsey was sitting in the squad car when Wood pulled up. He jumped out and went to talk to him, to find out what was happening.

"You know how it is. When the shit starts to fly, it goes right on down the line. The old 'pecking order' of things."

"But what's it about? Why me?"

"Here he comes. Ask him yourself, just be ready to duck." Halsey looked around, out the back window of his car. "Hey, look at that, Wood. You're getting a ticket. Boy, this must be your day!"

"Yeah," he said. "Tell me about it."

Danahy strode out of the hotel. "Move your car, Wood."

"Why? I already have a ticket."

"Move it, I said!"

"Hey, Jack. Will you do me a favor and get in the car with me? I want to talk to you."

Tight-lipped and grim, Danahy yanked open the car door, grabbing the ticket from the windshield first.

"Is all this about the other night?" Wood asked. "If so, I'm the one who ought to be pissed. You let me have it pretty hard."

"I'm not pissed at you; it's myself I'm pissed at—for letting you get away with that little scam of yours so long. I figured I could look the other way for a friend and what happens? Some poor little bastard's going to lose his job. For you. Nothing's going to happen to you, except the lieutenant'll have a slightly bigger hate-on for you. But that's not going to affect your life."

"Open the glove compartment, will you?"

"Why? You want to show me where you keep your ticket collection?" He opened it, looked at the CB radio fitted inside. He slipped the ticket in behind it.

"Turn it on, Jack."

He glared at him. "C'mon, Wood, I don't have time for this." He shook his head and turned it on anyway.

". . . in progress. All units in vicinity of Broadway and—"

He turned it off. "How long have you had that?"

"Can we go get some coffee? I've been up since five thirty this morning, I've cut myself shaving, I think I've locked myself out of my apartment, my best friend is mad at me, and I still haven't had a cup of coffee!"

"You also got a twenty-five-dollar ticket and it's starting to rain. C'mon, I'll tell Halsey to wait for those other people to get back to the hotel and question them."

They took the last booth and ordered coffee. "Where'd you get the police crystal for the CB? It's illegal for you to have one, you know."

"I know. But no one'll lose their job over it."

"It still doesn't account for you getting to the scene of a crime before the police. Not a single officer can remember seeing Angel Fornetti going into the theater that night."

"Ought to teach them to be more attentive."

"That wouldn't hurt either. However, in this case, the reason they didn't see him is because he'd already gone inside the theater. They remember seeing you though. Because you were there before they were. You were probably on your third roll of film! Gallagher wants to know why."

"And you're going to tell him what a nut I am for old movies, remember? *It Happened One Night* was playing there. I was a block away when the call came in on my illegal radio, which you're going to confiscate today and give to him. And I hope the turkey chokes on it. Now, what else can I do to make you love me again?"

"Unplug 'Deep-er Throat.'"

He reached into his jacket pocket and took out the beeper. "Here," he said, passing it to him. "Take this, too."

"I don't want your goddamned beeper," Danahy said, shoving it across the table.

Wood turned then, without knowing why, and looked behind him in the direction of the counter.

"What are you looking at?" Danahy asked.

Wood was frowning. "I'm not sure, but you know that girl— the friend of Freddie's the old lady described to me? There's a kid over there, at the counter. It's just a hunch. Stay put."

She was huddled in the corner, leaning against the wall, coat collar turned up hiding most of her face, and wearing large sunglasses. He could see a bruise on her cheek, just underneath the glasses. She was jabbing at the ice in the bottom of her glass with a straw.

As Wood approached, she shrank further down into her coat, turning her face away toward the wall. Her mouth was bruised and swollen. She took a napkin from the counter to cover it.

He sat down on the stool next to her. "Hello, Winter," he said quietly, not looking at her. He sensed her stiffen. She said nothing.

"I'm sorry about Freddie."

She turned then, swiveled around, away from him, and got up to go. He reached out, stopping her, his hand on her sleeve.

"There's a cop over there in the booth, Winter. Would you rather talk to him or to me?"

"Get your honky hand off of me. How do I know you're not a cop?" But she made no move to leave.

"Look." He pulled out his wallet and handed her a picture of Donnie.

She looked at it. "Where did you get that?" she gasped.

"Turn it over."

She did, a deep frown crossing her face as she read the name written on the back. "Who's Donna Wood?"

"That's my daughter. Scary, isn't it?"

"Who are you?"

"My name's Homer Wood. I'm a news photographer. Look, Winter, we don't have a lot of time. You were described to me by someone who knows you were there that night. Which means someone else knows, besides me. The cop sitting over there is a friend of mine. He'll let us walk out of here if I ask him. My car's out front. You'd be smart to get out of this neighborhood, don't you think?"

"I—I—don't know. I—can't—" She was fighting tears. "How do I know you're not a—creep?"

"By looking at me."

"If I don't go with you—you'll give me to that cop?"

"No, but you can't hide around here, you know that. I'm going to go over there now and tell him. Then we're going to walk out of here together."

He went to the back booth where Danahy was waiting, watching him. "I may have something for you. Call you in a couple of hours."

"Wood, goddamnit—I told you, no!"

"Look, she may talk to me, but she sure as hell isn't going to talk to you. Whatever I get, I turn over to you and walk away. Okay?"


"Do you like Chinese food?"

Winter nodded.

"My daughter's favorite thing to do is to go down to Chinatown, eat Moo Goo Gai Pan, and play the pinball machines. How does that sound to you?"

She smiled ironically. "I've never played pinball."

Winter was ahead by five thousand points when Wood ran out of quarters. He went to get more change and ducked into a phone booth.

"Sergeant Danahy there? Wood calling."

"Jack? Got a pencil? Write this down. Name, Frederica Charles; age, twelve; residence, Hillside, New Jersey. Father owns a furniture store in the same town. Got it?"

"Wait a minute—!"

"Can't. Call you later." He hung up quickly, thinking himself lucky the phone didn't explode in his hand.

A group of teen-aged boys had taken over the pinball machines. Wood looked around. The place was empty except for a five-year-old standing on a stool playing an electronic car-racing game. Winter's coat was hanging on a hook against the wall. He walked to the back, toward the ladies' room, and found the door wide open. No one was inside. He swung around, ran to the pinball machines, and grabbed the nearest boy by the arm.

"There was a little girl here when you came in—"

"Hey, man, what's your problem?" He pushed Wood's arm away roughly.

"*Was* there?"

"Yeah," he said, challengingly. "She split."

"What's the matter?" another boy taunted. "Lose your little nooky?"

Wood's face was white with rage. "You rotten little punks! Did you bother her? What did you say to her?"

Another boy, older than the others, looked up from the machine.

"Hey, asshole, the kid just split, understand? She went back there to use the phone or something and then she ran like a bat outta hell—"

In a second Wood was outside in the drenching rain looking up and down the street. It was deserted. He decided to get the car. Silently he cursed himself for having made the phone call. The girl obviously had seen him in there and gotten frightened.

The narrow winding streets of Chinatown made it impossible to navigate and watch for her at the same time. His windshield wipers in this kind of downpour were useless. Finally he gave up and headed uptown, doubting he'd find her there.

He drove around, aimlessly, looking in every coffee-shop window he passed, and was about to turn around and go home when he thought he spotted her. A child's figure, standing in a doorway of an office building. He had to back down a side street the wrong way, but there she was, shivering and soaked in just her skirt and blouse. And those ridiculous high-heeled shoes.

He jumped out of the car and made a dash for her. It was raining harder than ever; he took off his jacket and wrapped her in it and carried her to the car, scooping her up the way one would an injured animal from the side of the road. She was shaking violently. He put her in the seat beside him and turned the heater on full blast. Then he headed home.

He found he had a spare set of keys in the glove compartment, for which he said a word of thanks; his first break of the day. But the instant he put the child down to unlock the outer door, she bolted. Half crawling, half running, she got several feet away before he caught her; both of them soaked again. This time he held onto her hand as he opened the door. She couldn't have weighed more than ninety pounds, but she was wet and struggling so hard that Wood was barely able to make the four flights of stairs with her tucked under his arm.

He took her straight into the bathroom and ran a tub.

"Get out of those wet things," he said.

"*No!*"

He handed her a large bath towel. "I mean after I go out and close the door." Wood went into the living room and sat a moment, thinking. It was only three o'clock, but it seemed a long time ago that he woke up in Shawna's bed. He went to the phone, certain she wouldn't be home yet. Still she might have left a message on her machine.

"Is that you or your machine?" he asked, surprised.

"Tuesday's my day off. I thought I told you."

"No, you didn't."

"I'm sorry you left so early—we could have had breakfast or coffee." Her voice was marvelous.

"I never eat cat food for breakfast, and you don't have any coffee."

"I do too. I'm having some right now."

"Shawna? I wonder if you could help me. I've got a child here and she's sick—"

"Not Donnie?"

"No, no. I can't really tell you much over the phone, but she's got to get some help. Not just medical help. I know it's a lot to ask."

She paused for just a moment, then said, "I'll be glad to, if I can. Do you need anything? And oh, I don't have your address."

He asked her to stop and pick up some canned soups and gave her directions to give to the cab driver. He hung up, thinking how absolutely wonderful she was.

Winter was half asleep in the tub. He felt her forehead; she was feverish. Gingerly, he lifted her, wrapping a large bath towel around her.

"C-cold." She began to shiver again.

"I know. Here, let me help you put these on." He had found a pair of Donnie's warmest pajamas, with feet.

He turned down Donnie's bed, adding extra blankets. "Better?" he asked, after she crawled in and pulled the covers up around her. She nodded. "Can you swallow a couple of aspirins?" She shook her head, then in a weak voice, she asked, "Are you gonna call the cops?" She curled over on her side, and without waiting for his answer, fell asleep.

Wood looked at her. The bruises on her face seemed somehow worse in innocent sleep. We're going to find them, Winter, he promised her silently. And then he thought of Danahy. Wrong again, Sergeant. On both counts. He remembered his own wet clothes, and went to change, but first he went to the phone and took it off the hook. He wasn't ready for Danahy yet.

When the doorbell rang, Wood listened on the intercom to make sure it was Shawna, then buzzed her in and met her on the stairs.

"What've you got there?" he asked, taking two of the heavy bags.

"I go crazy in a supermarket. I can't find anything so I buy everything. That's why I try to stay out of them. Hello."

"Hello," he said, stopping to look into her eyes. "Thanks." They went up to the apartment.

"She's been sleeping," he said, opening the door.

Shawna went to the bed and looked at the girl. "My God."

"I'm sorry, I should have warned you."

She put her hand to her cheek. "She's burning up. Have you got any alcohol?" Then she was all business, getting a sponge, a pan, towels—finding everything she needed, knowing just where to look. She handled the girl with such sure, gentle hands, as she took off her pajama top and began to sponge her down, that Winter barely woke up. Shawna kept talking to her, though, in soft, reassuring tones, getting her to turn this way and that, sponging her, drying her, and dressing her again, all in less than fifteen minutes. She even got her to take two aspirin. Once or twice Winter blinked at her, not really seeing her, but smiled at her dreamily. Shawna covered her again, tucking her in securely, swaddling her in the blankets like a baby.

Wood's function was that of an assistant, handing her things as she asked for them. Mostly he just watched her.

They sat in the kitchen, on barstools, and talked. He told her everything, leaving nothing out, except of course what Danahy had said about her, and she listened attentively, showing no shock, only enormous compassion.

"Now I understand the reason for all that deadly silence at the dinner table when I went on about adolescent sexuality. God. Well, what's your plan?"

"I don't have one. I just know I have to follow through."

"Yes," she said simply. And he felt a surge of love for her, stronger than any he'd ever known.

They heard Winter murmuring, then she called out. They went to her, Shawna sitting on the bed, her hand resting on the blanket where Winter's shoulder was, Wood at the foot of the bed. Her eyes were closed.

"I don't feel good. Mama—? I don't feel good—"

# PART 2

"I DON'T FEEL good. Please don't make me go to school today. I got a fever, I think. Really, Mama, I do. Feel."

"Don't call me Mama. I'm not your Mama. Your Mama was a nigger like you. A lazy nigger— Now you just get yourself out of that bed, or I'll call your father in here. He'll give you something to cry about."

"Mama—*please*—"

The tall, straight, colorless woman was across the room in three steps. She slapped her in the face, then turned and was gone.

Shivering, body aching with fever, Mary Ann dressed quickly and slipped out of the house. Her brothers were laughing in the kitchen as her stepmother made them breakfast. The smell of eggs frying made her stomach turn over.

She huddled in a corner of the bus, resting her cheek against the cool windowpane, and closed her eyes, shutting out the hated gray houses, endless rows of them, street after same ugly street.

It was early spring. The classroom windows were open. Mary Ann pulled her thin sweater tightly around her. The pretty blond girl in the seat next to her was watching her. Mary Ann looked away. If only she looked like that. Long straight hair the color of corn. And white skin that was almost pink. She looked down at her own light tan hands that her Mama used to say were the color of butterscotch. "Keep her out of the sun or she'll turn to chocolate," her father said, "like your nigger mother."

The teacher's voice droned on and Mary Ann shut her eyes, willing her mind to take her somewhere else.

To the time when she was little. She was nestled in her mother's lap; her mother was drawing little circles on a piece of paper with lines connecting them. She called it "Mary Ann's family tree."

"Here's your great-grandmother up here. She was black."

"*Black?*" Four-year-old Mary Ann asked in amazement.

Her mother laughed. "Well, brown. Like chocolate. Great-grandfather was white. Here's grandmother, my mama, who's butterscotch like you."

"How come my brothers are vanilla?"

"'Cause they're not sweet like you."

"That's how come they don't suck their thumbs like I do!"

That same year, not long after, her mother looked very white lying in her bed, bottles of pills lined up on the table next to her. Shadows under her eyes. Thin, so thin, Mary Ann could trace the blue lines under the skin on the back of her hands.

"Page *eighty-four*, Mary Ann."

Startled, Mary Ann looked up and tried to focus her eyes on Miss Andrews, who was standing; waiting.

"Open your book."

She did, but the words all blurred together.

"Read aloud from the bottom of page eighty-four, please."

"I can't," she whispered.

"What?"

There was laughter everywhere around her, and Miss Andrews's voice pounded in her ears. "Then what are you doing in the sixth grade?"

"I don't think she feels well, Miss Andrews."

The teacher sighed. "Frederica, take Mary Ann down to the infirmary—why parents don't keep their children home with all that virus going round—"

The pretty blond girl's hand was gentle on Mary Ann's arm as she helped her up from her desk. Eyes lowered, she allowed herself to be led across the classroom and out into the hall where she stopped a moment to rest against the wall.

"Are you all right?" the pretty blond girl asked.

Mary Ann nodded, but then burst into tears, turning her face to the wall, helplessly ashamed.

"Don't let them call home. Please don't. I can't—"


"Here, try to drink some tea, okay? We're not going to call anybody; you're safe here."

She opened her eyes, blinking at the man standing at the foot of the bed, the strange room. She wondered with alarm what she'd been saying aloud. Had she told them . . . ? The memory of that night flooded over her, pulling her down and under.

Freddie's scream from the next room. Oh, God, what are they doing to her? Then silence, terrible silence.

Shawna put a cool washcloth on her forehead, saw the tears running in little rivulets out of the corners of her closed eyes, falling into her hair. She dabbed at the tears, feeling an unspeakable sorrow for this strange and beautiful child.

Mary Ann stayed out of school all that week. There was a math test her first day back, right after lunch. In the cafeteria Mary Ann sat alone eating a ham sandwich and studying in her workbook. The pretty blond girl came and sat next to her.

"She's giving us problems, not division. Look." She opened her own workbook, which was neatly organized in precise pages. Her handwriting was clear and even, unlike Mary Ann's jerky scrawl that ran off the page mid-sentence.

"Here's the first one." Her name was carefully written in plain block letters at the top of the page—"Frederica Charles"—and the date, April 24, 1977.

"That's a pretty name," Mary Ann said shyly.

"I hate it. Don't you think we should be allowed to pick our own names?"

"Yes." Mary Ann smiled at the idea. "What would you pick?"

"Well, I wish people would call me Freddie, but my mother thinks it's undignified."

"I'll call you Freddie," Mary Ann offered.

"Are you Chinese?"

Mary Ann looked at her, but Freddie's blue eyes were completely without guile. "No," she said.

"That's too bad. I know a Chinese kid called Kim. I always thought that was a neat name. Well, let's think about one for you." Mary Ann pulled her sweater around her and buttoned it at the neck. They spent the rest of the recess attacking the math problems together until the bell rang.

Once or twice during the test Freddie glanced over at Mary Ann, who, when she caught her looking at her, screwed up her face and shook her head despairingly. Watching to make sure Miss Andrews wasn't looking, Freddie mouthed, "Which question?" Mary Ann cautiously held out four fingers, pointing them at the floor. Freddie scrawled the answer on a piece of paper and slipped it across the aisle to Mary Ann.

"Let's go get a Coke," Freddie said after school.

Mary Ann hesitated. "I can't."

"Sure you can. Just say you had to stay late at school to make up work you missed when you were sick."

"No, I really can't." Mary Ann looked embarrassed.

"I'm treating—to celebrate. I decided from now on no one calls me Frederica anymore. Only nerds like my parents and teachers. C'mon. When we think of yours, you can treat."

Freddie's spirit was irresistible, her certainty of purpose absolute. Mary Ann followed her into the drugstore, where Freddie immediately claimed the first booth. Mary Ann shivered. Freddie handed her her sweater. "Take it, I'm hot. I guess you're still getting over your virus, huh?"

"No, I'm always cold."

Two boys at the counter were watching them. "They're in the seventh grade," Freddie whispered.

"Hi, Frederica. Who's your friend? She looks cold—we thought we'd sit with you and warm you up."

"My name is not Frederica. It's Freddie. And this is—*Winter!*" She looked over at Mary Ann, who was trying the name out in her mind. Winter—white snow, clean and unspoiled. She smiled at Freddie. "And if you want to sit with us, you can buy us Cokes and drink a toast to our new names."

It was after five when Mary Ann got home. Dorothy, her stepmother, jumped to her feet, grabbed her by the arm, and swung her around, catching her as she got to the stairs. "Where've you been?"

"I had to stay late at school—to do make-up work."

"Liar." She slapped her. "Where were you?" Mary Ann's dark eyes shone with hatred. She pressed her lips tightly shut.

"Go to your room and clean it. It looks like a pigsty. Call me when you think it's clean, and I'll come look at it."

Halfway up the stairs Mary Ann turned. Her stepmother was watching her, an ugly sneer on her thin, bony face. "Your father will find out where you've been when he gets home."

Mary Ann shuddered and walked up the rest of the stairs holding onto the banister. They were going to do it again, she knew.

Wearily, she set about straightening her starkly bare room. Dorothy changed all the beds in the house but hers. Her brothers' clothes were laundered and ironed and neatly put in their drawers for them. They raised hell if they couldn't find matching socks. But then they were white; she was the nigger. She went out into the hall to find clean sheets when she heard the front door slam. It was Thursday, her two brothers worked until six. Oh, no, God, it was Wednesday—tonight they worked till nine. She was alone with her father and Dorothy. She heard them talking. Then the heavy footsteps on the stairs. Unthinking, she squeezed herself into the linen closet and pulled the door shut. Darkness enclosed her, shutting out air. Camphor stung her eyes, filled her lungs.

The footsteps passed, stopped at the door to her room. Quicker, lighter footsteps, Dorothy's, followed. She held her breath, trembling uncontrollably. The closet door burst open. There, silhouetted against the light from the hall, stood her father. Without a word he pulled her, feet barely touching the floor, to her room and threw her onto her bed. She landed on her stomach and buried her head in the pillow.

"Your stepmother wants to know where you went after school today." His voice was husky, deep.

"To—to a drugstore—for a Coke," she said into the pillow.

"Where'd you get the money for a Coke?"

"I—didn't—"

"What?"

"I was—treated—" Her muffled voice was dead, toneless.

Dorothy shouted, "Who treated you? Boys? You know what they want when they treat a little nigger to a Coke—what's your father told you? Answer!"

Mary Ann was silent. She heard the buckle of his belt being undone, heard the sound of the leather being whipped out of his pants.

"Take off her pants." His voice was huskier now.

She gritted her teeth as she felt Dorothy raise her skirt about her waist and yank off her panties. Then she did what she'd taught herself to do every other time. Before the first stinging blow came, her mind took her away, far away to a grassy green place next to a cool clean river where she and Mama sat underneath a tree and watched the white, white clouds floating in the sky above them, giving them the names of animals, sometimes making up new ones like rabbit-cat or . . . Mama, they're hurting me—make them stop. No, look at that one, it looks like a cow with a horse's head; let's call it moo-horse!

It was over. She waited until she heard the door close, then pulling a blanket over her, she curled up, making herself as small as she could, and quickly folded the pillow over both ears to shut out the sounds she learned to expect afterward. Their room was next to hers, and the walls were thin. She used to think with some satisfaction that her father was hurting Dorothy after. Until some other sense from God-knows-where told her differently.

Mary Ann, now Winter, and Frederica, now Freddie, became best friends. Sisters, they decided. Freddie was never told why but accepted the fact that Winter always had to go straight home after school, so lunchtimes and recesses were precious moments to share their secrets and dreams. Freddie was first in her class and won a gold pin for perfect attendance and promptness. She was also the prettiest girl in the school; a prettiness she knew how to use well. Women teachers liked her because she seemed unaware of her beauty. With the men teachers, including the principal, she was different. She let them know that she knew exactly how pretty she was and somehow let them in on the secret. Winter worshiped her. "You're going to be a movie star," she told her one day. Freddie looked at her friend sternly. "Listen, you're really dumb, you know that? You're prettier than I am, but you're so dumb you don't even know it."

Winter listened, unbelieving, but intrigued. Freddie thought hard. "We have to find a way to get your parents to allow you to come over to my house after school. No one's home except my crazy old grandmother, and she just sits and watches soap operas all day."

"Where's your parents?" Winter asked.

"Away, as usual. We could do things with your hair. And my mom's got all this beauty stuff—we could fix ourselves up—" Freddie stopped. Her friend looked hopelessly resigned. "Well, at least help me think!"

The next day during the recess Freddie was nowhere to be found. Winter spent the entire forty-five minutes alone wondering where Freddie was. Her seat was empty when class began.

"Mary Ann Richards? You're wanted in the principal's office." The children watched with interest as Winter crossed the classroom to the door.

Freddie was seated in the chair opposite the principal's. She winked at Winter as she walked in.

Mr. Wallace's chair was pushed back from his desk, feet resting on an open drawer. He had long sideburns which he kept touching, smoothing them down.

"Mary Ann, I understand you and Frederica are interested in learning filing." Winter's eyes darted in the direction of Freddie, who was concentrating her full attention on the principal. "And since both of you have been spending some time in your fathers' offices and are planning to help out your fathers this summer—" Winter's eyes opened wider. "I think it would be a fine idea, with your parents' permission, of course, to stay two afternoons a week and help out Miss Hannah. Provided, of course, your grades don't suffer. I admire you both for your practicality. I've prepared a letter for each of you to take home for your parents' signatures. That's all, girls, hurry back to class now."

Out in the hall Freddie broke into a run and once out of earshot, she collapsed with laughter. Winter was still stunned. "I wish you could have seen your face!" Freddie howled.

Wood and Shawna were sitting on the sofa drinking coffee. Winter was laughing softly. They both got up and went to the bed. Her eyes were still closed. She was grinning. "It worked, it really worked." She laughed again.

"Winter?" Shawna said quietly. "How about some soup now?"

Winter looked up; her eyes were focused somewhere else. "That old Miss Hannah was so deaf and blind, she never knew if we were there or not—and Wallace—he left every day on the dot of three . . . probably out looking for little girls . . ."

Incredibly, Winter's father, who worked as a postal clerk, was pleased, even impressed. Freddie had asked to borrow Miss Andrews's typewriter, which she used to change the number of days that they'd be helping Miss Hannah from two to three. Freddie had no problem. Her parents were away, and her grandmother just sat in front of the television all day with the shades drawn, so she never knew whether it was day or night anyway.

Now they were free! The first afternoon they rushed into Mr. Wallace's office on the dot of three, immediately after their last

62

class, and worked diligently for less than an hour, until he left for the day. Then they'd show Miss Hannah all that they'd done and she'd nod vaguely at them and they'd leave. That gave Freddie and Winter a full hour to spend as they wished. Usually it was at the drugstore, where they knew they'd be treated to a soda, but sometimes they just enjoyed walking through town.

Mr. Wallace seemed to like having them around. Especially Freddie. Sometimes Winter would notice him watching Freddie, following her with his eyes, with a peculiar expression that made Winter look away. Not Freddie. Whenever she caught him looking at her, she'd just look back at him, turning the full force of her clear, blue eyes on him; innocent, and at the same time, intense. As though he were the most interesting person in the whole world.

And once, when Freddie accidentally bumped into him when she didn't know he was standing behind her, he blushed, his face turning a blotchy red, and he suddenly left the office. That's when Freddie devised the new plan. They'd spend their recesses in his office instead of the afternoons. He was hanging around too much, anyway, and it was getting harder and harder to leave. She told him they were rehearsing for the school play, for graduation.

"Freddie, aren't you ever afraid they'll catch you lying?"

"Winter, look at me. Ask me something. Anything."

"Uh—how old are you?"

"I'm fourteen and a half. I was born on December twenty-fifth, the same day as Jesus Christ, our Lord. Now, do I look like I'm lying?"

Winter shook her head. "How do you do that?"

"It's easy. Just watch me and copy me. Always look at people like this." And she did that thing with her eyes again that Winter didn't think she could ever do.

At home Winter would lock herself in the bathroom and practice in the mirror. When she thought she had it right, she tried it on her father one night at dinner. He was telling a story of an argument he had with his supervisor, one they'd all heard many times before. It was a very long story, and Dorothy and the boys ate silently, waiting for him to finish, never looking up from their plates.

But Winter fastened her eyes on him and listened with rapt attention. Instantly she saw how it worked. Her father didn't even notice her nervousness. He became more animated and told another story, then another; ones she hadn't heard before, and he was telling them only to her. It was the first time in years he really smiled at her. And, as if that weren't enough, when Dorothy interrupted to tell Winter to clear the table, her father told Dorothy to do it herself.

It was early May. There was an excitement in the air as the afternoons grew longer and the end of the school year began to feel like a reality. Freddie and Winter were beginning to spend more time at Freddie's house, experimenting with her mother's makeup. They'd find pictures in fashion magazines and choose the models they wanted to look like, then they'd lay the open page out on the bathroom sink so they could compare and correct.

One day they decided to go into town wearing their makeup. As Freddie lived outside of town, in the suburbs, they had to take a bus. They were nervous about it, but they looked so pretty, they had to let someone see. They gasped when they saw Mr. Wallace sitting alone in the back of the bus, and were ready to jump off at the next stop. After all, weren't they supposed to be at rehearsals? He was happy to see them, though, and didn't seem to remember they were supposed to be anywhere. He called to them to sit with him and told them how pretty they looked.

They sat on either side of him, near the window. Freddie kept leaning over him to talk to Winter or to point out something through the window, resting her arm on his thigh. And every time the bus came to a stop, she'd fall against him, and he'd laugh out loud and put his arm around her to steady her. Winter didn't understand what was so funny, but when he laughed, his face got all blotchy again.

Then he took them for a milk shake. Not to the drugstore, a different place they'd never been, and let them buy magazines. When it was time for Winter to go home, they walked her to the bus and waited until she got on. Winter looked out the back and saw them, Mr. Wallace and Freddie. They were walking away, his arm around her shoulder.

That same week Freddie arrived, Friday morning, carrying a large leather shoulder bag on her arm. She sat at her desk, slipping the bag under her legs, and flashed Winter a secret grin. She waited until Miss Andrews turned to face the blackboard, then she reached across the aisle and slipped a folded piece of paper into Winter's hand, and waited, watching her as she opened it.

Winter smiled. It read: "Hooray, hooray. The tenth of May. Today's the day we break away!" She looked at Freddie, puzzled.

Miss Andrews turned to the class. Freddie promptly raised her hand.

"Yes, Frederica?"

"Miss Andrews, I'm supposed to go see Mr. Wallace at nine thirty."

The teacher looked on her desk. "I didn't get a memo about it."

"Maybe he forgot to send one. I'll be sure to bring a note back with me, Miss Andrews."

Miss Andrews looked at the clock on the wall. It was nine fifteen. "All right. Why don't you begin then? Come to the blackboard and show us how you divide this number, breaking it down first, as we did yesterday."

Freddie performed remarkably as usual, accepting with good grace Miss Andrews's approval.

"Run along now. It's nine twenty-five."

Winter prayed she wouldn't be called on. Once or twice it looked as though she might, and she held her breath until the teacher's eyes traveled past her to someone else.

Finally Freddie came back and handed Miss Andrews a note. She waited while Miss Andrews read it.

"Mary Ann, you're to go with Frederica to Mr. Wallace's office." Winter got up. "And take your things." Freddie went to her own desk and gathered up her shoulder bag and books. Miss Andrews nodded as the girls left the classroom.

Freddie was walking very fast down the hall, and Winter had to run to keep up with her. She was headed for the main door.

"Where—hey! That's the *door!*"

"Yep, and watch us go through it."

They were a full two blocks away from the school building before Freddie slowed down. It was a brilliant, clear day; it would be warm by noon. She took a long, deep breath.

"Where're we going?" Winter asked in amazement.

"Shopping. For your father's surprise birthday party."

"*What?* It's not—"

"Yes it is. And your father's never had a real party before, and he's such a wonderful man, he's worked so hard, and we decided he deserved one. Close your mouth, silly, or you'll catch a fly—and Mr. Wallace said we were the most thoughtful little girls he's ever seen, *and* he's excused us for the whole day to buy the decorations and make the cake—and here comes the bus."

"Freddie, are you crazy? That's the New York bus!"

By the time the bus pulled into the Port Authority, Freddie had shown Winter the contents of the bag. Two silk blouses, each freshly pressed and carefully folded, two pairs of dress-up shoes with a slight heel and strap across the instep, makeup, and a curling iron. And thirty dollars.

"Emergency money my parents left. You don't have a phone in your house, and no one expects you back until five. It's eleven now, we'll get a bus back at three thirty—that'll give us plenty of time."

"What're we going to do?"

"Well, first we're going to find a ladies' room and fix ourselves up, then we'll see New York. Happy tenth of May!"

Winter had never seen New York. She grabbed Freddie's hand as the driver called out, "New York—last stop!"

In the ladies' room they searched for an outlet and plugged in the curling iron before changing into the new blouses and shoes. Then, setting out the makeup on the sink counter, they began to do their faces, just as they'd practiced at Freddie's house.

"Where're you girls from?"

They looked up. Reflected in the mirror, they saw a black girl perhaps in her twenties wearing a tight sweater, her hair arranged in shiny ringlets around her face. She was smoking a cigarette.

"Hills—" Winter started to say.

"*Chicago*," Freddie cut in. "Why?"

"In town on holiday?"

"We're going to the theater—with relatives," Freddie answered matter-of-factly. "It's her birthday." She unplugged the curling iron and began to do the ends of her hair.

"Yeah? How old are you?"

"Sixteen," Freddie answered quickly. The black girl was leaning against one of the stalls watching them.

"How come you're using honky makeup, girl?"

"Let's go," Winter said, glaring at the girl.

"Wait, fix your hair first." Freddie removed the barrette from Winter's hair.

The black girl dropped her cigarette on the floor and ground it out with the heel of her boot, never taking her eyes off the two girls. Then abruptly she turned and left.

"She gave me the creeps," Winter said. Freddie shrugged, examined them both in the mirror. "We have to look sixteen in case there's truant officers around." Winter frowned. "Don't worry, we do. You look gorgeous!"

They walked through the terminal, looking for the street exit.

"Look," Winter nudged Freddie.

The black girl in the tight sweater was standing with a tall, thin man, also black; they were watching the girls as they headed for the exit.

"They're following us!"

"Don't be silly. They certainly don't look like truant officers. New York is full of creeps, you know. Don't walk so fast, it's important not to look scared. Let's buy a *Cue* magazine and decide where to go."

"Freddie, there's two other men watching us, too. Please let's get out of here."

"Okay, we'll get a cab. Boy, are you a worrier."

They found one right away. "Schrafft's, please," Freddie instructed the driver.

The driver turned to look at them. *"Which* Schrafft's?" Winter looked out of the window in time to see the black couple stroll out of the main entrance.

"Park Avenue!" Winter blurted out.

"Look, girlies—"

"Fifty-eighth and Madison," Freddie said, as imperiously as she could.

The lunch crowd hadn't started to come in yet, so Freddie and Winter were given a center table where they could study the busy, well-dressed New Yorkers; shoppers, businessmen and women, even some models. Tall, lanky, beautiful girls with loose, freshly washed hair took the table next to them. Freddie pointed out how they rouged *under* the cheekbones. They carried large, important-looking portfolios, and they put Sweet 'n Low in their coffee. Freddie and Winter did the same.

"Let's buy sunglasses and wear them on top of our heads."

"And lip gloss!"

A handsome man in a gray pinstriped suit walked over to the models' table and, kissing each on the cheek, sat down to join them. Freddie and Winter strained to hear some of the conversation.

". . . and there he was—in the back seat of *my* car—*stoned* out of his gourd . . . screwing some broad that was at the party. My own chauffeur!"

Freddie and Winter giggled. The businessman stood up and, reaching into his pocket, pulled out some money. They gasped as they watched him put a crisp, new fifty-dollar bill on the models' table, then walk past Freddie and Winter. They could see close up his tanned, handsome face and slightly graying hair. They could catch the lovely smell of his cologne.

Freddie sighed. "Don't talk to me, I think I'm in love."

They went into a drugstore. Each bought a pair of sunglasses, trying on several different sizes and shapes. They settled on ones that were identical. Window shopping along Fifth Avenue, they stopped in front of I. Miller's to admire the shoes, then decided to go in and try some on. The salesman, realizing what they were up to, led them to seats in the back and, humoring them, brought out a wide selection of the dressier, most expensive shoes. The girls pranced in front of the mirror, admiring themselves, then sat down to let the salesman remove one pair and put on another.

Freddie looked directly into his eyes and smiled. "You're really nice to let us try them on. What's your name?"

"Mr. Van Dyke. George."

"Well, Mr. Van Dyke, when we're famous models we'll come back and buy all our shoes from you." She stretched her legs. "Do you think we have pretty legs?"

He blushed and got up. "You—both have—beautiful legs. Excuse me, I have to go now." He left them abruptly.

Outside on the corner they jumped up and down, squealing

with delight. "You see that, Winter? See how he liked us—I bet we could go back in there and get him to give us a pair free!"

They hooked arms and walked across the street to Bergdorf's. "Shall we go in?"

Suddenly Winter caught sight of a clock in the window. She screamed. "Freddie! Look what time it is!"

Panicked, they ran to the curb to stop a cab. It was almost three. Freddie begged the driver to hurry.

"It's all right, Winter," she said, trying to calm her. "They leave every half hour; we won't be that late."

"But how're we going to change? And wash our faces—I can't go home looking like this!"

By the time they boarded one of the crowded buses, Winter was near hysteria. Freddie helped to get some of her makeup off with a tissue, wetting it with her tongue first and rubbing at it. Then she held her sweater up in front of her and, shielding Winter from the looks of other passengers, helped her to slip out of Freddie's silk blouse and put her own back on.

"Look, why don't you come to my house? We could think of something—"

"No." Winter was resigned now. As they neared the town of Hillside, Freddie, not knowing what else to do, just held her hand. Winter had about a half-hour's walk from the bus stop. She was a block away from home when she noticed they'd forgotten to change out of the new shoes. Heart pounding, stomach knotted, she opened the front door with cold, trembling hands.

"Whore! Little nigger whore!" Dorothy shouted as her father beat her that night. It was the most painful and lasted the longest of any beating she'd ever had.

Winter didn't go to school the next day; instead she was taken by her stepmother to the neighborhood clinic to be examined. Her father wanted to know if she was still a virgin. Dorothy, when asked about the red, raw welts all over the child's buttocks and thighs, explained defiantly, "She stole a pair of shoes."

The doctor asked Dorothy to leave the room while he completed the examination. Then he called for the nurse. The last thing Winter remembered before she fainted was the nurse putting her feet in some steel contraption and forcing her knees apart.

The next morning Winter got to school early and waited for Freddie outside on the steps. She sat, half crouched, over her books, knowing how terrible she must have looked. There were dark circles under her eyes this morning when she looked at herself in the bathroom mirror, and her face was ashen. A couple of classmates walked by on their way into the school building, looking at her curiously; and a black boy who sat behind her in class, one she'd always avoided, came up to her and said, "Hey, sister, you look all strung out today, baby. What's happenin'?" She glared at him, shrinking further behind her books, which she held onto like a barricade. "Go away," she said.

"That's what wrong with you, girl. You don't like hangin' out with your brothers and sisters; you don't dig that we're the only people you c'n trust."

"Get away from her, Jimmy." It was Freddie, running up the steps. "Leave her alone. Winter, what's wrong? Are you sick?"

"*Winter!*" the boy laughed. "That's a good one. Why not Snow White?" He turned, still laughing, and walked away.

She started to cry then, hiding her face. The words came out garbled, mixed with her sobs. Freddie couldn't understand what she was saying. "Do you want to come home with me?" she asked.

Winter shook her head, crying harder.

"C'mon." Freddie helped her up and led her down the steps to the park across the street. They sat on a bench.

"They beat—me—and, oh God, they hurt—me. Freddie, they pushed—my legs into these—things—and it hurt. I don't know—what they—put—in me—" She was rocking back and forth as she talked.

Freddie's eyes widened and filled with tears as she listened.

"I can't go back there, Freddie. I'll never—never go back. I won't—" She took a long, deep breath and looked at Freddie. "See?"

Winter opened her bag and showed her what was inside. She had crammed into it all the things she could: blouses, underwear, a sweater, all rolled up together. Then she showed Freddie the money. Forty dollars she'd taken out of Dorothy's underwear drawer. Household money for the week.

"Wait. I have to think," Freddie said. She looked around for a place to leave Winter, where she wouldn't be seen. There was a children's playground at the other end of the park.

Freddie left her there on a bench, behind the fence, and told her not to move, that she'd be back in a half an hour. She put her arms around Winter and hugged her tightly. Then, quickly, she dashed across the park, into the school.

Freddie was back as promised in just a little over half an hour. Her face was serious and a little angry, even, Winter thought. Freddie took her hand and, without a word, began walking toward the bus stop. Strong, purposeful steps, stopping only once to get out money.

The bus to New York was practically empty. Freddie was quiet for a long time. Then she announced in a voice that was grim and final, "Winter, we're running away."

Freddie had the address of the YWCA written on a piece of paper with Mr. Wallace's name printed across the top. They went directly there.

The elderly, stern-looking woman behind the desk flatly refused to register them. She told them they were under age and needed an adult with them, staying in the hotel with them. When she asked for their names, they left. If Freddie was upset, she didn't show it. "Let's go get something to eat," she said, and they walked west, looking for a place to go.

They were all the way to Eighth Avenue before they found one that wasn't too crowded or didn't look too expensive. Three teen-aged girls were sitting at one of the tables with a baby propped up in a little carrier.

Freddie and Winter took a table near them and kept watching as one of the girls gave the baby a piece of toast, which he grabbed and waved in the air, trying to find his mouth. They all three laughed, and he began to wiggle his feet and make funny gurgling sounds. The girls were pretty, not made-up like models, but had cute hairdos and nice clothes. And they seemed happy and sure of themselves. Freddie and Winter wondered how old they were.

One of them, the one with short curly hair and a turned-up nose, got up and came over to their table. They were surprised to see that she worked there and had come to take their order.

"What a cute baby," Winter said. "Whose is it?"

"My sister's, the one with the pony tail, but everyone says he looks like me. She always brings him here to lunch, so I can play with him." She wrote down their order. "You can come look at him if you want to; he loves attention." When she came back from placing their order, Freddie stopped her.

"Do you happen to know a hotel where we could stay?" She told her what happened at the Y.

"A lot of places are like that," she said. "Maybe not the big hotels, but they're expensive. Come on over and I'll ask my sister."

They introduced themselves, and the girls told them they could pull their table over next to theirs. Gelsey was the baby's mother. Merrie was her sister who worked there, and Christine was a friend. She was the prettiest and looked older than the others. She was also the one who seemed to know the most.

"If you've run away from home, you'd probably be afraid to tell me, and you'd be right not to, so I won't ask. But if you have, you've got a problem. No decent hotel will take you, and you're too young to get a job. The only safe place for you is a home like Under Twenty-one or the Open Door, one of those. They'll take you without asking any questions and they're free. Not much fun, maybe, but neither are the alternatives."

"Do you all have jobs?" Winter asked.

They didn't answer right away. "I'm sixteen," Merrie said, "that's why I could get a job as a waitress."

"What about you?" Freddie asked Christine. "You're older than that, aren't you?"

"No. I look it, but I'm not. I just pick up work here and there."

"What kind of jobs? Couldn't we do that, find something, I mean?"

She shook her head. "Look, come back here tonight around nine o'clock if you haven't found a place to stay. Maybe we can ask around and find something for a night or two, anyway."

"Gee, that's really nice. Thanks."

They went for a walk after lunch, then decided to see a movie. They wanted to go to Radio City Music Hall and see the Rockettes. So they waited in line for the two o'clock show and afterward took the NBC tour at Rockefeller Center. It was almost five when they stepped out of the building and headed downtown on Seventh.

Winter noticed a man watching them. She couldn't be sure, but she thought she'd seen him when they first came out of the NBC building. Freddie turned to look. He was tall and thin; a black, dressed in a light tan suit with a matching hat. He came to within ten feet of them and stopped, leaning against a doorway, and smiled at them.

"Look at all those gold chains around his neck," Winter said. "One of them must be his birth sign, the big round one with a crab on it. What sign is that?"

"I don't know. He's probably a fairy," Freddie said, looking for a phone booth. "My parents have some friends here in New York. I think I'll call them up and tell them I'm here on a class trip and need a place to stay. They know my parents are away—" She hunted in her pockets for a dime.

The telephone directory was missing from the phone booth, so Freddie dialed information and asked for the number of Mr. and Mrs. John Davis.

"No, I don't know the address, Operator." She waited. "Oh." She hung up the phone. "She said there were almost a hundred Davises in New York and half of them with the initial *J*. Damn."

"You don't know where they live?"

"I might remember if I saw the address written. They always send us Christmas cards and birthday cards—last birthday my mother made me write and thank them."

"May I be of assistance, ladies?" It was the man who'd been watching them. He lifted his hat and bowed low from the waist.

"Doesn't this city have any books in the booths?" Freddie said distractedly.

"You're lucky to find a phone that works in one of those booths. Did you try information?" His speech was clipped; it sounded almost British.

"Yes, but there were too many people with the same name. I need to look in a phone book."

"There's a coffee shop just down the street that has one. The owner's a friend of mine. Follow me, ladies," he said, putting his hat back on and leading the way. He minced a bit as he walked. Freddie and Winter exchanged amused glances.

He held the door to the coffee shop open for them and showed them to a booth, then he excused himself and disappeared, returning a moment later with the Manhattan directory under his arm.

"May I order something for you while you're looking? They have a magnificent milk shake here."

The girls looked at each other and nodded. "Sure," Freddie said, taking the book.

He snapped his fingers at a waiter, rings flashing on his long, slender hands. "Three magnificent milk shakes, please—black and white—that seems appropriate, doesn't it?" He laughed, showing very white, very even, teeth.

Freddie opened the phone book to the *D*'s and found the Davises with the first initial *J*. "Boy, there are a lot." She traced the addresses with her finger.

"Where are you lovelies from?"

As Winter started to answer, Freddie cut her off. *"Connecticut."*

"Are you here on holiday?" he asked.

"It won't be much of a holiday if I can't find these people . . ." Freddie's head was buried in the phone book, blond hair skimming the pages.

The waiter brought the milk shakes. "Thank you, young man—wait." He reached into his pocket and pulled out a large handful of bills, folded neatly into a gold money clip; on it was a little crab, also gold, with sapphire eyes. Winter nudged Freddie under the table. He selected a crisp twenty-dollar bill from what looked like several fifties and hundreds.

"Break this for me, will you? There's a good chap."

The girls were staring, dumbstruck at the money.

"Do you like my little crab?" He put the whole thing, money and clip, on the table in front of them. "Cute, isn't he? He was a birthday present."

Neither of them made a move to touch it, just continued to stare, mesmerized by all that money.

He watched them, laughing softly. Suddenly the waiter rushed forward, handed him the two tens, and whispered something in his ear. He listened attentively, then looked above the girls' heads at the window overlooking the street. At the same time he reached for the money clip and slipped it into his pocket.

He stood. "Excuse me, ladies. I'm late for an appointment." He motioned to the two tens on the table. "That's for you, in case you can't find the phone number you're looking for. If you're around later, I'd like to take you to dinner."

"Around where?" Freddie asked.

"Anywhere. If you're around, I'll find you! Au revoir for now!" And he was gone.

They both spoke at once. "Wow—did you see that!"

"He gave us twenty dollars just like that!"

"It was a deposit," a voice said.

They looked up to see a woman standing at their table. She appeared to be in her forties, plumpish, wearing a tight-fitting skirt and sweater, and a long, dark wig. Her face was heavily made-up; her false eyelashes moved as she talked. She looked at them with a hard, stern expression.

"Nice neighborhood you kids picked to play in. Cute play-mate, too. He can show you lots of tricks, which is what he had in mind until he was tipped off that the little matzoh ball from the pimp squad was outside watching for him to make his move. You know how to do cartwheels? Because that's what he'll have you doing for him and his friends if he finds you tonight—only without any clothes."

Freddie and Winter were gawking at her, their mouths open.

"Either of you nitwits getting the picture yet? No? Well, you just better take that money and beat it while you can. 'Cause if that pimp don't get you, the prossies sure as hell will. Now scram, before I call the runaway squad."

Sergeant Mark Cohen of the pimp squad had been standing outside the coffee shop waiting, leaning against his car, while his partner got some sandwiches across the street. Sergeant Cohen had been carrying around a big hate-on for Pretty Joey for a very long time, ever since he'd seen a sample of his handiwork on the face of a fourteen-year-old girl who would never grow up to be beautiful. Now, as he watched him move in on these little kids, his stomach turned over in rage. God, how he'd love to nail him.

He followed the little kids until they were well out of sight of the coffee shop, then called to them, catching up and walking alongside them. Startled, they walked faster and almost broke into a run, so that finally he had to flash his badge. One of them, the darker of the two, looked as if she might faint.

"Hey, I'm sorry to frighten you. Look, you're not under arrest or anything. I just want to talk to you."

They stood, frozen still, staring at him.

"I mean it. I'll tell you what—reach into my back pocket and take out my handcuffs and"—he backed up to a parking meter— "cuff me onto this. Only be sure to put a quarter in. I wouldn't want to get a ticket."

The blond one almost smiled, but her friend wasn't having any.

"Hey, you," he said to the dark one, "want to take my gun? It's hand carved—out of soap. The real ones scare me—make too much noise. My name's Cohen. My mother wanted me to be a doctor, but I couldn't stand the sight of blood, so I became a cop, and you know what they did? They assigned me to homicide. Can you believe it? My first dead body I went bananas and got sick all over the lieutenant, so now they got me out on the street watching pimps. From a distance, which believe me, I prefer. But, thing is, if I don't see enough from a distance, they make me get closer, which makes me nervous." He rolled his eyes around comically. "Oy, does that make me nervous."

Finally they laughed a little. The blond one said, "Okay, but we don't know anything. Just that some lady called that man a—what you said."

"Did he say anything to you?"

"No, he said he'd take us to dinner," Freddie said.

"But we didn't say we would," Winter added quickly.

"Good." He thought a moment. They've just gotten into town, and not a day over thirteen, if that. How to get them off the street now, before it was too late? They'd already made contact with the meanest, kinkiest pimp around, who won't forget their faces, who'll watch for them, wait for them to run out of money. He ran down a mental list of the guys on the runaway squad he knew he could trust. Tumelty would be good. He checked his watch. Not quite three. Tumelty usually came on at four.

"Hey, girls, how about a Carvel? Please say yes. My partner hates them and today's his day to choose, so I'll have to settle for Baskin-Robbins, and I'm really in the mood for Carvel. Okay? Great. I'll tell him."

He put his two fingers to his mouth and whistled. The girls clapped their hands over their ears. "Loud, huh?" Then he waved and signaled to a man across the street.

"Okay, ladies," he said, taking each of them by the arm and doing a quick soft shoe. "How about a little walk? Nice day for a walk, good for the cir-cu-lation."

He ordered doubles for all of them, then went to the phone and tried Tumelty. He was told he'd come in early and was already out in the field.

"Raise him on the beeper, will you? It's important. Tell him to cruise around Ninth and Eighth between Fiftieth and Fifty-third until he finds me. He'll see me, I'm walking."

The girls seemed to be arguing. They stopped when they saw him.

"C'mon," he said, "I want to show you my favorite store." They walked two blocks, Sergeant Cohen talking constantly, telling old vaudeville jokes, until they came to a pet shop. "Look," he said, and stopped. The window was full of puppies climbing all over each other, nibbling on each other's ears and tails, rolling topsy-turvy, one on top of the other. Except for one who slept soundly through it all. The girls watched, entranced, and wanted to go inside, when a car slowed and came to a stop.

"Sergeant Cohen?" A young man got out of the car and came toward them. "I was asked to find you, to give you a message. Detective Tumelty's tied up in a community-affairs meeting that may last a couple more hours, so someone else on the runaway squad sent me over to see—" He stopped when he saw the expression on the sergeant's face.

Cohen looked at the girls. "Runaway squad" was the trigger. The blond one grabbed the other by the hand.

"Thank you for the ice cream," she said. They backed away a few steps, turned and broke into a run, full out down the street.

Cohen grabbed the young cop by the collar. "That was beautiful, just beautiful, you schmuck! Who the hell do you work for anyway? Never mind," he said, releasing him with disgust, "I don't want to know. Just hope I never run across you again."

It was getting dark, couples were strolling along Fifth Avenue, dressed to go to dinner. It was a clear, still night, warm for May. They passed a bookstore and looked at the records in the window and decided to go in. People were browsing, taking their time; it was a nice place to be. Freddie and Winter looked through the records, then went to the mystery section and began reading the jacket copy quietly to each other; reciting the plots, each topping the other's dramatizations.

"Wait—here's one: 'A lonely spinster takes to walking the streets of New York at night, looking for—'" They giggled.

"Can I help you?" A young, serious-looking salesman approached them.

"Oh—we're looking for a book for her spinster aunt who's in the hospital," Freddie said, turning her blue eyes on him.

"Does she enjoy mysteries?" he asked Winter.

"I—think so," Winter answered.

"See, she used to like to walk around the streets of New York at night—and, well, she got mugged," Freddie explained.

"Perhaps something lighter would be more appropriate," the salesman suggested.

"Uh—maybe. Is it okay if we just look?" Freddie asked, smiling warmly.

"Of course. Let me know if you need any help."

"Thank you."

Freddie noticed a man watching them. His hair had some gray in it, but he didn't look old. He was smiling at her, enjoying the joke. Freddie smiled back. He had a nice face, almost handsome. And he was wearing a beautiful jacket, camel's hair or maybe even cashmere. He walked toward them.

"Maybe you should buy her aunt a cookbook. If she got interested in cooking, it might keep her off the streets at night."

"Oh, I never thought of that! Winter, maybe she was out looking for restaurants that stayed open late or something."

"Let's see if we can find a spinster cookbook," he said. They walked over to the cookbook section. "There's every other kind . . ."

"What kind of food do spinsters like, I wonder. How about Japanese? Raw fish, and—"

"Ugh."

"*Raw* fish?"

"Yes. There's a restaurant right around the corner from here that serves it. I was on my way there. Want to see it?"

"You're kidding, aren't you?" Freddie said.

"No. They prepare it right in front of you. C'mon, I'll show you. You can see it through the window."

Winter screwed up her face. "I don't think I could look at it without getting sick."

"Yes, you can, chicken," Freddie said, pulling her toward the door.

The man laughed, walking behind them. He let them through the revolving doors first.

"Your name's Winter?" he asked. She nodded. "Pretty name."

They started down Fifth Avenue. "And what's yours?" he asked Freddie.

"My name's not so pretty," she answered. "It's Freddie." They turned the corner at Fifty-fourth.

"Neither's mine," he said. "It's Franklin. Here we are." They stopped in front of a small, brightly colored restaurant. "Now if you look in there on the left—see that counter?"

"Freddie, look! He's cutting up fish—are they really raw?"

"Want to go in?" he asked. "You can sit at the counter and watch him do it."

"No!" Winter said.

"Yes," Freddie said and led the way.

A small, friendly-looking Japanese man in a white jacket smiled and bowed at them. Then, inspired by an audience, he began slicing the fish rapidly, expertly, never missing a beat. The girls watched, wide-eyed. He sat them on small wooden planks.

"You want taste?" the small man asked, his eyes twinkling.

"I do," Freddie said.

He passed her a wooden plank with a single slice of pinkish fish wrapped around a mound of rice and decorated with a miniature paper umbrella. He gave another to Winter, then handed them each a pair of chopsticks.

Franklin ordered a sake from a pretty lady in a kimono. "How about a Coke or ginger ale—in case you need to wash that down?" he asked the girls.

They asked for Cokes and examined the fish carefully. The little umbrellas opened and closed; they toyed with them.

"You try?" the small man asked, waiting for their verdicts. "Fingers okay."

"Okay." Freddie took a deep breath. "I try." And closing her eyes, she bit into the fish. Winter waited, hers poised in midair, for Freddie's reaction. Freddie chewed slowly, eyes still tightly shut, then swallowed.

"Hey, know what? It has no taste. Really."

Winter did the same, copying Freddie's gestures. Franklin grinned, sipped his sake.

"It *doesn't* taste," Winter agreed, "but it *feels* funny."

"Well, then, don't feel it, dummy. Eat the rest," Freddie said.

The lady in the kimono brought the Cokes. "You like to order now?" she asked Franklin. He pointed to the hibachi and explained to the girls how they cooked the shrimp and steak, then showed them a beautifully arranged platter that was about to be served to the table behind them. The girls looked impressed; they hesitated only a moment, checking with each other silently, then accepted enthusiastically.

"Table or booth?" the lady asked.

"Booth, please."

Franklin sat across from the girls. The waitress brought their drinks. "What's that?" Freddie asked, pointing to the oddly shaped white porcelain bottle.

"Sake," Franklin said. "Japanese wine. It's strong. Want to taste it?" He handed her the tiny white cup, which she took and sipped.

"It's warm. I don't think it's strong. Here—try it." She passed it to Winter, who sniffed it and passed it back to Franklin without tasting it.

Freddie shook her head. "She'll never try anything."

"Unlike you," Franklin said.

"Freddie's never scared," Winter said. "I've never seen her afraid of anything."

Freddie reached over and took the sake cup back. Then she raised it and said, "I'm the Bionic Teen-ager!"

Dinner came: shrimp tempura—huge deep-fried shrimp which they picked up with their fingers—then hibachi steaks and fresh vegetables, lightly breaded and fried.

"Boy, what a good dinner!" Freddie exclaimed.

"Where do you girls have to go? Where do you live?"

Freddie smiled mischievously. "She lives in New Jersey, I live in Connecticut—or is it the other way around?"

Winter nudged Freddie with her knee and shot her a look.

Franklin glanced at them. "You must have a train to catch then."

"It's okay. We have time," Freddie said. "We might even go stay at Winter's aunt's apartment tonight."

Franklin laughed. "How old are you? No, Freddie, don't you tell me. How old are you, Winter?"

"Six—sixteen. Almost."

"Do you often come to New York alone?"

"No—"

"Do you need a place to stay tonight? My office has a couple of couches. They're quite comfortable. I could have the security guard let you in."

Freddie stood up. "Would you excuse us—we have to go to the ladies' room, okay?"

Franklin smiled. "Sure, it's right back there."

Winter got up and followed.

"Freddie, what if he's that man from the runaway squad? He's asking an awful lot of questions," Winter said in a hushed voice.

Freddie was combing her hair. "He can't be a cop. He looks too rich."

"But maybe he does this in his spare time—like for charity or something. It's possible, Freddie."

She put her comb down and turned to her. "It's also possible he wants to get us alone. Ever think of that?"

"Uh-oh. Hey, let's get out of here, okay? Freddie, please, I'm scared. Don't tease me, I really am."

Freddie was thinking. "How much money do we have?"

"Twenty dollars and thirty-five cents."

"I have an idea. You stay in here and wait for me. If it takes too long, go into the phone booth and pretend you're making a phone call. Don't come to the table, though, okay?"

"Oh, Freddie—"

"You need some more lipstick. Don't worry—"

"Where's Winter?" Franklin asked, rising as Freddie slid into the booth.

"She's still in there. Listen, Franklin—is it okay if I call you Franklin?"

He nodded, smiling a little half smile. She fastened her eyes on him and waited until she knew it was working. The half smile faded and his cheeks began to color.

Then she spoke, never taking her eyes from his, never even blinking. It was almost a whisper. "I would stay in your office because, see, I can tell you're really nice. I don't know why, but I can always tell." She reached across and touched his hand resting on the table. "You have funny hairs on the back of your hand, like my father did." She brushed her fingertips against his hands. "Look, they even stand up when I do that. Isn't that funny?" She held her hand up and spread her fingers. "Look how big your hand is compared to mine—"

He put his hand up, matching palms.

"My father said I was always going to have small hands. His

were big like yours. Winter's afraid you'll report us or something. Would you?"

"Report you for what?"

"We're not runaways or anything. We're just on vacation. We were going to stay at the Y, but the lady there wouldn't let us in alone; she must've thought we were *twelve* or something. I tried just now in the ladies' room to talk her into staying at your office. I don't know why she's so scared."

Franklin paused, then he said, "There's a YWCA a few blocks from here. I'll take you over and get you checked in."

"You will?" She jumped up and leaned across the table and kissed him on the cheek, near the mouth.

While he paid the check, Freddie went to find Winter, who was sitting in the phone booth, waiting. Her face lit up when Freddie told her the plan.

"How'd you do that?" she asked in wonder.

They passed a horse and buggy on the way. "Ooh, I want a ride in one!" Freddie cried out.

Franklin checked them in, explaining to the woman at the desk that Freddie was his niece in from out of town with her friend, and giving them both last names. He paid with his American Express card. Freddie was given his last name—Cartwright.

At the elevator Franklin gave them each ten dollars and told them he'd pick them up after work, at six o'clock, to take them for a horse and buggy ride through Central Park. Then he kissed them each goodnight, little pecks on the cheek, and started for the door.

"Wait!" Freddie called and ran to him. She stopped a moment and looked up at him, into his eyes. "I forgot to say thank you."

He looked back at her, his cheeks coloring again. "You're welcome," he said and left.

It was the first time Winter had ever been in a hotel room.

"I love it. It's the best day of my whole life."

"He really liked you," Winter said.

"Of course he did."

"How do you do that?"

"I already showed you. You have to practice, that's all."

"Show me again," Winter said.

"Okay, look." She opened her blue eyes wide, but not too

wide, and fixed Winter with a look, smiling ever so slightly. "Go ahead. Try it on me."

She tried, but couldn't keep a straight face.

"You can't laugh, dummy, or you'll spoil it!"

"I know, but I can't help it. My eyes get all watery, not blinking like that."

"Okay. Look, I'll be Franklin and I'll tell you some really boring story about my day at the office. Now you just keep looking at me. It's okay if you have to blink a little, but not too much. Okay, here we go."

Freddie crossed her legs and put them up on a chair near the bed, leaning back on her elbow. "So I said to my secretary, I said, 'Hey, honey, how 'bout comin' over here and takin' a little shorthand . . .'" She puffed on an imaginary cigar.

"You look like Groucho Marx!" Winter said. Freddie threw a pillow at her, and soon they were jumping up and down on the beds, tossing pillows at each other until the desk called to say there were complaints about the noise.

The next day Freddie and Winter got back to the Y just before six, having spent a glorious day going in and out of boutiques on the side streets in the East Sixties. Often Freddie would tell a salesperson they were waiting for her mother so they could have a little more time to examine carefully the expensive clothes. The money was used up on lunch and two pairs of pantyhose.

Franklin arrived a few minutes after six, rushing to announce that he'd hired a horse and buggy waiting outside. The girls climbed in. Franklin sat between them.

"Where would you like to go?" he asked.

"Central Park!" they shouted. "And can we go up Fifth Avenue, too?"

"No," Franklin said, "we can't go *up* Fifth, but we can go *down* Fifth."

The sun was beginning to set; a golden light shone on the trees, bounced off of the buildings on Fifth Avenue. Winter began to shiver.

"Is that the only sweater you brought?" Franklin asked.

Freddie started to take hers off to give to Winter. "She's always cold," she explained.

Franklin reached down and pulled the heavy blanket up

around them, tucking it around Winter's shoulder. "Better?" he asked. Then he pulled her closer to him, letting her snuggle against him.

"What about me?" Freddie asked.

He laughed and put his other arm around her. Freddie reached across Franklin and poked Winter, making her giggle. Then Winter reached over and tickled Freddie, who laughed. "Let's see if he's ticklish," she said and put her hand under Franklin's jacket, playing her fingers along his stomach. Winter did the same.

"Hey, come on, you two, cut it out," he said, laughing, giving them each a little poke under the ribs.

"You have a fat stomach," Freddie said teasingly. "Feel, Winter."

"I do not!" He sucked in his stomach. "Now feel."

"That's better," Freddie said, "but I bet you can't hold it in like that for long."

"Yes, I can," he said, not breathing.

"No, you can't," she said and began tickling him again until he gave in. He pulled them closer to him. Freddie whispered to Winter and ducked her head under the blanket, holding it open for Winter.

"What're you doing under there?" Franklin asked.

"Secret!" Freddie's muffled voice answered. "Look," she whispered, pointing to Franklin's pants.

"What?" Winter asked.

"Ssh. *Look*," she whispered again. Then Winter saw where Freddie was pointing, to the bulge in his pants. She stared at it in amazement.

"What're you two little squirrels up to?"

Their heads bobbed up from under the blanket. "I was showing Winter your fat stomach," she said, grinning at Winter.

Freddie kept her hand on his stomach as the buggy bumped along, through the park. Little by little her hand slipped down until it rested on his belt.

"Hey, look at that dog catching a Frisbee!" Franklin and Winter turned to see a group of boys throwing a Frisbee, a large, spotted dog chasing it and catching it in his mouth.

Freddie's hand dropped down to the hardness. She left it there.

He froze, his head still turned in the direction of the Frisbee game. Winter had swiveled all the way around in her seat to watch.

"I once saw a Golden Retriever who could body surf," Freddie said. "No kidding. Really, he'd dive right into the biggest wave and ride them in. I used to watch him every morning last summer in Atlantic City."

"Are you going there this summer?" Winter asked.

"My parents are, with my brother. But I think I may stay in New York."

Franklin was looking straight ahead now, not saying anything; not moving.

"Winter, put the blanket around you again, or you'll get cold," Freddie scolded.

She did, and Freddie reached for Winter's hand, placing it on Franklin's zipper, which was halfway down.

Winter's eyes opened wide in surprise as she felt Freddie's hand pull the zipper the rest of the way down. She looked at Franklin, whose face was flushed, almost red. He didn't look back. Then she looked at Freddie, whose expression was perfectly natural.

"What are you going to do this summer?" she asked Winter.

"I—I don't know—"

Then suddenly there it was. It was out; stiff and hard, standing straight up, the skin oddly smooth, stretched tight. Winter started to pull her hand away, but Freddie grabbed her wrist, held it and pushed her hand against the naked thing, making her feel the skin of it.

"Why don't you stay in New York with me, Winter?" She fixed Winter's fingers around it, clasped her own hand over Winter's, and forced Winter's hand up and down. Winter could feel the skin move.

He leaned his head back, helplessly, and closed his eyes. The hands moved faster, and his whole body seemed to stiffen. "Oh, God," he said, and slumped against the seat, his body limp.

Freddie released her grip on Winter's hand. Winter pulled it away. It was wet and sticky.

"Maybe we could even go to the beach one day. I'd love to see Coney Island, wouldn't you, Winter?"

*  *  *

Freddie was in the bathtub, encircled by her wet hair floating in the water. Winter sat on the closed toilet seat.

"We shouldn't have done that, Freddie. We could've gotten into trouble."

"How?"

"What if he wanted to—you know?"

"Where? In the middle of Central Park? Besides, once you do that to them, it's all they want anyway."

"Did you ever do that before?"

"Of course." Freddie stood up. "Hand me that towel, will you?" She began to dry herself, watching her reflection in the mirror. "We have the room for the rest of the week, isn't that terrific? And twenty dollars each besides."

"But what if next time . . . I mean, he might think we'll do more."

"He can think all he wants. We won't." She looked at her tiny breasts in the mirror. "We should do exercises to get bigger. Look, put your hands in front of you—like this—that's right. Now push your hands together as hard as you can. If we do this every day, by the end of the summer we'll look like Raquel Welch!"

It rained the next day; they spent the morning in Bloomingdale's and bought earrings that cost ten dollars a pair, plus tax. Then they went to the perfume counter. Freddie sampled the Tea Rose, then slipped the bottle into her bag. She phoned the Y for a message from Franklin, but there wasn't one, so they stopped and had a pizza before heading back to the Y to watch television. They were almost out of money again, but, if they were careful, it would get them through the day tomorrow.

The phone rang at ten in the morning.

"Hi!" It was Franklin. "How about lunch? Someplace special, because I don't have to come back to the office this afternoon. Be downstairs at twelve thirty, I'll pick you up."

Their spirits were high. It was a clear, sunny day, they had new earrings to wear, and they decided to ask Franklin if he'd like to buy them each a present of a new blouse. After all, if they were going to be taken to special places for lunch and dinner, they'd need something special to wear.

He was waiting in the lobby, near the entrance. He hugged them both as they stepped out of the elevator and rushed to him.

"What's all of this?" Freddie asked when she saw the shopping bag in the back of the cab.

"Surprise!" he said. "Have you ever seen a penthouse before?"

"No," they said in unison.

"You're about to. With a terrace, so you can look out across the park and see the whole city."

"Yours?" Freddie asked.

"A friend's. He's going to cook us lunch. Look what's in here"—he opened the shopping bag—"little steaks, salad makings, wine. My friend loves to cook. Wait till you see his kitchen—"

"Oh, Franklin—we can't. Not in these clothes! We've been wearing them for three days. I think we should wait till we can go home and pack some nice things, don't you, Winter?"

Winter was about to object, but Freddie shot her a look, then, smiling at him and gazing into his eyes, she said, "We'll do it another day. Ask the driver to take us back to the Y, please."

Franklin looked agitated; he said his friend had gone to some trouble to plan lunch. He looked out of the window, thinking. They were headed up Madison, in the Sixties.

"Stop," he said suddenly to the driver as he reached into his pocket for his billfold. "Do you think they'd have your size in there?" He pointed to a boutique.

"Oh, yes, I'm positive they do," Freddie said, watching him leaf through the bills. "Why don't you give us two of those." She fingered two fifties and looked at him, her eyes dancing with mischief.

He grinned at her. "Pretty expensive lunch. Shall I come in with you and help you pick something—?"

"No, you wait here and keep an eye on the groceries; we want to surprise you." She was already out of the cab. "We'll be out in a jiffy—hurry, Winter!"

Inside the boutique Winter stopped at the size-six rack, but Freddie grabbed her by the arm, pulling her to the back of the store where a saleswoman was standing.

"Excuse me, ma'am, but is there a back door?"

"Well—yes, for deliveries. Why?"

"We'd like to use it, please."

"It's kept locked—why—?"

Freddie glanced toward the street, nervously. "A—man's been following us—for blocks. He's probably waiting right outside for us now to come out and my mother's waiting for us for lunch. Maybe it's nothing, but—we were frightened."

"As well you should be. I think I should call someone and report it."

"Listen," Freddie said, panicking, "my mother gets furious when I'm late. If we could just get out the back door, we only have one more block to go—"

The saleswoman opened the door with her key. "Well, all right—if you're sure you'll be all right."

"Yes. Thank you!" she called as she scurried out the door with Winter close behind.

The alleyway led to another, then back out onto Madison.

Freddie stopped, flattened herself against the building, and held Winter back with her arm. She peeked out to look for the cab.

"Freddie, what are we doing?"

"Do you want to be trapped in some strange man's apartment?"

"Oh. No."

"In a minute he'll get out of the cab and go looking for us in the store. Be ready to run when he does. Hey—" she laughed, "know what? When he asks the saleslady about us, she'll probably call the police!"

"Oh, boy, is he going to be mad. Freddie, we've got his hundred dollars—"

"Have we got change for the bus?"

Winter searched in her pockets. "Yes."

"Okay. When he goes inside, we're going to run like hell to Fifth and get a bus downtown."

"What if he sees us?"

"There he goes—wait—now! *Run!*"

They shot out of the alley into the street, to the corner, where they turned without looking back, and ran to Fifth. A bus was just pulling away from the curb. Freddie knocked on the door until the driver opened it. "What's the matter, kids—boogie man after you?"

"Thanks," they said breathlessly and squeezed their way to the rear to look out the window.

"We made it," Freddie said and sank into a seat.

The bus stopped opposite the Plaza Hotel and they got off. The hotel seemed a good place to change the fifties, and they wanted to have a look at it anyway. It looked just as it did in the movies: flowers everywhere, musicians playing romantic violin music in the Palm Court, marble floors, and crystal chandeliers. They were certain they'd spotted at least four princes and two or three movie stars.

Freddie went to the cashier, who peered at them from behind a glass enclosure as he examined the fifty-dollar bills.

"You girls guests in the hotel?"

"No," Freddie said, "we're having lunch with my mother in there." She pointed in the direction of the Oak Room. "She just sent us out to get change—to tip the captain. We promise you it's not counterfeit."

He smiled then. "I'm sure it's not. There you are: enjoy your lunch."

That seemed like a good idea after all. They went to the Oak Room and presented themselves to the captain, changing their story slightly.

"We're meeting my father, so we'll need a table for three, please."

"Did your father call for a reservation?" the captain asked.

"I'm sure he must have. Davis is the name, John Davis."

The captain ran down the list of names in his book. "I don't have a Davis down here." The girls looked at each other, disappointed and somewhat confused. "Well, let's see what we can do," the captain said and put them at a table near the front, where they could watch for Freddie's father.

Awed by the quiet elegance of the room, they studied the menu in silence, wondering if they'd made a mistake. If they weren't careful, they could spend half their money just for lunch. The captain came by and asked them if they wouldn't like to order an appetizer while they waited. They both chose oysters on the half shell, then Freddie asked the captain where the phone was. When she came back, she mumbled something to the captain about her father being delayed in a meeting, and she would have to check back in another fifteen minutes. She sighed, shrugging her shoulders as if to say, "Oh, well, what can you do."

"But we have money, anyway," she assured him. When they'd finished their oysters, Freddie got up again.

"What're you doing?" Winter asked.

"I'm going to go find us a father."

Freddie smiled as she left the table, returning in a few minutes with an elderly gentleman with wire-rimmed glasses and gray hair. The captain greeted him, addressing him as Mr. Davis, and complimented him on his daughter's charming manners.

Mr. Bovers, a toy manufacturer in town for a convention, was hugely amused. He ordered an outrageously expensive lunch for the three of them and, as a grand finale, a flaming baked Alaska for dessert. He showed them how to play a mathematical game on the table using matchsticks and sugar cubes, then he invited them to his room to see the new dolls he'd brought to the convention that would come out in time for Christmas.

"But it's such a beautiful day," Freddie said, "and there's something Winter and I've been wanting to do ever since we got here—"

"What's that?" asked Mr. Bovers.

"Go for a ride in one of those horse and buggies," said Freddie.


"I won't, Freddie. I just won't! If we go back to the Y, Franklin might come and find us. He could be so mad, he might do something to us!"

"Winter, I'm sick of you being scared all the time. If you're such a damned baby, you shouldn't have left home in the first place!"

They were walking along Sixth Avenue, a few blocks from where the horse and buggy stopped, and they'd said good-bye to Mr. Bovers.

Freddie was angry. "Look, we had a hundred before and now we have a hundred and twenty-five. That's enough to stay in New York more than a week, if we want to. The room's paid for; he used a credit card. He can't have us thrown out. Besides, he can't even come up to the room, men aren't allowed. What's he going to do—rape us in the lobby? God, Winter!"

"He could be waiting outside or something . . ." Winter said weakly. She was trying hard not to cry, blinking the tears back, and biting down on her lip. "Look," she whimpered, showing Freddie, "I've got that stuff all over my hand again."

"Let's go into this hotel and use the ladies' room. Your eyes are all smudged anyway." They went into the International and walked through the huge, crowded lobby trying to find the ladies' room, when suddenly Freddie stopped and grabbed Winter's arm.

"Look who's here," she said.

"Who?" Winter whirled around, terrified.

"Not *him*, idiot. The pimp!"

He'd already spotted them and was coming straight toward them, grinning broadly.

"Good afternoon! See, I said I'd find you. Why, what's this? Do I see traces of tears, little sister?"

"N-no," Winter stammered.

"We were just on our way to wash our faces," Freddie said hurriedly.

"I'll show you where the ladies' room is." He put an arm around Winter's shoulder. "You have been crying, haven't you? Do you want to tell me what's wrong?" he said softly.

"Don't touch her—we know what you are!" The words were out before Freddie had a chance to stop them. She looked at him, suddenly frightened.

"Look at you—you're both upset, aren't you? Let's go sit down over there on the couch, and you can tell me what's happened." He smiled. "Come on now, it's a public place. What harm can possibly come to you here?" His voice was gentle, soothing, in its lovely, singsong accent. He was already leading Winter, who'd begun to cry again, to a couch at the far end of the lobby. Freddie followed. He sat down between them and took a snowy linen handkerchief out of his breast pocket and dabbed at Winter's eyes. Freddie watched nervously; agitated and helpless to do anything now that Winter was sobbing. The black man's arm was around her, comforting her, and Freddie couldn't see her face.

"You're—a—you're a—pimp—" Winter said, in between sobs.

He threw back his head and laughed. "Where did you get such an idea? How do you even know about such things?"

"A lady—a—prostitute told us—and so did a—"

"*Winter*—" Freddie glared at her, stopping her.

"It's all right. Let me show you who I am." He took a wallet out of his breast pocket and gave them each a card. They looked at it: "Tommy Thomas, Fashion Photographer." Underneath the name was a phone number and an address on Park Avenue.

"Does that name mean anything to you?" he asked.

They shook their heads. "I thought not. In this business only the models get famous, the photographer's name is written in very small letters. You know who Twiggy is? Or perhaps you were too young to remember when she was really at her peak?"

"I remember," Freddie said.

"So do I."

"Well, I did her first cover—in this country. Since then I've been doing work mainly for the young magazines, like *Seventeen, Mademoiselle*—in fact, guess who I'm meeting here in"—he looked at his watch—"fifteen minutes. Provided she isn't her usual tardy self, that is. Skippy. Skippy Addams."

He waited for their reaction. "You'll recognize her when you see her. She's on the cover of at least one magazine a month, and she's got five television commercials going now. That's why I was watching you two. You're incredible types, do you know that? I have an assignment from *Seventeen* coming up, and they've been begging me to find some fresh, new faces for their August back-to-school issue, and while it may not be as dramatic as pimps and prostitutes—" He laughed again. "Well, I just wanted to have another look at you." He patted Winter on the head. "I hardly expected to find you in tears. Go wash up now, I want you to look pretty when Skippy comes. I'd like to see what she thinks."

They got up and walked, as if hypnotized, through the lobby to the ladies' room.

He was still sitting there when they came out. But now there was a breathtakingly stunning girl sitting beside him, talking to him in an intimate, engrossed sort of way, leaning toward him and resting her hand on his arm. He must have already told her about them, because she looked up as Freddie and Winter came walking out. Her hair was white-blond and hung straight, well below her shoulders, with a shaggy fringe of bangs that came right to her eyes, almost brushing her thick, black lashes when she looked up.

She was pencil thin and the way she was sitting, one arm stretched along the back of the sofa, the other reached over to him, her long legs crossed in front of her at an angle, she looked as if she must have floated down from somewhere and landed, like a long, silk handkerchief, beside Tommy.

He stood to introduce them. Her name wasn't Skippy, it was Candy. Skippy, she said, was shooting a shampoo commercial, and God knows what time they'd finish. As soon as she spoke, her one imperfection showed; a front tooth that was slightly chipped, reminding Freddie immediately of the famous model,

Lauren Hutton, who never bothered to have the gap between her front teeth fixed. Maybe it made them seem more normal.

They'd probably seen Candy dozens of times in magazines; they were sure they had.

She got up, and incredibly she stood every bit as tall as Tommy. All around them people were stopping to look at her. Freddie and Winter flushed and smiled, caught accidentally in her golden spotlight.

"Tommy, why don't we go over there?" She pointed to the promenade at the other end of the lobby where there were sofas arranged around little tables. "So we can have a drink."

She led the way, walking quickly, taking long steps that Freddie and Winter had to hurry to keep up with. Freddie grabbed Winter's arm to whisper, "Bet everyone's wondering who we are too."

Candy sat down and took a long, brown cigarette out of her bag and waited while Tommy lit it with his gold lighter. She was wearing a black halter dress, cut low so that when she bent forward, most of her breast showed. Her shoulders and arms had a glossy tan, as did her legs, but interestingly, there didn't seem to be the usual white bathing-suit lines anywhere on her chest. Freddie wondered if Winter had seen that too, when Candy bent over.

"Candy, order the girls a Shirley Temple," Tommy said. "I've got to make a phone call. And a split of champagne for us."

When he'd gone, Candy smiled at Freddie and Winter. "Did you really ask Tommy if he was a pimp?"

They both blushed. Freddie answered, "No—I mean—some lady saw us talking to him and she told us—terrible things—"

"Where was that?"

"At a coffee shop on Eighth Avenue. And she said she'd call the runaway squad if she ever saw us around there again."

"I bet she called that cop too," Winter said.

"We almost got arrested!" Freddie said, suddenly pleased with the way it sounded.

"What did she look like?" Candy asked.

"She was fat and wore a wig—"

"And false eyelashes," Winter added. "Huge ones."

"Did she look around forty?"

"At least!"

"A dark wig, with bangs?"

"Yes," Winter said. "Do you know her?"

She nodded. "Sounds like Big Alice. Poor thing, she's really"— Candy tapped a long fingernail to her head—"out to lunch. Her father has the newsstand there on Forty-eighth where all the pimps and hookers hang out, and I think he must bring her with him to keep an eye on her or something. Anyway she's been around there so long, she imagines she's a prostitute and every man she sees is a pimp. She's always calling up the cops. They all know her, and I guess they feel sorry for her, but—boy, someone ought to put that lady in the funny farm, going around scaring little kids like that."

She held her hand out to stop a waiter and ordered their drinks.

She told them how lucky they were that Tommy was interested in them. "He's the most wonderful, generous man in the whole world. We all adore him." Then she paused, drawing on her cigarette. "He said you were all upset when he saw you tonight. Is that what upset you?"

Freddie and Winter hesitated, uncertain whether or not to tell her. Winter spoke out. "It was me. I was afraid to go back to the Y because the man who got us the room—paid for it for a week— gave us a whole lot of money, and we ran away from him."

Candy held her hand out to slow Winter down. "Wait a minute. You ran out on him after he paid you? No wonder you're scared, you should be."

"He didn't pay us. He gave us money to buy clothes with," Freddie said, a bit indignantly.

Candy raised her eyebrows and shrugged, perfectly willing to dismiss the subject.

"What do you think we should do?" Winter asked.

"I think you should tell Tommy. He'll know what you should do." She looked at Freddie. "You know, I wasn't much older than you when I came to New York. I lived in a hole-in-the-wall town upstate, and I didn't know anyone here. I didn't know where to go. See, I wasn't a runaway, I was a throwaway. When I was thirteen, my mother gave me a hundred dollars and told me to get out. Her boyfriend used to like to watch me when I was taking a bath, and she caught him once. Of course, she said it was my fault.

"Anyway, it was Tommy who took care of me and taught me how to dress. But most of all, he taught me that I wasn't the worthless piece of garbage my mother made me feel like I was."

Freddie stole a glance at Winter, who was listening, hanging on every word, infatuation showing all over her face. What a nerd, Freddie thought.

There was another man with Tommy when he came back. He was a nice-looking man, a little like Franklin. When he got closer they both noticed what a smooth, pink complexion he had, almost like a baby's. He seemed to know Candy very well. She got up to kiss him. Tommy introduced him to Freddie and Winter. His name was Mr. Blue and, Tommy explained, he was an editor of *Seventeen*, the one in charge of selecting the girls who would appear in the August issue.

"So these are your new discoveries," he said. Freddie and Winter held their breath as he looked them over, appraising them carefully. Even Freddie stammered when he asked them questions.

"I have an idea," he said, "why don't we all have dinner, and afterward maybe I could persuade Tommy to take some test shots of you. If you're willing, of course."

Willing! Neither Freddie nor Winter could manage a bite of food, they were so nervous. Tommy ordered another bottle of champagne and let the girls each have a glass. Candy proposed a toast to their new careers, and Freddie reached over and grabbed Winter's hand, squeezing it tightly. Winter smiled at Freddie, beamed at her, thinking how it was all just like in the movies. A fairy tale come true. How she'd love to be able to see Dorothy's face the first time her picture was in a magazine, only she wouldn't. Winter never wanted to see any of them again. And now she wouldn't have to.

She came out of her champagne reverie and saw Freddie looking at Tommy with a curious frown. She was asking him why they weren't going to his studio on Park Avenue to take the pictures.

"Because, beautiful," he said, "Mr. Blue already has everything all set up in a hotel suite around the corner."

"Where?" she asked.

Winter wished Freddie would stop asking so many questions before they changed their minds.

"Right here on Forty-eighth Street. If the magazine's going to use you, they'll have to have the test shots right away."

Freddie grew quiet. After a moment she put her napkin on the table and started to get up. "Well," she said, "Winter and I better go to the ladies' room and fix ourselves up then."

Mr. Blue put his hand on her arm. "I've got everything you need there, and Candy can put your makeup on. She's an expert."

"Sure," Candy said. "I'd be happy to."

"Thanks," Winter said. "That's really nice."

"I have to go to the ladies' room anyway. Come with me, Winter."

"Hey," Mr. Blue said, with a little laugh, "that's not very nice, to have both my guests leave at once."

"That's okay," Winter said quickly. "I don't have to go."

Freddie just stood there, fixing Winter with her stare. "But I need her to help me with something." Winter didn't catch it. She was smiling at Mr. Blue.

"I'll come with you, Freddie. I need to powder my nose too." Candy excused herself and got up.

Mr. Blue poured Winter more champagne while Tommy called for the check. "You know, Winter," Mr. Blue said, "you're both beautiful. But of the two of you, you have the more interesting face. More unusual, don't you think, Tommy?"

The waiter came right away with the check. "Uh-huh, I do," he said as he handed the waiter a hundred-dollar bill. Mr. Blue went on studying Winter's face, holding her chin and tilting it slightly. She blushed, noticing that people at another table were watching. "In fact—you know, Tommy, I'd like to try something —with the lighting on her. Why don't we start over there now, because it may take a little longer—"

Tommy was already on his feet. "What about Freddie?" Winter asked.

"Candy'll bring her over. She knows where it is. C'mon, little star, never keep beginnings waiting; they don't come that often."

Winter kept looking back over her shoulder as they walked through the lobby to the front door to search for Freddie, hoping she'd come out in time to go with them.

"They'll catch up," Tommy said. But they were walking fast, west on Fiftieth Street, then down two blocks to Forty-eighth.

The hotel looked awful; run-down and dirty on the outside

and even worse in the lobby. It was badly lit, and paint was peeling from the walls. And not a soul was around, except the desk clerk, who never looked up as they walked to the elevator. Winter didn't like it. She wished they'd waited for Freddie.

"This city's really going to the dogs," Mr. Blue said as they got into the elevator. "This used to be a great little hotel years ago. A lot of actors and actresses stayed here. It's very convenient, right in the middle of the theater district. I've kept a suite in this hotel for I don't know how long . . ." He kept up a steady stream of talk all the way to the fourteenth floor.

Winter tried to hide her disappointment. Why would such an important man choose such an awful place to work in? She wondered what Freddie was going to say when she saw it. The suite was at the end of the hall, fourteen-oh-six. Mr. Blue took out his key, then he said to Tommy, "You open it, I want to carry the star over the threshold." Winter tried a feeble laugh as he picked her up and carried her inside.

She heard the door lock behind them, and then the lights went on. He put her down, and she looked around. It was worse than the lobby; dirtier. Unwashed glasses everywhere, stains and cigarette burns on the carpet, the sofa was torn and one of the cushions was missing. But worse than that, there was a terrible, sickly sweet smell in the room. Smoke was coming from the adjoining room where, she could see from where she was standing, bright lights were blazing. She coughed.

"Christ, why don't you guys at least open a window?" he called into the next room. Then he threw the window open all the way. "What the hell are they smoking in there anyway? They can afford better than that. How's that? Better, Winter?"

She nodded, hating the place, hating the whole thing suddenly. Even Tommy and Mr. Blue. They didn't notice though. Tommy went to the open door. "How's it going? Almost ready?"

"Another ten minutes and we will be," a younger man's voice answered.

There were bottles and ice on a card table. Tommy took the dirty glasses into the bathroom. "I think Winter ought to have a drink, to relax," he said over the sound of water running. "Models always work better when they're relaxed."

"No. No, thanks, I don't want one. I—I'm starting to get a headache. Maybe—"

"Just nerves. Everyone's nervous the first time." He handed her the glass.

"What's that?" she asked.

"Water. Here, swallow this. It'll make you feel better and take away your headache."

"I—"

Mr. Blue smiled at her. "Winter, my sweet, by tomorrow your whole life will be different. You've just got opening-night nerves, that's all. Take that and wash it down with the water, then you'll be able to have a drink and relax, and you'll sparkle for the camera."

She closed her eyes and put the pill in her mouth and gagged on it. It tasted bitter. They were waiting. She tried again and this time it went down. "Why isn't Freddie here yet?"

"She's probably got Candy talking her head off. They'll be here soon. How do you feel?"

"Okay—I guess."

Mr. Blue went into the other room and came back with the missing cushion. He put it on the couch. "Here, honey, why don't you stretch out a few minutes, until they're ready."

"No—I'm fine. Really." She was beginning to feel strange. Warm and fuzzy, sort of. Mr. Blue was walking her to the couch. Not really walking, though, because she couldn't feel the floor.

Her head was at one end of the couch, her feet at the other, but over Mr. Blue's lap. How did his lap get there? He was stroking her legs. His hand was warm, but it felt strange, as though the skin on her leg wasn't her skin; yet it had to be, it was on her leg.

"We're ready in here," a voice called out.

"Good, we're ready in here too." And he was carrying her in his arms. She didn't weigh very much, she thought. Then there were lights, blinding, so that all she could see was Mr. Blue's face smiling at her. He was saying something but there were other voices at the same time, so she couldn't tell what he was saying.

He put her down on something soft, that she sank into. Funny patterns on the ceiling. Wiggly lines. She tried to figure out what they were.

Hands on her. Underneath her skirt, pulling at her panties. "No!" They were doing that to her again, forcing her legs apart. The nurse would put them in those steel things again. So cold.

She felt her arms. They were bare. Why was she naked?

"She's making too much noise. Joey! Come here." A hand clamped down over her mouth. Black. She wrenched her head away and bit into it, as hard as she could.

"Goddamn! The little bitch!" She was being held by her hair. A sudden sharp pain on her face, blinding her for a second. Then another.

She heard a noise from far away. A hammering, getting louder and louder. Freddie's voice, calling her. Thank God. Oh, thank God, Freddie. The hands were gone and she could scream out to her. She raised her head, and with all the strength she had, she screamed.

Freddie screamed back, "Winter! Where is she! No—get away! No!" Then a horrible fading scream. Then nothing.

# PART 3

"wood?" shawna was shaking him gently. He'd fallen asleep in the chair. "Wood, I don't like the way she's breathing. She might need to be in a hospital."

Wood got up to look at her. Her face had become pale, and there was a bluish tinge to her lips. Shawna felt her pulse. "It's slow," she said and felt her face. "Fever's down." Then she called softly to her. The child lay still.

She folded the covers down. "What're you doing?" Wood asked. Shawna was pressing lightly, with just a little pressure, on her stomach and diaphragm. "Checking for injuries . . . abdomen's soft." She put the covers back over her, then bent over her face and carefully lifted each eyelid. "Pupils are the same size, no sign of concussion. I don't understand it. Five minutes ago she was breathing normally. Then suddenly it became very shallow."

"What could that mean?"

"The color, the weak, slow pulse, the breathing, are symptoms of shock, generally. Do you have another blanket?"

He went to get one. She called Winter's name again. This time Winter's eyes flew open. She stared out, unseeing, and then a howl like that of a trapped baby animal pierced the silence, filled the room.

Shawna gathered her into her arms and held her there, letting the child scream into her breast. Quickly Wood wrapped the extra blanket around Winter's shoulders and watched helplessly, her screams ripping into him.

Shawna began to murmur to her, soft cooing sounds, as though to an infant. Gradually the screams began to subside and she was breathing again, gasping occasionally, sudden, sharp gasps that caught her and made her shiver.

"Winter, you can cry if you want. I'll hold you as long as you like, just like this, and you can let them go—all the tears inside you. You can give them all to me now. That's right, just pretend you're a little baby and you're safe and warm in a special, private place all your own where you can let all the tears out." She kept on crooning to her, rocking her, cuddling her.

Wood looked at Shawna. Her eyes were moist. She lowered her head and kissed Winter's brow tenderly, and the child's sobs became rhythmic. Finally they subsided. Winter's arms were wound around Shawna's waist tightly. She clung to her. "Mama," she whispered, "they hurt me."

"I know. That's all over now. No one will ever, ever hurt you again," she answered softly.

Wood went to the window and stood staring out into the desolation, all the mindless wreckage out there in the starless, black night.

It was after midnight. Winter had taken some soup, finally. Chicken noodle with an egg in it. She watched Shawna constantly, never taking her eyes off her, and smiled at her once or twice shyly.

"I'm on duty tomorrow, Wood." She looked over at Winter, then she said, "I think I'll call in sick." But she was beginning to look tired.

"You take my bed, in there. I'll sleep on the couch."

Winter moved all the way over to the edge of the daybed, making herself very small. "I don't take up much room, Shawna. Hardly any." It was the first time she'd said her name. She patted the space beside her. Shawna smiled and asked Wood if he had an extra bathrobe, then she looked at Winter, eyeing her cautiously. "You don't snore, do you?"

Wood lay awake most of the night. The few times he drifted into sleep, he awoke with a start, catching himself on the brink of a nightmare.

In the morning Shawna suggested taking Winter home with her. She was in need of a change of clothes, and Winter was well enough now to be moved. The fever was gone; she was just weak and very fragile. Wood took them in the car.

When he got back to his apartment, he replaced the phone on the hook, waited a minute to make sure it was working, then called Danahy. He and Halsey were on their way to New Jersey to talk to Freddie's parents.

"I want to come," he said.

Danahy hesitated.

"Look, I think I can be of help. Winter said a few things that might make it all come together. Jack, it's crazy not to use me— you've got nothing now. Maybe they'll say something that'll fit with something Winter said, and we can put some pieces together."

"You think you can sit there and keep your mouth shut? It's absolutely—"

"—against regulations. Hey, I'm the guy they all complain about being noncommunicative."

"How would I know? I was never married to you. I'll pick you up in twenty minutes. You did get us the identification on the girl. I guess we owe you for that. Now what about the other one —Winter?"

"I'll tell you when I see you."


Halsey was driving. Wood got in the back, setting his camera bag down on the seat beside him.

"What d'you think you're doing?" Danahy said. "They were just notified yesterday; they're not going to let you take pictures."

"You never know. Who identified the body?"

"The father—and an aunt. We have to go over to the ME's office first before we go to Jersey. You should come in with us— something I think you should hear. I mean as long as you're putting yourself in the position of withholding evidence—"

"I'm not—"

"You're concealing a witness, aren't you?"

"She's not a witness. Not a reliable one anyway. The kid was sick and delirious all day yesterday. I couldn't make any sense out of anything she said. That's why I wanted to hear what Freddie's family had to say, to see if I could put any of it together."

"Where's the girl now?"

"A friend's taking care of her."


As they walked up the steps to the entrance, Halsey asked Wood if he'd ever been to the Morgue before. Wood said he hadn't.

"Oh. We'll have to arrange a tour for you then."

"That's all right. Thanks anyway."

It was a modern, six-story building with a facade of blue and white glazed bricks and wide glass doors that opened into the outer lobby, where comfortable chrome and vinyl-upholstered chairs were arranged in groups.

The first thing to catch the visitor's eye was a marble wall eighteen feet long, with an inscription, written in Latin, that ran across the length of it in small, evenly spaced brass letters: TACEAT COLLOQUIA. EFFUGIAT RISUS. HIC LOCUS EST UBI MORS GAUDET SUCCURRERE VITAE.

Wood stopped to look at it. "How's your Latin?" Danahy asked.

Wood made an attempt. "Let talking—stop. Let laughter—?"

"'Let conversation cease. Let laughter flee. This is the place where death delights to help the living,'" Danahy read aloud. "My seminary days weren't a total waste."

Wood nodded. "It's good that's up there. Otherwise people would be sitting around here talking and laughing their heads off."

They walked through an efficient-looking business office where they were greeted by a well-dressed, attractive black woman who, with a brisk smile, directed them past the communications room, with its several streamlined desks and telephones, to the administrative offices at the end of the hall.

"Are you sure we're in the right place?" Wood asked as they passed another series of office cubicles for typists and stenographers.

A young man in a suit and tie admitted them into the office of the chief medical examiner and explained that Dr. Auslander would be with them in a moment. It was a spacious office, with large windows facing north. The walls were painted a dark, semishiny brown that set off the framed drawings that hung over the couch. Wood put on his glasses to look at them. Original Hogarths, titled, "The Four Stages of Cruelty." The last was of a boy killing a dog. The rest of the drawings were courtroom scenes, famous trials, at which the chief medical examiner had testified. A highly polished oak desk dominated the room, a tall leather chair behind it. Except for the bare floor it was an office befitting any executive of any large corporation.

Halsey was seated on the couch, Danahy on the chair facing the desk. They stood when the doctor came in. He was a small, birdlike man. He greeted them in a soft German accent and offered them a diet soda, which he got for himself out of a little refrigerator mounted into the bookcase.

Putting a straw in the can of Fresca, he went to his desk and pulled out a folder marked, "CUPPI—Frederica Charles."

"This is the case you wanted to talk to me about? Let's see . . ." He began to read, ". . . fracture of skull, legs, and arms. Contusions of brain. Intermeningeal hemorrhage, lacerations of lung, liver, aorta, heart, and spleen. Fall from height. Circumstances undetermined pending police investigation."

Wood sat in the chair next to Danahy's. "I was curious, Doctor, about how many deaths a year do you get resulting from a fall from height?"

"I'm not very good at statistics, but I would take a guess—three to four hundred. I could have someone check for you and tell you exactly."

Wood nodded appreciatively. "Of them, how many would you guess were homicides?"

"Less than one percent. Ninety percent are jumpers, the rest, accidents."

"All classified as CUPPI's?"

Auslander sucked on his straw. "Yes."

Danahy's eyes were fixed on the drawings on the wall over the sofa. Halsey was watching with interest.

"So if I wanted to kill someone, throwing them out of a window would be a pretty good way."

"As good a way as there is." He smiled at Danahy. "Your friend writing a mystery?"

Danahy rubbed at his chin. "He seems to be in the process of creating one," he said.

"Well, injuries resulting from a fall from height will look exactly the same whether the person jumped or was pushed—or accidentally fell. The person could have been struck on the head and rendered unconscious, then thrown out of a window, and that injury would still be consistent with all the others sustained by the body hitting the ground. The same would apply to almost any bruises." He tapped a well-manicured finger on the folder in front of him. "This—Charles girl could have been beaten to death first and we'd have no way of telling."

"That's interesting," Wood said quietly.

Danahy looked at Halsey and closed his eyes as Auslander went on.

"Unless we find something like what we have here—" he reached down to the bottom drawer and took out another folder. "Female, white, sixteen years old," he said, "fell from the roof of an apartment building, nineteen stories—this is my autopsy protocol." He waved the paper in the air. "Except that she was strangled first, which we could see immediately from the hemorrhaging in her eyes. This case was classified homicide. It's going to trial next week. But here the cause of death was strangulation, not fall from height. The murderer, or perpetrator as the men like to say, might just as easily have buried the body in the backyard as thrown it off the rooftop."

Wood turned to Danahy and Halsey. "Shame Freddie wasn't strangled first. She'd be classified a homicide and you guys would be working on Department time. Gus, there were signs of a struggle in the hotel room, weren't there?"

"Yes," he answered, "but not in the living room where the window was wide open. We found signs of a violent struggle in the adjoining bedroom, where the windows were sealed shut because of the air-conditioner."

"It doesn't matter anyway," Auslander said, sipping the last of his soda and buckling the can in half. "The samples of blood found on the bed were not the same type as that of the victim." He referred back to the Charles folder. "We also found traces of fresh semen on the bed, strands of hair that had been pulled out by the roots—"

"What color hair?" Wood asked tightly.

"Dark, almost black. Negroid. About twelve inches in length. It's my opinion that whomever that hair belongs to was brutally beaten and raped."

"Is it also your opinion, judging from the freshness of the blood and semen stains, that the rape and the death might have taken place at the same time?"

"Very likely. Yes."

Wood leaned forward in his chair. His hands were clasped together, resting on his knees. "Dr. Auslander, if you were a detective instead of a physician, wouldn't you have to figure something—pretty *heavy* was going on in that hotel room?"

Auslander snorted. "Of course. That's why—"

Wood moved closer. "I mean, I realize you don't want to dismiss the possibility that the little girl might have tripped over the corner of the rug trying to get to the window for a breath of fresh air and fell out accidentally. Or that she may have gotten suddenly depressed that her friend was in the next room being raped and decided to commit suicide—"

"That's exactly why I classified it a CUPPI. The circumstances are undetermined!"

"*Undetermined*, hell! You're classifying it *unimportant!*"

Auslander looked at his watch. "Gentlemen, I'm due downstairs. If you'd care to walk along with me, I'm willing to continue this interesting discussion." He stood and walked briskly to the door, Wood close behind him. Halsey and Danahy exchanged looks.

"Shee-it," Halsey said under his breath.

Wood walked beside Auslander as they headed down the hall toward the stairs. "But you're not a detective, you're a doctor." He jerked his thumb behind him at Danahy and Halsey. "*They're* the detectives—why should a doctor be allowed to speculate on the circumstances of death instead of just the *causes*, when they're the ones who're trained and have the experience to find out?"

They were halfway down the stairs and Auslander was quickening his pace. There were a pair of stainless steel swinging doors at the bottom of the stairs. Wood was aware of the faint smell of something that he connected with a veterinary hospital.

"Mr. Wood, I am a trained specialist in forensic pathology and considered by my colleagues to be a leading expert in my field. My opinions and testimony are sought by criminal lawyers all over the country." His hand was on the door. "And you're trying to tell me that a detective with a high school education and the ability to get three out of five questions right on a multiple choice test is better qualified than I?"

Wood looked to see where Danahy and Halsey were. They were just starting down the stairs.

Auslander pushed the doors open. "Not squeamish, are you?"

It was a huge room, perhaps thirty feet wide, tiled, immaculate, with bright overhead lights, sparkling stainless steel. Wood's nostrils were filled with a cool, sweet-sour odor mixed with strong disinfectant that stung his eyes for a moment.

Then suddenly he was looking at four naked bodies. Not four; five, counting a tiny child not more than two years old, but he looked away quickly, his mind refusing to see it. One woman, three men, all lying face up on stainless-steel tables. Scales, the type used in grocery stores, hung suspended over each table. He counted three more empty tables.

Auslander had walked over to where three men clad in green operating-room gear were standing, huddled around one of the tables. Wood seemed to want to count everything, to remember the numbers seemed important.

Halsey and Danahy had come in. Halsey said, "Think we're in the right place now?"

"They're not real, are they, Gus? I mean they're wax dummies they use to practice on—right?"

The needle on the scale moved as one of the doctors placed a soft, pinkish-gray object on it. Something weighed fourteen hundred grams.

"Listen," Wood said, "I'll meet you outside."

"Mr. Wood?" Auslander called without looking up. "Leaving so soon—I'd hoped we'd have more time to talk."

"Yes. Me too. Some other time, Doctor." As he turned to go, he spotted out of the corner of his eye something on the floor underneath the body on the last table at the far end of the room. He looked. It was a dog, lying on a towel. He bolted. Halsey was right behind him. "You okay, Wood?" he asked.

"Yeah. Fine. Just don't tell me about that dog in there, all right? I'll see you in the car."

They were headed south on the New Jersey Turnpike. Danahy turned to Wood. "Hey, I'm sorry about that. I swear I didn't know he was going into the Autopsy Room."

Halsey looked at Wood in the rearview mirror. "When they say 'downstairs' around there, you gotta ask them what's down there before you go."

"You know why they had that dog in there?" Dahany said.

"Oh, shit." Wood dropped his head down into his hands.

"The man had been dead several days before the body was found. His genitals were gone. The ME got permission from the ASPCA to put the dog to sleep so they could do an autopsy—to determine whether the man had been mutilated by someone, or if the dog, as often happens in cases like that, was starving and—"

"Hey, for Christ's sake, Danahy!"

"What's the matter, Wood? You wanted in on the investigation, didn't you? Or did you just want to come along for the car chases?"

They'd come to the town of Hillside. Halsey slowed down, looking for street signs.

Wood was sitting back, thinking. "So once the ME decides a case is a CUPPI—" Danahy cut in. "Only thing that can upgrade it to a homicide is a collar. How come you never knew that before?"

"I was wondering that myself."

"Good. You learned something today."

"Yeah—never to go anywhere with you guys before lunch."

The house was set back from the street, surrounded by neatly clipped hedges, and separated from the other houses by a well-manicured lawn. Ranch-style suburban homes, built in the sixties, Wood guessed.

"What about Auslander's findings in the bedroom? Any of that fit with what the other girl told you?" Danahy asked as they walked up the path to the door.

"She didn't tell me anything. But it does fit."

"Doesn't look like Freddie was doin' it for the money," Halsey said.

Cars were parked in front of the Charleses' house, six or seven of them, all fairly new.

"Looks like we might be walking into a wake."

"You've been in the Department so long, Halsey, you think all honkies are Catholic," Danahy said.

Mr. Charles opened the door. He was a small man, older than Wood expected, fifty perhaps, and there was something about him that was soft, almost diffused. His eyes were reddened. He looked at the three men, puzzled.

Danahy spoke. "We're police officers, sir, from New York Homicide. I'm Sergeant Danahy, this is Halsey and Wood. May we have a moment of your time?"

"Homicide?" He sounded as though he didn't understand the word.

"Yes. Since we were called in, we have to make a report. Just a few routine questions."

"We have friends here. Do you think it would be all right to just say you're police officers, not—"

"Of course."

"Come in. We'll go into the den. I'll tell Pearl to excuse herself . . ."

The den was just off the entrance hall opposite the living room. Wood hung back to get a look. There were eight or ten people in the room, talking in subdued tones. Their attention seemed to be fixed on a pretty, blond woman dressed in black, sitting in a large wing chair. Another woman was passing a tray of drinks and sandwiches. The one in the wing chair had to be Mrs. Charles. Even from a distance Wood could see Freddie's face in hers. He stopped a moment, a peculiar sensation coming over him. *He'd never seen Freddie's face.*

"In here, Wood." Danahy touched his arm.

The den, like the living room, looked like a page out of *House & Garden.* The furniture was color coordinated and carefully arranged; bird and animal prints in matching frames were symmetrically hung on the walls.

A boy in his early twenties was standing across the room talking on the phone. He had dark blond hair, fashionably long without being hippie length, and clear blue eyes. He was tall, a good athlete's body, evident even in the way he stood; straight, yet at the same time relaxed. His face was finely carved, strong. Strangely aristocratic, Wood thought, for this family. He turned around when he noticed Wood studying him and continued talking into the phone.

"Sit down, won't you? Would you like anything? Coffee or—a drink?"

"No, thanks, Mr. Charles," Danahy said.

"My name's Arthur. That's Michael, my son, home from college. He'll be off the phone in a minute . . ."

Arthur Charles, Wood noticed, never completed a thought. His words seemed to trail off in mid-sentence. "I'll go tell Pearl . . ."

Danahy was staring at an eight-by-ten framed photograph of Freddie that was centered over the fireplace. He looked at Wood, who'd seen it too. It was a recent one, the kind taken for a school yearbook. She was smiling into the camera; a warm, infectious smile that shone in her eyes. She was looking directly into the lens, making contact with it, in a way very few people, including models and film actors, know how to do. There was nothing affected about the picture, though; the girl was a natural.

Except for that, the resemblance to Donnie was frightening.

He moved closer, putting on his glasses to get a better look. Something else was different; a knowingness behind the eyes. Jesus Christ, he thought, as he felt his stomach muscles knot, it was sexual.

He was suddenly aware of someone standing behind him. He turned.

"Pretty, wasn't she?"

The boy was looking at the picture with hard, cold eyes. "She was also a superb liar. Would have made the master criminal of all time. Too bad she died." He started out of the room.

Danahy stopped him. "Wait a minute, we'd like to talk to you. You're Michael, aren't you?"

"Yes, and I'm a first-year law student at Rutgers, which means I've learned just enough to know I'm in no way obligated to talk to you. Besides, I've already told you everything you need to know about my sister. Excuse me," he said politely and left the room.

There was a stunned silence.

A moment later Mrs. Charles came in. Tall and erect, almost but not quite beautiful, and as cold and self-assured as her son, she stood looking at them, stony faced. Quite a pair for Arthur Charles to handle, Wood thought. And where, he wondered, did Freddie fit in.

Arthur came up beside her to introduce the men to her. She registered no surprise, nor did she step forward to shake hands when they rose to their feet.

"Please sit down. Arthur, do ask someone to bring them coffee."

"They said they didn't want any." She ignored him, and he went anyway.

"We're terribly sorry to have to come at such a difficult time," Danahy said.

She shrugged. "I guess they have to give you people something else to do besides write parking tickets." She sat in a chair, her legs crossed. "How can I help you?"

"Actually it's more like we're here to help you," Halsey said. "To find out what happened to your daughter."

She turned and looked at Halsey, staring at him in a way designed to discomfit him. It worked. He lowered his eyes, studying the pattern on the rug.

"We know what happened to her. She committed suicide."

It angered Danahy, the way she looked at Halsey. "We're investigating the possibility of a homicide," he said.

She paused. "I see."

Good going, Danahy, Wood said to himself. Hit her again.

He did. "When did Freddie first begin staying away from home?"

"Frederica's her name, not Freddie. She didn't—I mean—we didn't know about it. We were on a trip at the time. We work very hard, Arthur and I, to give the children all this"—she raised her hand in a gesture to include the house and its furnishings—"and badly needed a vacation. Michael, of course, was away at school."

An old lady came into the room balancing a tray unsteadily. She set it down on the coffee table, toppling the cream pitcher over on top of the sandwiches. Distressed, she tried to mop it up with the corner of her apron. Wood reached over to help her. She peered at him through thick bifocals and smiled nervously, uncertainly.

"It's all right, Mother, just leave it," Mrs. Charles said, her voice edged with impatience.

"I'm sorry," she mumbled, "I'll get some more." They watched her as she walked out of the room, reaching out to touch things for balance.

"Who stayed with Frederica while you were away?" Danahy asked. He already knew the answer.

"She did, my mother. She always lived with us."

Danahy nodded, then having made his point, pulled back a little. She was on the defensive now, he could get on with the questions.

Frederica had been a model child and a straight-A student up until a few months ago. Her grades began to fall off, and she began staying home from school sometimes, in the mornings. She baby-sat for the principal of the school, whose wife was in the hospital for an extended period of time. Some serious illness, she had heard. He often stayed at the hospital late, leaving Frederica with the twins, who were two years old and very difficult. She could never get them to go to sleep.

"We let her do it, though, because she was trying to save money—she had her heart set on taking dramatic lessons this summer."

Arthur had come back into the room in time to hear her last statement. His eyes clouded, and he looked away, his mouth trembling.

"Excuse me," Wood said. "Is there a bathroom I could use?"

"Of course. Arthur, show the young man where the powder room is."

Mr. Charles led him out into the hall, to a door at the foot of the stairs. It was locked. "Someone must be using it," he said. "There's one upstairs, first door to your left."

"Thanks."

"Wait a second. Can I give you something? I didn't want Pearl to see this." He pulled a soiled white envelope out of his pocket. "It came to our hotel in Bermuda just a few days before— addressed to both of us. Look at it later; you can keep it. Just make sure Pearl doesn't see it, please."

At the top of the stairs Wood opened the envelope. Inside was a black and white picture of Freddie, fully made-up, her hair curled in long ringlets around her face. She was standing in front of a theater marquee, not looking at the camera. The picture was obviously taken without a flash, since the light from the theater was more than adequate, and with a telephoto lens, since there was not the graininess in it of an enlargement. In the background, and partially out of the picture, was a well-dressed man who looked to be in his forties, and beside him, with just a tiny portion of her face showing, was Winter. The picture was pasted on a piece of paper. Underneath were the words: "Do You Know Where Your Children Are?" cut out of a newspaper and Scotch-taped on. Wood put the picture in his pocket and was about to go into the bathroom when he noticed the door on his right was ajar. He caught a glimpse of pink and white ruffles at the bottom of a bed. He opened the door further; then checking that no one was in the hall, he slipped into the room and closed the door behind him. It was Freddie's room.

Very quickly he went to the windows and raised the shades all the way to the top. The light was good. Using the miniature Minolta he'd taken out of his camera bag and put into his pocket before he got out of the car, he began shooting. The four-poster canopied bed with the matching ruffles, the small vanity table, the desk. It was painted white; on it was a framed photograph of her brother and another of Freddie and her brother together. He was in football uniform, she was on his shoulders, her arms raised in victory. He took a picture of the cork bulletin board above her desk, covered with magazine cutouts of teen-aged fashion models.

Her vanity table was crowded with tiny jars and bottles of cosmetics, perfumes, and an array of makeup brushes. They looked like samples. There was a sheet of instructions next to them, showing diagrams of different shaped faces, which Freddie had marked with arrows pointing to the oval-shaped one.

Suddenly he had a thought. He went to the dresser and opened the top drawer. She had to have one, and she had to keep it right where Donnie kept hers; in the underwear drawer, in the back, hidden underneath everything else. The book was there. On the cover, in large letters printed with a felt-tip pen, was the familiar warning, PERSONAL PROPERTY OF FREDERICA CHARLES. PRIVATE. KEEP OUT!!! He slipped it into his pocket and turned as he heard the door opening.

Michael stood in the doorway; a look of surprise and anger crossed his handsome features. "What the hell are you doing in here? Let me see your search warrant."

"I don't need one, Michael. I'm a journalist, not a police officer."

"In that case you need an invitation! Now get the hell out of here. Christ, you make me sick. All of you, you have no goddamned right to do this to us!"

"If you were my lawyer, you'd be defending me on the grounds of the First Amendment of the Constitution. Look, Michael, the story's going to be written, with or without your permission. It's news, you know that. I think your best chance of having it written fairly is with me. I can name you half a dozen reporters who would rip your family apart without ever bothering to talk to you."

Michael glared at him as he thought. Then he turned abruptly. "Come into my room, I don't want to talk in here."

His room was another page out of *House & Garden*, titled: law student, athlete, collector of trophies and pennants. All in brown and beige plaids, with splashes of color here and there. Perfect. Michael sat in a leather chair and pointed to one of the plaid upholstered ones for Wood. He looked at the boy, who was obviously suffering a great deal, and wondered why he didn't like him. It had nothing to do with his hostility. Wood could easily understand that. Come on, he chided himself, give the kid a fair shake.

"It's easy to blame the parents, isn't it?" Michael said, reaching up and picking one of the trophies off of a shelf and turning it over in his hand. It was a football trophy; he fingered it as he talked. "To ask what they were doing, going off to Bermuda and leaving a twelve-year-old kid alone with a senile old lady—well, let me tell you those two people worked damned hard for their vacations. We used to live in Newark until five years ago, in a white neighborhood that was ninety percent black. I was the only white kid in my class. I was the punching bag they used to practice on before they went out and busted up the neighborhood—including, by the way, my father's junk shop.

"I was ten when Frederica was born. A baby was the last thing in the world they needed, but maybe abortion was out of the question too. Anyway my mother was determined not to raise another child, especially a little girl, in that jungle we lived in. So she went to work in his junk shop—seven days a week, hours you wouldn't believe, to try to turn it into a furniture store. My grandmother lived with us then too.

"When Frederica was ready to start first grade, they registered her in school over here and gave my aunt's address. Mom wouldn't let her play with any of the kids in our neighborhood, and she wasn't supposed to tell her friends in school where she lived, so I guess she was alone a lot. I was no help, I was sweating my way into college on scholarship. I couldn't take care of her."

"Your parents certainly seem to have done all right. In terms of business," Wood said.

"They did all right in terms of Frederica too," Michael said quickly. "I mean what were they supposed to do—hire an English nanny to wash her mouth out every time the kid told a lie? She's a born manipulator. My parents didn't know how to cope with that."

"How about you? Did you know how to cope with it?"

Michael stood and stretched his back. "Well—there's your interview, Mr.—what did you say your name is?"

"Wood. Homer Wood."

"What paper do you work for, Mr. Wood?"

"I'm a free-lance photojournalist."

"This ought to be good for the *National Enquirer* then."

Wood got up to go, looking at the things on the shelf. "How do you like your Nikon? An F-two, isn't it?"

"Yeah, it's great."

"The attachments are a fortune, though. I just bought a Nikkor telephoto lens, cost more than the camera."

"I know. Unreal, isn't it?" Michael said as they walked to the door. "I paid eight hundred dollars for a four hundred-millimeter Nikkor."

Wood nodded as he left.


They compared notes in the car on the way back. Wood told them about his conversation with Michael, but not about the picture Mr. Charles gave him or the diary. He wanted to think about it by himself first. He was beginning to get a sense of who Freddie was; now his need to understand why she became who she was was overpowering.

Halsey was talking. "So Freddie grew up believing that what life is all about is wall-to-wall carpeting and no blacks living next door to you."

"That's right," Danahy said. "Pretty clothes, pretty people, and money. She bought her mother's dream. But she could have just as easily gone the other way and put it all down. Other kids do."

"I don't think she could," Wood said. "I think she had to buy it. Why else would they be too busy for her? There had to be a reason why she was coming home to an empty house every day after school—and if it wasn't wall-to-wall carpets and a white-on-white neighborhood, what was it? That they just didn't give a damn about her? Kids don't like to believe that."


Wood opened the diary the minute he got home, smiling ruefully as he leafed through the pages. It was full of the same teenage hieroglyphics as Donnie's, which she loved to show him, as much to test the effectiveness of her many codes and symbols, as wanting to share some of her secrets with him. He opened to a page near the end.

May 9, 1977,

*Found Pix!* If b.b. can go to n.y. so can l.s. Sentence for Blackmail: 20 yrs to life. Out in 10 with good lawyer. $20 to shut up on dirty pix—$10 to shut up on n.y. Considering following him (?)

May 10, 1977,

Did it! Terrific story to Big W. + hug. IT got big!! Interesting. n.y. with Little W. Lunch at Schraffts. Models and rich men. 5th Ave. Gorg. clothes—shoes, sweaters, bags, jewels. We want all. Will *have* all. Bought padded b's and eye gook.

> Hooray hooray, New York today
> Tomorrow we conquer the world!

The image of her body that lay fallen and broken flashed for an instant in his mind. He closed his eyes, blacking it out, and turned the pages back to several months before.

September 6, 1976,

The style was less tricky, the handwriting more scrawled.

I hate her. I hate him. He didn't look at me once the whole time at dinner—only her. She's pretty, but I'll be prettier. She's so stupid—I think one of her eyes is crossed and her nose is flat and I'll never love him again for looking at her like that. Mom liked her because she's rich. I hate Mom too.

September 11, 1976,

And a few pages later:

I'm going to sneak into his bed some night when he's sound asleep and sleep on his shoulder. Why can't I be like him? Why can't I *be* him and him be me. And I would love me more than anyone. And I would be happy.

The phone rang several times before he heard it. He answered it distractedly.

"Dad?"

"Donnie—?"

"Hi. What's wrong?"

"Sorry—I was just in the middle. Hi, honey, how are you?"

"Dad—did you forget? It's Mom's birthday. You were going to help me make dinner. I already made the cake—did you get a present?"

He looked at his watch. It was five o'clock and he had forgotten. Completely. He could still get a bottle of champagne and have it wrapped as a gift.

"Sure," he said. "What time do you want me?"

"Are you going to help me with dinner?"

"Of course."

"Then come now. Mom's going to meet Joyce for a drink after work, so it'll be a surprise when she gets home. Okay?"

"Good. Be there as soon as I can."

He put the phone down and thought about Shawna and Winter. Curious, these sets of females suddenly circling about in his life. And, in the center, Freddie, demanding to be explained. Her death demanding the recognition, at the very least, that she couldn't get in life.

He dialed and waited for the sound of Shawna's voice, realizing at once how badly he wanted to hear it. He was surprised when it was Winter who answered the phone.

"Is that you, Winter?"

"Yes, Mr. Wood. Shawna's taking a bath."

Compared to Donnie, she sounded about eight years old. "How're you feeling?" he asked.

"Better. I've been playing with Houdini."

"Oh, are you allergic too?"

"To cats? No, why? Wait—here's Shawna."

"Hi! Houdini's found himself a new means of transportation—he's been riding around on Winter's shoulder. Oh, thanks, Winter. Wait a minute, let me put my robe on." He heard Winter laughing in the background. "We just burned a pouch."

"What?"

"A frozen-food pouch. We didn't put enough water in the pot."

"You don't have a pot."

"I do now. And a coffeepot too. Are we going to see you?"

Wood explained about Barbara and Donnie and said he'd stop by after. "Shawna, I've got Freddie's diary. I need Winter to help me figure out some things. Do you think she's up to it?"

"No." She paused and lowered her voice. "That's the police's job, let them do it."

He waited. A silence hung between them. Wood was caught, completely unprepared for this kind of a reaction from Shawna. He realized he'd already made them a team in his mind. Now, suddenly, she'd shut him out.

"Wood, you asked me to help her. You can't ask me now to let you take her back to where she was when I found her."

"I'll see you later," he said finally and hung up.


Donnie had strung crepe-paper streamers across the dining room and hung balloons from the brass chandelier over the table. She had even baked a fair imitation of a birthday cake. Wood knew Barbara would be touched. It was a sensitive birthday, her fortieth and her first since their divorce.

Donnie had set out the ingredients for the dinner: lamb chops, baking potatoes, and frozen creamed spinach, all of which she'd gone to the market and bought by herself; charging it, of course. She was being very businesslike, assigning the salad to him while she put the potatoes in the oven and set the table.

She doesn't seem to need any recognition, he thought to himself as he watched her, or doesn't it always show?

"You've done a great job, Donnie."

"I know," she said matter-of-factly. "Don't use that lettuce, Dad, it's yuck-y. I bought a fresh one today."

Barbara came in looking pleased and flushed; pretty in her lightweight, camel-colored suit, almost the color of her hair.

"I haven't had a martini in six months. I just had two and I'm flying." She hugged Donnie and gave Wood a peck on the cheek.

Dinner went smoothly. Barbara allowed Donnie to take complete charge, complimenting her from time to time on her cooking. And Donnie told only one joke, which she saved for after the cake ceremony. Wood opened the champagne with a good bit of fanfare and they toasted Barbara; to her health, her happiness, and, Donnie added, "You sure don't look forty, Mom. Really." Then she left, to go to her room to do homework. "Science —bor-ring!"

Barbara took her glass of champagne and curled up in a corner of the living room couch. "What a nice evening. It was sweet of you to come, Homer. Thank you."

"You're welcome. Donnie planned it all, you know."

She laughed. "Forty must seem so ancient to her that she had to tell me I don't look it, to make me feel better."

"You don't, you know. Look it."

She took a sip of wine. "Really, Homer. Isn't that just a bit condescending?"

"I'm sorry. I didn't mean it to be."

She didn't seem to hear. Her head was resting on her hand, eyes far away, lost in thought. "I'm not sure when I began to no-tice—months ago, maybe more—when I walk down a street or sit in a restaurant, men look right past me. I mean they won't even bother to turn their blown-dry heads around for a second look, once you're past thirty. And you know what else? Every young, beautiful woman I see, I take as a personal affront. A defeat, be-cause I've been aged out of that market." She looked at him as she poured herself more wine. "Then I wonder why I didn't think of that when I so bravely demanded my freedom."

"Barbara, I think I hear the sound of two martinis talking—"

"With some champagne chasers. I'm embarrassing you, Homer. Indulge me, you can afford to be generous. I hear you've got a girlfriend. Donnie tells me she's very beautiful."

"Donnie's talking about someone I only just met."

"Oh, but we have antennae about our men, didn't you know that? Tell me, is she under thirty?"

"Jesus, Barbara!"

"And talented, independent, and terrific? Why the hell can't any of you fall in love with someone my age? Someone who re-ally needs you? You're only forty-two; it's not like you're an old man with something to prove."

He started to get up. She put a hand out to stop him. "There's something I need you to remind me of, will you—because some-times"—her voice broke—"I forget"—she frowned, blinking away tears that she didn't want to come—"what my reasons were."

He looked at her a long time. When he spoke, it was with a gentleness she didn't remember him having.

"My cameras, you said, were my weapons. Defense weapons

to keep between me and life. A way for me to be a witness to life, instead of a participant."

"Oh. Right. And every time I tried to talk to you, you made me feel like I'd just barged into your head uninvited." She nodded. "Have you changed?" she asked.

"I don't think people do, do they?"

She got up then and smiled at him. "I don't feel like apologizing for my little side trip down memory lane. It was self-indulgent and I enjoyed every minute of it. Anyway, I never met a woman yet who wasn't more articulate than any man about her pain. Even a fleeting one." She kissed him lightly on the cheek. "Good night, Homer Wood, I'm going to go get ready for my hangover now."

He smiled back. "I'll go say good night to Donnie."

Her door was closed. He tapped softly, then opened it. Donnie's head was bent over her desk.

"How're you doing? Need any—"

She turned around. Her face had been completely transformed by makeup, expertly applied; mascara, eye shadow, rouge, shadings to give her face the contours she didn't have yet. And deep, red lipstick. The desk was covered with miniature jars and bottles, in the center of which stood a round magnifying mirror.

Wood stared at her, felt himself turn to ice as she grinned at him, waiting for his approval. He was across the room in three steps; his hand shot out and caught the side of her face.

"Daddy!" she screamed.

His hand was raised again. "*Mommy!*" Astonished, he stopped, his hand poised in midair.

In a moment Barbara was there, standing between them, staring horror-stricken at Wood. Donnie was crying, clutching onto her mother, burying her face in her mother's skirt. Wood's eyes were riveted on the tiny bottles. One had toppled over and a flesh-colored liquid was spilling out, forming an odd design as it spread on the surface of the desk. He watched it for a moment, then turned and left.

He was outside on the street, lunging down Second Avenue to his car. He threw the car door open and got in, fists tightly clenched, and pounded them against the steering wheel. A moment later he horsed the car into gear, and, flooring the gas, he drove the four blocks to Shawna's.

She opened the door. Her smile faded immediately. "What happened, Wood?"

"I want to talk to Winter."

She paused. "All right. But talk to me, first. She just dozed off. Let's go in the bedroom. We've been playing checkers. She beat me three games in a row. Then we put together a jigsaw puzzle. The lady downstairs lent me a folding bed. Isn't that nice?"

"Look," he said as she closed the door, "there's an animal out there somewhere tearing apart twelve-year-old girls. Sometimes he even tosses them out of windows. Can you get that, Doctor? Don't give me that horseshit about it being a police problem. It's *my* problem. And I don't want to know why I feel it is, so get that 'how interesting' look off your face.

"Now *I* don't know who he is and *they* don't know who he is, but that kid in there does! It won't wait six months or six years till you can analyze her enough so she can talk about it. She's not the only twelve-year-old girl that needs protecting."

Shawna nodded, her face expressionless, and went to the door.

Winter was awake. She was lying on the bed, propped up on one elbow, working on the jigsaw puzzle, its pieces spread out on the table beside the bed. She had company; Houdini was watching from a vantage spot near her feet, and a floppy stuffed tiger sat on her pillow, the price tag still on him.

"Hi. I didn't hear you come in." She looked better. The bruises were faded, almost gone, and she looked rested. Her hair was tied back in a pony tail, and she was wearing Shawna's white terry-cloth robe with its sleeves rolled up. Wood saw for the first time what a lovely, delicate face she had. Her features were finer and less babyish than Freddie's, judging from the photograph in the Charleses' house, and with her taffy-colored skin and black hair she looked like a tiny Egyptian princess.

"Want to help with the puzzle?" she asked.

"He wants to talk to you, Winter." Shawna's voice was tight. Winter looked from one to the other. After a moment she understood and nodded solemnly.

"Shawna, one of us should take notes," Wood said.

"I will," she said and went and got her notebook and a pen. She sat in the canvas chair, and assuming an air that was both detached and professional, she waited for him to begin.

Wood took the diary out of his pocket and gave it to Winter. She held it, rubbing her fingers along the cover protectively.

"How'd you get this?" she asked.

He sat beside her on the bed. "I went to Freddie's house today. I found it in her bedroom—"

"Was it still in her underwear drawer?"

"Yes."

"Good, then they didn't find it. You won't let them see it, will you?"

"No, I promise."

She opened it and read one of the pages, smiling to herself. "Bet you couldn't understand it, could you?" She waited till he shook his head. "It's in code. I can't tell you what it means— they're her secrets. Boy, would Freddie be mad if she knew you had that."

He started to answer, but she cut him off. "I don't see what good it would do, anyway. She didn't bring the diary to New York, so there's nothing in there about that night. It's all stuff from before."

"We have to know about the stuff from before too, Winter. She was your best friend! Don't you want the man who did it caught?"

"Are you going to write about us in newspapers?"

"If I do, I won't use your name. I've never even tried to find out what your real name is. And I'd only write about it to make it worse for that man—there'd be no reason to tell your name."

"You can't," she said, her jaw set and her mouth tight. "Because no matter what happens to me, I'm never going home. No matter what." She was quiet a moment, then she looked down at the diary again. "What do you want to know?"

"There, May 9—who's b.b?—and what's that about blackmail?"

"Her big brother, Michael. Freddie found some dirty pictures in his drawer. Ones he took. So she blackmailed him for twenty dollars not to tell about the pictures, and ten more to keep quiet about him sneaking off to New York when he was supposed to be at school."

"Wait. How did Freddie know he'd taken the pictures himself?"

"Because they were mixed in with a bunch of others that she knew he took."

"It says 'considering following him.' What were you going to do?"

"Follow him to New York. We had a plan, but it didn't work. See—he was in a car with his friends and we were in a bus, so when we got to New York we didn't know where to look."

"What were you going to do if you found him?"

"Blackmail him again. Freddie, not me. He didn't even know me."

"Winter, why wasn't she afraid of her brother? I mean, you said you have brothers—wouldn't you be afraid to try something like that?"

"I would. But Freddie just wasn't afraid of anyone, that's all." She was looking at the cat, stroking him, keeping her eyes away from Wood's.

"You know what I think?"

"What?"

"I think Michael was more afraid of Freddie. That she had something else to tell about that frightened him more; something he wouldn't want anyone to know about. Did he ever do anything to her?"

She shook her head, concentrating all of her attention on the cat. She chewed her bottom lip. He looked up and saw Shawna move in her chair.

"It's important, Winter," he said quickly, before Shawna could stop him.

Her voice was barely audible. She spoke without looking up. "Freddie did something to him, something he told her to do."

"To touch him?"

She nodded, miserably. Then she looked at him. "What's so wrong—for her to do that? He was her favorite person in the whole world then. Why wouldn't she, if he asked her to?" Her voice was trembling. "I don't know what's so wrong about it; he was her own brother! It didn't hurt her or anything." She looked at Shawna. "Did it?"

"It had to do with feelings that Freddie was too young to understand, Winter," Shawna said. "And it could have confused her about love and natural, normal sex when it came time for her to understand."

"Who's big W. and little W.?" Wood asked, pointing to another page.

"Mr. Wallace, the principal. Little W's me. He had a terrible crush on Freddie." She smiled a little, looking at the entry. "That day, all she had to do was just give him a hug and he let us leave school." She looked at Wood. "That's *all* she did. She'd have told me!"

"There's something I have to ask—I'm sorry if it embarrasses you—but it's important to know. Was Freddie a virgin?"

"Are you kidding? God! She was only twelve years old."

Shawna got up to go into the kitchen to make some tea. Wood took Winter's hand and said gently, "Of course. I'm sorry."

"Tea or hot chocolate, Winter?" Shawna called from the kitchen.

"Tea, please."

"Wood?"

He sneezed, four times in a row, and got up, taking out his handkerchief and fumbling in his pockets for an antihistamine. Winter began to laugh. "Bless you," she said. He sneezed again, his eyes watering. He found the pill and went to get some water. "I'll be all right in a minute," he said, stifling another sneeze.

"It's all psychosomatic, you know. All allergies are," Shawna said, handing him a glass of water. He took it, giving her a dirty look, then kissing her lightly on the cheek.

"You know, with a little practice you could become a real pain in the ass," he said, and sneezed. They heard Winter giggling. "It's true," he said, walking back to the living room. "Here I am choking to death, and she's going to tell me that cat is my mother, right?"

Shawna came in with the tea. "Allergies are a fear reaction. That's why they use Adrenalin in severe cases."

"You mean Wood's afraid of Houdini?" Winter asked.

"Something Houdini symbolizes to him, maybe his mother. Cats are usually a female symbol."

"That's the worst load of—you mean people actually *pay* you to hear that nonsense?"

"He's reacting strongly, Winter. That means we struck a nerve," Shawna said in a conspiratorial tone.

"Reacting *strongly!* To that garbage? I—that's—" He was preparing for another sneeze. "It's—a—a—*choo!* Damn it!"

Winter and Shawna were both laughing. Winter hugged Houdini. "See what you started?"

"Mind you, Winter, this is what she learned in school, not

something useful, like how to cook. When I went to school, the girls all had to take courses in Home Economics and the boys took Shop. We made things with saws and hammers. See, they told us we were supposed to go out and cut down trees to build houses for you while you stayed home and cooked. What happened?"

"They lied," Shawna said. "What do you want to do when you grow up, Winter?"

"I want to be a famous model," she said. "So did Freddie." Her face became serious. She thought a moment, staring at the window, frowning. "Tell me something. If they caught those men, what would they do to them? Would they send them to the electric chair?"

"Men? How many were there?"

"Two. The photographer, if that's what he really was—maybe Big Alice was telling the truth. In fact I bet she was . . . and the one who said he was the editor or something, of *Seventeen*. And what about Candy? She lied to us, too. And the men in the room taking pictures—" She sat up straight and leaned forward, holding onto the edge of the bed, anger rising in her. "What will they do to them? Can they all be sent to the electric chair?"

"They can certainly be put in jail. And if we can help them find the one who actually killed Freddie, he'd go to jail for the rest of his life. I think that's worse than the electric chair, to die an old man, all alone and forgotten, in prison."

Winter thought about that. "Okay," she said. She stood up, tall and straight—a little soldier now, in a robe four sizes too large, its hem dragging an inch on the floor—and said in a strong, steady voice, "If I had been killed instead of Freddie, you know what she'd do? She'd go out there and find them herself and turn them over to the police, that's what she'd do. Then she'd go to court and be a witness and tell the whole thing to the jury and make sure they went to jail!"

The transformation was sudden and too extreme. It was almost as though she was trying to recreate Freddie for them, in herself. They knew from the words, the tone, and even the pose she struck that it wasn't Winter they were watching and listening to, it was Freddie.

The description of the events of that night were carefully detailed and told in minute-by-minute sequence; matter-of-factly, sometimes with a hint of irony.

Tommy and Candy became real for Wood; he saw them move and heard them speak; he felt their vibrations. The man called Mr. Blue was still without a face or a voice, just an amorphous idea, a vague, shadowy evil without form.

As Winter began to recite each awful moment inside those rooms, her voice went dead. The spirit of Freddie was gone, and Winter was alone again; her eyes were fixed on something, looking from a great distance at the small dark girl that was Winter, hearing but not seeing her friend screaming out her name—waiting for her to come find her and take her away from the hard hands holding her and hurting her. Waiting for Freddie to make it all right. Instead, only her scream—in the distance, and fading, fading. And then nothing.

Her eyes never flickered. "Then the next thing—I woke up on the floor of a bathroom. Not in the same room. A bathroom down the hall. I was cold."

There was a dead stillness. Slowly Winter lowered her head onto the pillow and said, in a voice small and far away, "I'm tired . . ." She lay there, motionless, her eyes open.

The floppy, stuffed tiger slid down on the floor. Wood went over and picked it up and, taking great care, he twisted and turned the price tag until it came off.


He was in his car, driving mindlessly, with no thought of where. He went through the park at Seventy-ninth Street to the West Side, then drove south on Ninth Avenue to the Forties. He pulled over and parked and began walking.

Strange, he'd never noticed them before. The night was full of children. Walking in pairs, some flashily dressed, others in blue jeans. They watched and they knew as they stood on street corners, talking and smoking; they saw out of the corners of their eyes the men who passed by, and there was an instant readout on their computers: john, cop, pimp, straight. They looked into the cars that pulled over and slowed, and disappeared into doorways when the readout flashed cop or runaway squad. They sat in windows of run-down rooming houses, exchanging signals with the men below who knew where to look.

And the pimps, strolling arm in arm with one of their ladies, strolling along with nothing to fear, no one to hide from. The young boys in tight pants and brightly colored body shirts and old, old eyes.

Wood was standing in front of the Rockmoor Hotel, at the very spot where Freddie had fallen. There was no trace left of the chalk outline on the pavement. He looked up at the canvas canopy, at the place where she'd fallen through. It had been roughly mended with some sort of masking tape. Less than fifty feet away was a newsstand, and in front of it was a woman. She was watching him. A plump woman with a dark shiny wig. He looked at her, trying to remember something Winter had said. A name. He walked toward her.

"Hello, Alice."

She looked back at him from underneath enormous false eyelashes. Her eyes held no trace of suspicion nor of curiosity. She waited for him to speak.

"Winter's all right," he said. "She's safe."

The eyelashes moved up and down once, but her expression remained unchanged.

"Who was he, Alice? Is he still around?"

"Of course he's still around. Why wouldn't he be?" Her voice was flat, matter-of-fact. "He's a big man now."

"Tommy—is that his name?"

"It's one of his names. He's known on the street as Pretty Joey. The cops know who he is."

"They do?"

"Of course. They can't prove anything, though, and he knows it. He can go bragging all over town about what he does to girls who give him trouble. He'd say he did it even if he didn't. And if he did, there's only one person who can prove it—that he has to be afraid of. You say she's safe. I hope you're right."

His face clouded. "What about the other man? Winter said—"

Alice was shaking her head. "No way," she said flatly and turned to leave.

"Wait—where does Pretty Joey hang out?"

She looked at him then and gave a short, mirthless laugh. "Why? You want to have a look at him? You're kinda cute, but you don't look like any Charlie Bronson to me. He'll probably be over at the Pig Pen tonight. They got a cutting room in the back. I hear they just got a shipment in."

He frowned, trying to understand.

"Your newspaper ought to give you guys a dictionary before they send you out on the street."

"How'd you know who I am?"

"Knowing's how we stay alive, honey. The Pig Pen's a bar on Eighth Avenue between Forty-seventh and Forty-eighth. They have a room in the back where they cut up coke. Pretty Joey gets mean when he's coked up, so if you plan to do any sight-seeing, leave your camera home."

"Alice—thanks."

"Yeah. Aren't I the hooker with the heart of gold . . ."

He watched her as she ambled down the street, her too-tight skirt wrinkling as she walked.

He had difficulty finding it. The name Pig Pen was obviously a term of endearment rather than the name posted above the door. There were three or four small dingy bars on the same block, all with names like Oscar's Happy Time or George's Gaiety. Wood went into George's. It was long and narrow; grotesquely lit from the green neon in the window. Several men, most of them black, were sitting on barstools, their backs to him. None of them turned to look at him, yet he felt he was noticed. Even the bartender refused to look up.

A television at the far end of the bar was turned on without the sound. Wood looked twice when he saw it was a football game. Football in May? Curious, he positioned himself against the wall where he could see it. The Giants were playing the Baltimore Colts. A sign flashed across the screen, "The Way It Was," and underneath the date, 1958. He remembered it well. It was the first sudden death play-off in pro football.

A movement at the far end of the room caught his eye. He turned and saw a tall thin black come through a door. He was dressed in a light chamois suit, a matching wide-brimmed hat, and a red silk shirt opened at the neck showing gleaming gold chains.

The man stopped when he saw Wood and looked at him for several seconds, as though deciding. Then he went to a table in the corner where two girls, also black, appeared to be waiting for him. One of them wore a platinum-blond wig, the other, a short, natural-colored Afro. Both had on filmy dresses, bared at the shoulders, with deep, plunging necklines, and flashy jewelry.

The one with the Afro reached out to him and pulled him down in the chair beside her. Then she lifted both her legs and draped them over his lap. He kept his eyes on Wood as he absently ran his fingers up and down the girl's legs.

The one in the blond wig glanced at Wood and, laughing, leaned over to whisper in the man's ear. She undid the top two buttons of her blouse; he slipped his hand inside and caressed her breast.

The look in the black man's eyes was challenging now. They glittered with hatred from across the room as he moved his other hand up between the other girl's legs and stayed there, the corners of his mouth curving into a smile.

Wood pulled his eyes away, breaking the connection. Almost instantly he remembered something Halsey once said. "Rule number one of the street: never look away first."

"*Shit!*" A voice exploded from the bar. Wood felt a rush of adrenaline.

"Did you see that? Livingston stopped Ameche! Some fuckin' play!"

Wood looked up at the TV, his head pounding, and decided to get the hell out.

There was the sharp scraping sound of a chair being shoved against a bare floor. Wood turned and looked to the back of the room. The man in the chamois suit was on his feet and coming toward him. The sound on the TV was suddenly turned up full. The announcer's voice crackled in his ear. The Colts had just blown a touchdown. The front door slammed shut.

The man was ten feet away. Wood studied the face, the green light bouncing off the glistening forehead. Four feet now—a good close-up. Delicate nose, soft mouth; almost feminine, but cruel. Eyes like black diamonds. Two feet now— there'd be a distortion; elongated nose, receding forehead, mouth too large; out of proportion. The lips began to move; the words sounded out of synch. Wood felt something pressing on his groin.

"My lady fancies a lock of your blond pubic hair to carry in her wallet. For luck."

The pressure on his groin increased. He felt something sharp. There was a sudden ear-splitting crash and the front door banged open, resounding against the wall as it hit it. The same moment Wood heard something clatter to the floor at his feet. As he knelt to see what it was, the man in the chamois suit made a dash for the back door.

"Freeze, you fuckers!" a voice called out.

"Cover the back!" another yelled.

Wood was pushed aside. There were three of them. They were enormous; they filled the room, blitzing it, sweeping aside anything that got in their way. Two men got up from the bar and stepped in front of them, feigning innocence, as though they were just on their way out. The first linebacker in swung at both of them, aiming for their heads. Wood got a glimpse of something in his hand that resembled a brown leather bag, but it was moving so fast, he couldn't be sure. Both men went crashing back into the bar, knocking over stools, and crumbled like plaster statues onto the floor. Three more linebackers stampeded through, slamming tables against the wall that blocked their way, to get to the back door before the pimp got away. Only one of them had his gun drawn; for the others, their bodies seemed weapons enough.

They were dressed in skin-tight jeans and sneakers, and they all had long, healthy, sun-streaked hair. A couple of them wore moustaches. Wood was reminded of the surfers on the beaches of Waikiki and wondered if that's where they went for fun.

"You all right, buddy?" one of them asked. Wood looked down at the knife lying inches away from his feet. He stared at it, a wave of fear sweeping over him. He closed his eyes for a second.

"Get him out of here," another one shouted. "I want a make on him."

A linebacker with a moustache led him out. Wood turned to look at him. "Who are you guys?" he asked.

Outside five or six uniformed men were holding back the passersby gathering on the sidewalk. An empty taxicab was left at the curb, stopped at an angle, its doors wide open. Another screeched to a stop behind it, and three more men, identical to the first three in size and dress, jumped out. The police officers made way for them.

"What've we got?" the first one out of the cab asked, looking at Wood.

"Assault. A mack pulled a knife on this guy. We lost him out the back."

"Who's this?"

"I don't know. I'm taking him over to Midtown North."

Wood reached for his wallet and was immediately restrained. "Hey—wait a minute—don't you want my ID?"

"Later, pal." He started to lead him to a patrol car.

"Wood! Is that you?" He turned around, relieved to hear a familiar voice. It was Frankie, a patrolman he'd known for years. "What the hell were you doin' in there?"

"You know this guy?" the linebacker with the moustache asked.

"Yeah, that's Homer Wood. He's a journalist."

The linebacker shook his head. "Oh, for Christ's sakes. Press." He spat the word out. "You guys really are stupid, aren't you? Hey, Al, guess what? He's press."

"Shit. Take him anyway and get a statement from him. Then he can sit and look at pictures—see if he can identify the creep he made us lose. Fucking press gotta be good for something."

"C'mon, may as well walk. It's only a few blocks."

"Don't I get a ride in your taxicab?"

"Reporters are lousy tippers. You doing a narcotics story?"

"No. I was looking for a pimp."

"You found one. Were you also looking to get yourself cut up?" They were almost to the precinct, Wood quickening his pace to keep up with him.

"You guys really saved my ass. Thanks."

"You're welcome, but it didn't look like it was your ass they were after. My name's Jenkins, Vinnie Jenkins—Anti-Crime Unit."

"What's with the cabs?"

"They give them to us. Makes us less visible on the street. We're trained to handle street violence."

"I see what you mean," Wood said. They were walking up the steps. Jenkins nodded to the officers on their way out.

"My boss, the sergeant back there, gets really pissed off when you people write about how we go out busting heads every night. He's kinda sensitive that way." He held the door for Wood.

"Well, I, for one, will certainly do my best never to hurt his feelings," Wood said, following Jenkins up the stairs and along the dingy colorless hall to an empty office.

"Look," Wood said, "I could save us all some time. Does the name Pretty Joey mean anything to you?"

"No, why?"

"It's just a hunch, but I'd like to see a mug shot of him."

"The guys in the pimp squad know all those names. I can call downstairs and see who's around," he said and picked up the phone. "This is Jenkins, Anti-Crime—anyone from the pimp squad down there? We're trying to get a make on someone. He is? Ask him to come up for a minute, will you?" He hung up. "Sergeant Cohen's coming up. He knows them all."

They heard him whistling before he came in. "Is this the reporter that got bitten by a pimp?"

Jenkins laughed. "Sounds like an opening line for a vaudeville routine."

"My uncle was in vaudeville. Every time my aunt asked him if he wanted a cup of coffee or a sandwich, he used to say, 'No thanks, I just had my pants pressed.'"

"I don't get it," Wood said.

"Nobody did, but he kept on saying it. So, tell me your story." He sat down and listened intently to Wood's account, beginning with Freddie and Winter, but leaving out the fact that he still had Winter with him. Cohen knew Big Alice. "Her information's usually good. I saw those two kids a couple of days before it happened, on Eighth Avenue, and I lost them. Some loss that turned out to be, huh?" He went to the shelf and took down one of the mug books. "I saw Pretty Joey making his pitch to them and, boy, what I wouldn't give to nail that snake. My Aunt Sadie would have a heart attack if she knew what I offered God." He opened the book and put it in front of Wood. "Just turn the pages till you see one you like."

Wood stopped at the third page. "Here he is—*Ernest Harrison Kingsley, Junior?*" He looked at Cohen unbelievingly.

"Yep. With a name like that you could get in anywhere, right?" He took the picture out of the book. "Vinnie, take this downstairs and tell them to get it out right away." He turned to Wood. "And you think this might be the guy Winter described— that was in the hotel room that night?"

"I know it is."

"Then we better notify Homicide." When Jenkins had left,

Cohen said to Wood, "You wrote the story in the *News*, didn't you? It was good. Angry, the way I like to see a story like that written."

"Thanks."

"But you still shouldn't have gone in there after him yourself. Your anger should stay in your own work."

"Sergeant—"

"Call me Mark, I'm not pretentious. I'm not tall enough. Look, I know the feeling, but if you'd come to us with that description, we could have picked him up for anything, for spitting on the sidewalk, but we'd have had him. Now he's chasing an assault rap; he'll dig himself a hole and surface in Chicago or somewhere six months from now."

"Shit."

"Our only hope is that he was really coked up, like Jenkins said. If so, he might be around tonight. What's the matter?"

Wood wasn't listening. His eyes were searching out something in the past, something he was remembering. His voice was barely audible. "The hunter and the hunted . . . they're both the same person."

"What?"

"I'm not sure whether it's from a poem—or something that was told to me a long time ago. 'As love is connected to lover, so is enemy connected to enemy.' It's all the same thing, don't you see? I didn't go in there looking for him. Not to get him, anyway. I was pulled there, by the same force that pulled him across the room to me. I didn't know who he was and he didn't know me.

"But we know each other now. I *know* this man. I've seen his eyes, and he's seen into mine. The hatred between us is a powerful connection."

Cohen was staring at him as he spoke. Wood got up and paced the floor. Then he turned to him, eyes blazing.

"If you were to put me out on that street tonight, Mark, I'd find him. You know what else? He'd find me too. What do you say? It's worth a try, isn't it?"

"I say you're a raving lunatic. You already fucked up once. Now you want me to let you go back out there and walk around reciting poetry? I'd have to be crazy."

Wood looked at him.

Cohen looked back and a slow smile spread over his impish

face. "Wait—I'll get my hat and go with you," he said in his vaudeville voice.

Jenkins came back. "Done, Sergeant. Hey, where's he going? He's got to make a statement."

"Later," Cohen said. "We're going to go take a little walk."

Jenkins looked from one to the other and caught on. "That's a great idea. You two will make a hell of a team. The sergeant can't shoot a gun, and the reporter doesn't know how to get out of the way.

"I have a better idea. Instead of walking, why don't we call a cab."

The three of them were on their way out when Cohen spotted Patti. "Hey, little one, what're you doing?"

A young girl in sleeveless denim overalls was standing talking to another officer. She turned around. Small delicate features, long bushy hippie-type hair that looked dyed, and a fresh, amused sort of face, a cross between an elf and a rock singer.

"I just came on duty. What's up?"

"Come on, we'll tell you in the car."

Patti Brown was in fact twenty-one, a detective who worked as a decoy for the police pimp squad. The shoulder bag she carried was decorated with an assortment of patches: one of Snoopy on skis saying, "Don't Eat Yellow Snow," and Mickey Mouse on another, copulating with Minnie. The bag was large enough to hold a minitape recorder, a spiral notebook, a gun, an extra pair of shoes. She climbed in the back next to Wood and took out her notebook. Finding the page she wanted, she passed it up front to Cohen. "Want to see my latest? I got this down in the women's cells."

He took it and explained, "She collects graffiti—everywhere she goes, ladies' rooms, men's rooms." He read, "'Where tyranny is law, revolution is order.' What're we doing, arresting philosophers now?"

"I don't think a hooker made that up," Jenkins said.

"It sounds like Susan B. Anthony. I'll have to look it up," Patti said. "Read the next one, Mark."

"It's a list:

One. Get out.
Two. Make up with Mom.
Three. Pick up Bobbie.

Four. Get clean.
Five. Go shopping."

"That one blew me away," she said. "So, what's the scam to-night?"

They told her in shorthand, using terms Wood had never heard before. He laughed. "Do they give a course in street talk at Berlitz?" They were driving along Eighth slowly, Cohen and Jenkins watching the street as they talked.

Patti knew who Pretty Joey was, but she didn't think he knew her, especially with blond hair. He'd never made a pitch at her anyway. "I don't think I look young enough to interest him . . . maybe if I take these out." She reached inside the top of her overalls and removed a pair of foam-rubber falsies, putting them in her bag. "I can't stand them; they keep moving around." She sat up straight. "Now I'll pass for twelve, right?" Then she took her hair and separated it into two bunches, tying them each with rubber bands. "How's that?" she asked Wood.

He smiled at her, amused. "Could've fooled me."

"Hey, Patti," Cohen said. "Does your mother know what you do for a living?"

"No, I think she thinks I'm a meter maid."

They stopped on Forty-ninth between Seventh and Eighth, just past a topless bar.

"Let's try in here," Cohen said. Patti took a small beeper out of her bag and switched it on. Cohen had one too. "If I make contact and can't get the target to walk out with me, I'll buzz three times; once, if there's anything interesting going on. I'm going to go in through the back, see what the action is out there tonight. But you come in the front. Let's not upset them if we don't have to, okay?"

"Patti," Jenkins said as she got out of the car, "the boys just got a fresh shipment tonight. If he's there, he'll be upstairs and flying high. Watch it."

"Snow in May? Far out."

They watched her walk down the street. "What a girl," Wood said. "Where'd you find her?"

"She just turned up one day and said she'd been assigned to my squad," Cohen said.

"What's her story?"

"That question's off limits, Wood. You'd have to get that from her." When ten minutes had passed, Cohen checked his receiver.

"What did she mean about the action out back?" Wood asked.

"The dancing girls take their customers out to a van they keep parked in back and give the customers a quickie for twenty-five bucks. Sometimes a pimp will hang around, looking for new material or to rough up one of the prossies and grab her money."

"Couldn't that get dangerous for Patti?"

Jenkins turned and looked at Wood. "She probably could've gotten a job at Bloomingdale's if she wanted to."

"Right," Wood said.

Five minutes later the buzzer sounded. Once. "Let's go," Cohen said.

It was another long and narrow bar, queerly lit and airless, with closed doors that looked sinister to Wood after his visit to the Pig Pen. He half expected that at any moment a door would fly open and a pimp would charge him with a knife. But Jenkins and Cohen strolled in, nodding casually to the girls who were relaxing at the bar between shows, and greeted the fat Spanish lady bartender with a perfectly friendly, "Hi, Maria, how's it going?"

And she smiled back at them, her stained teeth looking mottled in the strange light, and said, "Quiet night, tonight." She eyed Wood and Jenkins, committing their faces to memory. "Want a beer?" They shook their heads and thanked her.

There were only four customers at the bar; beaten-down night types with gray faces, waiting for the next show to begin. Wood glanced at the girls in their bikinis and hoped it wouldn't start until after he left. Their bodies were chalky white, soft and lumpy like bread dough; tired looking, joyless bodies. The thought of watching them dance bare-breasted to junk music was about as unappealing an idea as he could think of.

"Who's upstairs, Maria?" Cohen asked.

"Some boys, playing poker." She nodded toward Wood and Jenkins. "They Vice?" Cohen shook his head no. She shrugged. "Then go have a look. Just don't bust it up," she called after him as he opened the door. "I gotta get my ten percent."

Jenkins followed, leaving Wood alone. He could feel the girls looking him over and felt uncomfortable, as though he ought to explain what he was doing there. The customers at the bar kept their backs turned to him. He started to wander down toward the back of the room, wondering where Patti was, when the door opened and a small, fragile girl with long dark hair braided down her back came out. She was walking toward him. At first Wood guessed she might be only fourteen or fifteen, but as she got closer, he realized that, like Patti, she'd gotten herself up to look that young. They were probably the same age. The girl was looking at him with wide, dark eyes. Suddenly the door of the back room opened and Patti came out. She looked as though she might be signaling him but without his glasses he couldn't be sure. One of the bikini-clad girls got up and started for the back, stopping to say hello to Patti.

"You got a new patch on your bag," she said.

Patti pointed to Snoopy. "My kid sister sent me this, from Colorado. Cute, isn't it?"

"I'd love to find one like that for my little boy. He'd flip."

"I'll ask my sister to send me one, next time I talk to her."

The small dark girl was standing beside Wood. "Hi," she said.

He looked at her and smiled hesitantly. "Hi."

"Can I buy you a drink?" she said.

"No—thanks, I—"

"I don't mean here. I have a room at a hotel around the corner. We could party for an hour, the drinks on me." Her eyes were serious and penetrating. He stared at her, astonished, unable to think what to say.

"Okay, June," Patti's voice broke in. "Let's go." The girls at the bar turned their backs to them and began making conversation with the men.

"You too, mister." And Patti's hand was holding Wood's arm firmly, guiding him to the door. The girl, June, scowled and walked on ahead, swinging her shoulders defiantly. "Keep walking," Patti said as they got outside. "The cab's parked down the street a ways, behind that truck. I just hope they had the sense to leave it unlocked."

"You mean you don't have a wire coat hanger in that bag?" June asked.

Patti laughed briefly. "Not a bad idea." Then, suddenly, she grabbed June's arm as a tall, heavyset black turned the corner and came walking directly toward them. June saw him too and jerked her arm away. "Get your hands off me, cunt!" The man walked past them, shooting Patti a murderous look, and spat on the pavement. Wood swung around angrily, his nerves already on edge, and took a step toward the man.

"Get in, Wood!" Patti was holding the door on the driver's side open. He looked at her, surprised at her tone. She shook her head. "June and I'll get in the back," she said and slammed the door.

"Sorry, Mr. Wood," she said when she got in. "But if you're going to be a hero, you could spoil it for us." She turned to June. "Do you think he recognized you?"

"I know he did. I'm glad you saw him first; he's not one of my favorites."

"I didn't know he was still in business," Patti said.

"He's only got one or two girls working for him now. Small-time macaroni."

Wood was by now thoroughly confused. "You sure had me fooled back there, June. I'd have never guessed you were a cop."

"I'm not. I'm a hooker."

Cohen and Jenkins came out and got into the car. Wood moved over and Jenkins got behind the wheel.

"Start driving, Vinnie. June shouldn't be seen talking to us. I had to make it look like an arrest so I could get her out of there. She's got very interesting news for us about Pretty Joey."

As they drove around, June told them that Pretty Joey had gotten some heavy backing to move inside. Cohen explained to Wood, "That means to open a whore house."

"A very special whore house," June said. "Rated G. Over sixteen *not* qualified to work there."

"Jesus. Who's the backer? Anyone I know?" Cohen asked.

"No. All I heard is that he wears a business suit and he's got a lot of bucks. Pretty Joey will bring in the girls and take out twenty-five percent of the profit. The backer's doing it mainly to support his habit."

"Which is?"

"He likes to play with little girls."

"I see," Cohen said. "Did you hear when all this is going to happen?"

"Soon. In a few days. They already have the apartment. Huge, eight or nine rooms in a fancy old building on Park or Fifth."

"Shit. You know what that means, don't you?" Cohen said.

"Yep. We'll never be able to touch him," Jenkins said. They were quiet. Jenkins drove distractedly.

"Why?" Wood asked finally.

"We have a law that says we can't," Cohen answered. "It's

private property. We'd need a warrant to get in, and you can't get a warrant without evidence they're engaging in prostitution. As a good reporter, your next question should be: why don't you send in an undercover cop? That would be a terrific question unless you already know that cops aren't allowed to undress. You might not have known that, but the guys who run those places sure as hell do. The girls aren't allowed to say hello until the customer drops his pants."

"I was hoping we'd be able to flush him out tonight with Patti, but not if he's shopping for teeny-boppers."

"I'm positively middle-aged," she said, sighing.

"I'm over the hill too," June said. "Sorry. If I hear of anything else, I'll let you know. You can drop me off anywhere here, fellas."

They thanked her. As they drove off, Wood looked out the back window and saw her stopping a man on the street.

Cohen saw him looking. "Turn around, Wood," he said, "and look somewhere else."

Jenkins headed in. Wood and Cohen sat quietly; they were both frustrated. But Wood even more so, thinking about how he'd blown the assault arrest and knowing that if he hadn't, they'd have Pretty Joey wrapped up now.

"Forget it," Jenkins said, reading his thoughts. "It happens to the best of us. Believe me, every one of us could tell stories worse than that. And we get *paid* not to make mistakes."

"Hey," Cohen said, "you guys are depressing the hell out of me—anybody want a beer?"

They went to Red's, where Cohen stopped first at the phone booth to check in, peeling off the "out-of-order" sticker which Red kept over the coin slot; another of his courtesies, to make sure the men always had a phone available. When Cohen finished, he came to the table and sat down. He seemed disturbed. "Wood, Lieutenant Gallagher's looking for you."

"What for? I didn't kill anyone. I just screwed up an arrest."

"You didn't tell me you're keeping the other girl under wraps. He heard that it was her information that sent you out looking for Pretty Joey. He wants to question her. Where've you got her —and why?"

"Mark, I didn't tell you for a reason. And the reason's getting better and better. Like you said to me in the car, turn around and look somewhere else. Excuse me, I've got to make a call."

"Peel the sticker off—"

"I know. But I thought Red only did that for reporters."

He spoke quickly, keeping his voice lowered. "Shawna, I want you to get Winter out of there as fast as you can. Somewhere you can spend the night, probably tomorrow too. Don't answer your phone again. When you get to wherever you're going, call this number and speak to Andy, no one else. Tell him where you are, but not to beep me. I'll call him. And tell him it's an emergency, this is the last time—555-1144, got it? I'll explain later, okay?"

As he hung up, he saw the two detectives come in. He recognized them as Gallagher's men. He walked back to the table slowly, keeping his back to them. Cohen and Jenkins had spotted them too.

"Hang around," Wood said to them. "I never got my beer. I think I may change that to a scotch when I get back."

The detectives seemed apologetic; embarrassed, even. Wood assured them he was glad to have an opportunity to interview the lieutenant, especially knowing how the man felt about the press. "And so thoughtful of him to send a car."

Lieutenant Gallagher was in his shirt-sleeves, straightening his desk, when Wood was shown in.

"Look at this report," he said, not looking up at Wood. "How the hell am I supposed to make any sense out of it? I keep telling them—you've got to have a system. Look at this. Do you see a time written anywhere?" He shoved the paper in front of Wood. "I brought that clock from home," he said, pointing to a large railroad-station clock with a sweep second hand. "I get a call, the first thing I do is look up there and write down the time. Simple, isn't it? Someone asks you what time you were notified of a homicide, what're you going to say—'around three in the afternoon'? Jesus Christ."

The phone rang and he picked it up. "Yeah?" He listened. "We don't have *any* cars? Well, get one from Robbery. Robbery doesn't have one, call Sex. Maybe they got cars." He banged the phone down. "Paper-clip mentality is what I call it. How do you run a homicide squad without cars? What're the men supposed to do? Take a bus?"

He called to the outer office. "Hey, Connelly, bring me a glass, will you? A glass—*the* glass. We have one lousy glass in the whole office. I hate paper cups, can't drink out of them."

Connelly brought in the glass, turned to go.

"Thanks—hey! Do you think maybe I could have some water in it too?" He shook his head as the flustered young detective took it and returned quickly with water.

"Thanks," Gallagher said. Then to Wood, "Want a vitamin C?"

"No thanks," Wood said.

Gallagher put one in his mouth and swallowed it down with the water. "Where's the girl?" he asked simply, using the same tone he used to ask for a glass of water.

"I don't know," Wood answered.

"Yeah?"

"I told a friend of mine to take her somewhere safe. I don't know where she's taken her yet."

"Oh." He swallowed another one, then a third. "Funny thing, isn't it? How you can just take a dislike to someone—no reason. Chemistry, maybe."

"Yeah, maybe."

The lieutenant thought a moment. "I never liked you."

"Hmm. Well, I won't take up any more of your time—"

"Sit down. I want to show you something." He took a piece of paper and tore it into three pieces, folding each of them in half. He passed them across the desk to Wood.

"Write down the name of a flower on one. Go ahead, any flower. First one that comes into your head."

Wood looked at him, then he took out a felt-tip pen. "Is it okay if I write it in green?"

"Fine."

"I mean, I probably have a blue one in here somewhere too." He felt in his pockets.

"No. Green's fine. Don't let me see what you're writing."

Wood covered the piece of paper with his hand, checking to make sure Gallagher couldn't see.

"Got it? Now write a color on the next one and a number on the third one. Any number from one to five."

"Okay."

Gallagher pointed to the papers. "The flower's a rose, the color's blue, and the number's three."

Wood nodded and passed the folded paper to Gallagher. "Gee, that's terrific, Lieutenant. What else can you do? Know any card tricks?"

Gallagher reached behind him for the phone and passed it to Wood. "Call Red's place and get the message you were waiting for. You have to dial nine to get an outside line." He went back to straightening his desk.

"Listen, I'd really like to stay and play some more games with you, but I've got to be going. Maybe you could come to my little girl's birthday party next month—the kids would really get a kick out of it."

"Connelly!" The young detective came rushing in. "Take Mr. Wood downstairs and book him—for obstructing justice." He got up and put on his jacket. "I'm going over to Clarke's and get a cheeseburger."

Wood stood up. "Come off it, Gallagher. That's false arrest and you know it. Besides, what is that crap about obstructing justice? You haven't even got a homicide, you've got a CUPPI—"

"That's right, I have a CUPPI. You're nosing around trying to make it look like a homicide. And one thing I don't need is someone trying to turn a CUPPI into a homicide without the collar to go with it!" His voice got louder. "See that chart up there? That's my clearance for the last five years. See those numbers? Last year I had a seventy-five percent clearance, the year before a sixty-eight, and the year before that a seventy-seven! That's the highest in the whole fucking city. And you know why? Because I don't go around *creating* homicides; I try to solve the ones I already have!"

"Come off it, Gallagher. The ones you already have—you mean the ones you call homicides. And you won't call anything a homicide that doesn't have a ready-made collar to go with it. Otherwise it might louse up your box scores at the end of the year."

"I don't *make* CUPPI's, goddamnit. Medical examiners make CUPPI's."

"What the hell does he know? He's a doctor, not a detective. All he knows is someone went out of a window, hit the ground, and the spleen burst and the brain hemorrhaged and that's what the person died of—a busted spleen, right? And if a body's delivered to him with a knife stuck in the back, he can tell the person died of a knife stuck in his back, right? That's his job. It's your job to find out how the knife got into his back!"

"Do you have any idea how many people jumped out of windows last year? Or fell out?"

"No, Lieutenant, tell me. How many twelve-year-old girls

jump out of a window of a hotel room that a pimp just happened to be in at the time. I'd really like to know about that, Lieutenant, that would make one hell of a story."

"Hey, you don't like the way the system is set up, go out and run for DA. Or better still, become the grand jury yourself. But don't tell me what my job is. No half-assed magazine photographer's going to turn my CUPPI into a homicide and then hide the fucking collar from me."

"I don't have the fucking collar!"

"You have the witness—that's the same thing! You don't get a collar without a witness!" Gallagher's voice was booming.

Connelly was backing toward the door, cowed by the shouting match.

"Pick a number from one to twenty," Wood said.

"Ten!"

"Right. Give me ten hours to produce the girl. Let Connelly here follow me if you don't trust me."

"Connelly couldn't pin a tail on a donkey *without* a blindfold."

"Aw gee, boss—"

"That's all right, kid. Someday I'll tell you the story of how I arrested a German Shepherd my first year on the squad." He looked up at the clock. "You be here in my office at ten in the morning, Wood. On the button. I'll be leaving here at ten thirty to go down to the DA's office. And Wood"—he paused at the door and looked at him—"I have no interest whatever in trusting you—or not."

Wood and Connelly watched him disappear down the hall.

Connelly turned to Wood. "He really means it," he said.

"No shit," Wood said and left.

Wood was relieved to find them still at the table. He hoped they would be; he needed both Cohen and Jenkins. They could be trusted, he felt. Neither of them were strict party-line men— they could bend the regulations if they wanted to.

The thought had first come to him when he left Gallagher's office, and he allowed himself to play with the idea in his mind, knowing that it was absolutely unthinkable. He grabbed a taxi to pick up his car, not entirely sure where he'd left it. He described it to the driver, telling him to watch for the one with a ticket on the windshield, just in case there were more than one 1964 battered Volvo in the area. Then he sank back and let himself ride with his thoughts; ride like an empty overturned kayak swept helplessly along the swirling rapids where he and his grandfather used to go trout fishing.

By the time he was in his car driving to Red's, he felt he was speeding headlong, tossed out of control, straight for the waterfall.

Now, finally, sitting across the table from the men, his face flushed, eyes burning, dots of perspiration formed, like a miniature moustache, above his lip. He downed a double scotch and told them his plan.

They sat for a long time after he stopped talking; Mark concentrating on the circles the wet glasses made on the tabletop, Jenkins drawing insane doodles on a paper napkin, puncturing it from time to time with the point.

"I'll leave you to talk it over. I have to make a call," Wood said. Neither of them raised their eyes as he stood.

Shawna had called Andy and given him a number. He called it and found out she'd taken Winter to her dormitory room at the hospital. Winter, she said, was down the hall watching television. The original version of *King Kong* was on the late show.

"What's going on, Wood? You sound strange."

"Listen," Wood said, "I'll be out of touch until late morning."

"Won't you tell me what's happening?"

"Can't. Talk to you tomorrow." He hung up then, resting his hand on the receiver while he thought. Then he picked it up again, told the operator to charge the call to his home, and dialed Danahy's number.

Charlene answered in a voice husky with sleep. He apologized for waking her and asked to speak to Jack, explaining that it was urgent.

He waited a few moments while an extension was picked up and the other one clicked off.

Wood talked a full five minutes without hearing a single sound from the other end. "Jack, are you listening?"

"Yeah—I'm listening."

"I was afraid you'd fallen asleep, you were so quiet."

"Fallen *asleep*, you crazy maniac. I'm sitting here in a chair in my study listening to you, and I'm speechless!"

"Good. Stay that way till I finish." He outlined the plan then, leaving out Cohen's and Jenkins's names until he found out whether or not Danahy was going to agree to go along with it.

"Those two cops, whoever they are—they said they'd do it?"

"Not yet. They're deciding now. If you—"

"Don't play games with me, Wood," he said sharply. "Where're you calling from?"

"A phone booth—on the East Side," he lied.

"You're beginning to think like a detective. Don't tell me where you are, I might have you picked up and hauled off to Bellevue. You also haven't told me where and what time you plan to stage this little caper. More good thinking. That means you've decided to do it with or without me." There was a long pause; it sounded like he was pouring a drink. "Apart from the *real* issue, do you realize I could lose my job?"

"Jack, only you can evaluate the risks, and how you'd feel about taking them."

"I suppose you've already—"

"That's my problem."

Cohen and Jenkins were deep in conversation when Wood came back. He interrupted them. "Jack Danahy from Homicide will do it," he said.

"Good. That'll cover our asses some," Jenkins said.

Cohen got up. "Let's get out of here. We've got a night's work ahead of us."

The interns' lounge at the Payne Whitney psychiatric clinic was empty. Winter sat alone, wrapped in Shawna's robe, watching television on a green vinyl couch, her feet curled under her. Although Shawna had borrowed some clothes for her to wear, she felt cozy in Shawna's bathrobe and put it on the minute they got to the hospital. Winter didn't understand why they had left in such a hurry, but Shawna explained she'd already taken off so much time she really had to be on duty tonight.

Winter was watching a movie about a family; they were sitting around a fire in a house in the country. A father was reading to his two daughters, one of them Winter's age, the other a little younger. They were nestled close to their father, listening to him. A little boy, about five or six, was lying on the floor on a cushion, playing with a toy car; a large, shaggy dog slept at his feet. The mother, a pretty, blond-haired, blue-eyed woman, was bringing a tray of hot chocolate and cookies to the children. She put it down on a coffee table, then sat next to one of the daughters and put her arm around her. The little girl leaned her head against her mother's shoulder, and the mother stroked her forehead as they listened. Then the little boy crawled up onto her lap, cuddling there, his thumb in his mouth. The little girl looked up at her mother and said, "I love you, Mommy." "And I love you, darling," the mother said and kissed the top of her head.

Winter felt a pain, like a great crushing weight on her chest. There was a sudden burning in her throat, and her eyes swelled with tears, spilling down over her cheeks, dropping onto her hands.

A commercial came on. Winter put her head back and shut her eyes, squeezing out the tears, and tried to think what it must be like to be dead. Mama, she called out in her mind, please find Freddie and take care of her. Maybe she isn't used to being dead yet and she's wandering around all alone out there, not knowing what to do. Maybe she's worried about me and doesn't know how to hear my thoughts like you do. Mama, teach Freddie how to talk to me like you used to when you first went there. She concentrated as hard as she could until she could see first Freddie's face, then her whole body. There! Freddie, where'd you get that dress? Did they give it to you? Freddie smiled her secret smile, her eyes clear and shining, blue like the summer sky, shining right down on her. Freddie, tell me what to do, I don't know what to do now. You always have good ideas, you have to tell me. Please don't go.

"Winter?" Shawna was standing beside her. She put her hand on her head, smoothing down her hair. "How about getting some sleep now? Is *King Kong* over?"

"I changed the channel, Shawna—it got too scary. Can I just watch this movie? I'm not tired, I slept this afternoon."

"All right. I'm still catching up on my work. Come in when it's over—you remember where my room is?"

"Yes. Down that hall and through the glass doors, four-twelve."

"Okay, here's some change for the Coke machine, in case you get thirsty."

Winter nodded. "Thanks." The movie was back on. The father was on a train, a sound she loved. She half closed her eyes and pretended she was on the train with him. He was her father, that tall handsome man with his gentle voice and kind eyes, and they were going on a trip, just the two of them.

He was talking. She opened her eyes and saw he was talking to a beautiful dark-skinned woman who was sitting next to him. She was really beautiful; darker than Winter. He was lighting her cigarette. She smiled and thanked him, then took off her hat, which was large and shaped almost like a man's, except she was wearing it at a little angle, tilted over her eye. Now she smoothed back her hair. It was pulled tight into a knot at the back of her neck.

Winter's hands went to her hair, smoothing it back and holding it in a knot. She listened carefully. The woman was a model, just back from Paris. She said some things in French which he didn't understand and that made the woman laugh. He laughed too. Then they were walking through the car of the train. How tall she was, almost as tall as he. She was wearing a black suit with a soft pleated skirt that moved as she walked. The train lurched and he took her arm to steady her.

Next they were in the dining car, sitting across from each other, and she was smiling at him, an enormous smile that showed even, white teeth and dimples. Dimples! Winter smiled and felt her cheeks to see if she had them, pressing her fingers in the place where they ought to be. The woman was holding a drink in her long slender hands, and Winter could see she had a lot of little gold rings on almost all of her fingers.

He lit her cigarette again, this time touching her hand as he did. She had a wonderful way of blowing smoke out in a narrow, gentle little stream, pursing her lips ever so slightly. Winter did the same with an imaginary cigarette, copying her every gesture, sitting up straight now and paying close attention to the way she cocked her head to one side, catching a stray hair, tucking it back into the knot, then suddenly throwing her head back and laughing—a deep, throaty laugh that Winter would have to practice.

The screen went black and they were in bed together! Even though they were partly covered with a sheet, it was clear they were naked. Her hair, loose, was spread out on the pillow. How could the man do this? What about his children and his nice, blond wife? They all loved each other so much.

The two people kissed again and again, in close-up. Winter could see the man's tongue going into the woman's mouth. He was on top of her and the woman's eyes were closed, her long black lashes curled against her cheek. She liked it. She liked what he was doing to her. She was whispering in his ear and there was a small smile on her lips. Her hands were resting on the back of his neck, caressing it with her nails.

Another commercial came on. Winter got up and turned off the television and went to the window. The street was nearly deserted, except for a couple of taxis and an ambulance turning into the driveway of the hospital. Beyond the street she could see the river, shimmering and still. She watched, thinking, could she ever become like that woman? Tall and elegant, making men fall in love with her even when they were married to someone nice and loved their children? More than that, she wondered could she ever be in bed with a man, naked and kissing—liking to do that same thing—that awful, horrible thing that she kept feeling again and again, making her want to scream out until it went away. Was it really possible to make yourself like it?

She heard the door open behind her and Shawna came in. "Winter," she called softly, "come to bed now. I'm on duty and I have to go downstairs, but I'd like to tuck you in first."

"Where will you sleep? There's only one little bed."

"I'll get a nap in the morning. I'm used to it." She had a clipboard and a pencil in her hand and looked for the first time like a doctor.

"Okay," Winter said.

Alone in Shawna's room Winter was unable to sleep. Her mind was racing, thoughts tumbling one after the other, and she felt propelled to get up out of the bed. She found the light over Shawna's desk and turned it on, and she was at once amazed at the amount of papers and folders piled high on the desk. How hard she must work. A notebook was left open lying on top of everything, a pencil clipped to the page. Suddenly Winter caught a glimpse of her name written across the top of the page. Feeling more curious than guilty, she picked it up and began reading. The words were meaningless: "low level object relatedness . . . borderline personality organization . . . weak ego boundaries . . ." Then her eye fell to the bottom of the page. "Recommendation: minimum three months observation at Payne Whitney under care of Dr. McKinley . . ."

She put the book down. They were going to keep her here! A psychiatric hospital, a mental institution. That's why Shawna was so strange about rushing to get here; they've put her in a crazy house. How could she be so dumb?

Freddie had helped her after all. She had made her stay awake so she could see the book, to warn her. She made her change the channel on the TV so she'd see that movie about the black model to show her what she could become. Now she had to think. She had to get out of here, but first there were some things she had to do. She picked up Shawna's phone and dialed the operator. "Could you connect me with the police, please?"

"Is this an emergency?"

"No, I mean yes, it's important—I guess it's an emergency."

"Dial 911," she said, and the phone went dead. She went to the door to see if anyone were in the hall, then dialed, her hands trembling.

A man's voice answered. "Police emergency," then something she didn't get, it was so garbled, then, "can I help you?"

"Are—are you a police officer?" she asked.

"What is the nature of the emergency, miss?"

"I want to tell someone about—a—a murder. See—I was—"

"Are you calling to give information about a homicide?"

"Yes—"

"Hold on please." He went away a minute. Then, "What is your name and present location?" he asked.

"No—I just wanted to talk to someone—on the phone."

"I see. How old are you?"

"I'm twelve—"

"Is there an adult with you?"

"What for? I can tell you myself; I was there!"

"What is the number you're calling from?"

She banged down the phone. "Oh, boy!" Then she took off Shawna's robe and got dressed quickly. Money, she thought, and looked in Shawna's closet. Her bag was there. Fumbling nervously, she found the wallet and took out twenty dollars.

"Dear Shawna," she wrote. "I have taken twenty dollars from your bag. I'm sorry I had to do that but I can't let you keep me in a mental—" She tried to spell institution. After crossing it out twice, she wrote, "hospital. I'm sorry you think I should be here for three months. Tell Mr. Wood some day I will find those men myself. I'm not afraid. Love, Winter. PS. I promise to pay you back the $20.00. PPS. Thank you and Mr. Wood for everything."

It was seven thirty when Shawna finished and got back to her room. Not finding the note right away, she went down the hall to the lounge to look for Winter, thinking she might be watching early morning cartoons on television. When she didn't find her there, she decided she must have gotten hungry and found her way to the cafeteria. Feeling not the least bit alarmed, she went back to her room to write her reports and wait for Winter.

The note was lying on top of the notebook. As she picked it up, she realized the notebook was left open to the page she'd been writing on about Winter. Winter's note was right on top of it.

"Damn!" She banged the desk with her fist, sending papers flying across the floor. Then she ran to the window, as though catching sight of her getting into a cab would help. God! Why had she lied to her? To frighten her about Wood's call would have been better than to let her think she was being committed, for Christ's sake.

Half wanting to run out and search the city streets herself, she tore through the pages of her phone book looking for Wood's number. She'd never in her life been able to remember anyone's number. Often she forgot her own. She dialed, letting it ring eight or nine times before she gave up. Then she rummaged through her desk drawers, her pockets, finally her bag for the piece of paper on which she'd written down that other number. What was his name? Dicky? No—*Andy*. She called and asked for him. It was a police switchboard of some kind; Wood had been oddly mysterious about it, and the man, Andy, talked almost in a whisper when she called last night to leave the number for Wood. The noise in the background made it difficult to hear him. The wait now seemed interminable.

"Yes?" he said abruptly.

"I'm sorry," she said, "but I have to reach Homer Wood. It's urgent."

He cut her off before she could explain. "Listen," he hissed, "I can't do this anymore."

"Please, it's important. A child's life is in danger," Shawna shouted, not caring how melodramatic it sounded.

He paused, obviously used to such phrases. "I'm just going off duty. Give me your number, I'll try to raise him before I leave."

"Okay, but look, in case he can't reach me, would you tell him that *Winter is gone*. Got that?"

"Jesus, lady, I'm supposed to give him weather reports now? What kind of a code is that?"

She thanked him and looked up Sergeant Danahy's number, which she'd somehow put in her book under C, for Charlene.

It was she who answered, sounding delighted to hear from Shawna and ready to chat. Shawna quickly explained that she needed to get a message to Wood, and was hoping that Jack might know how to reach him.

"That's funny," Charlene said. "Wood called here very late last night and he and Jack talked for a long time on the phone, then Jack got dressed and drove into town. He wouldn't tell me anything."

Shawna sat and thought. An alarm had signaled in her when she put that information together with the way Wood sounded on the phone last night. She wished she were a better detective.

Barbara was startled to see Wood standing at the door at eight in the morning. He looked a wreck, as if he'd been up all night; his clothes were rumpled, he needed a shave and certainly a shower. She wondered if he'd been drinking, his eyes looked so odd.

"Homer, what is it?"

"Nothing. I've been working all night, that's all. I need to talk to Donnie."

"Oh, Homer, must you? She was so upset last night I couldn't get her to sleep until almost eleven. Can't it wait until she comes home from school?"

"I'll straighten it out with her. Do you mind if I go wash up first?"

"No—of course not, you know where the clean towels are. There's a razor there somewhere too. But listen, I've got to get to the office early, my boss is preparing a brief for trial tomorrow morning. I was going to drop Donnie on the way."

"Go ahead. I'll have breakfast with her and take her to school." His voice was flat and had a harshness that made Barbara hesitate. "What's the matter?"

"Nothing."

"Okay," she said.

Donnie was sitting on the edge of her bed putting on her shoes. She scowled when she looked up and saw Wood.

"Have you come to take away my makeup? Because it's not fair. I sent away for it with my own money that I saved out of my allowance. Besides," she said, near tears, "they're only samples, you know, and there's hardly any left!"

"I'm not going to take them away, honey." He sat down on the bed next to her. "I want to talk to you." He thought a moment, unsure how to begin. "Do you know what prostitutes are?"

She jumped up. "God! All I did was try on some makeup!"

"Forget about the damned makeup! I'm asking you—do you know what they are?"

"*Yes.*" She rubbed at her eyes with the back of her hand. She looked frightened. "Why're you asking me?"

"Because I want you to help me do something—"

She looked at him cautiously, still teary-eyed. "What?"

"Let's go make some breakfast and I'll tell you about it." He put his arm around her shoulder and hugged her, to reassure himself as much as her.

As he poured himself a cup of coffee, he noticed a slight tremor in his hand. Donnie reached into the cabinet and got out a bowl for cold cereal, peeking at him from time to time out of the corner of her eye. They sat at the kitchen counter.

"There's a man—a really evil man that the police are trying to question about the death of a young girl—"

"The girl that was pushed out a window? She was a prostitute, wasn't she?"

"I'm not sure. People are saying she was."

"She was my age, wasn't she?" Donnie asked, eating her cereal.

"How do you know so much about it?"

"I read your story in the *Daily News*, that's how. And I saw the picture you took. She looked kinda like me, didn't she?"

He nodded. "That's what gave me the idea. The police can't pick the man up they want to question, unless they have a reason, so we thought we'd help give the police that reason."

"Is he a pimp?"

He frowned at her. "Yes." He sipped his coffee, finding it difficult to swallow. "What he does—is go up to a young girl and talk to her, to try to get her to—uh, work for him."

"I know. And then he keeps all her money and if she doesn't give it to him, he throws her out the window or something, right?"

He shook his head. "And I was wondering how to explain it."

"Oh, Dad, everyone knows about that. What was her name?"

"Freddie."

"That's funny, we both have boy's names, sort of. That's really weird. So what do you want me to do?"

He took a long breath. "I want you to come to a coffee shop with me and a lot of cops—including Uncle Jack—and just sit there. The—man usually goes there for breakfast. If he sees you sitting there all by yourself, he'll probably come up to you and start talking. You'll have a microphone hidden on you and the minute he starts asking you anything incriminating, the cops can arrest him."

"I'll be wired for sound? Oh, wow!"

"Uncle Jack and I will be watching and listening from the kitchen with several other cops. They'll have men out front in the restaurant too."

"That's dumb, he'll see them!"

"No, they'll look like ordinary customers—"

"Dad, a criminal can always spot a cop. I think I should be alone with just you there. Tell Uncle Jack to give you his gun—and when he starts to get funny with me, you come up behind him and say, 'Freeze!' and if he doesn't, you can shoot him—"

"*Donnie.*" He was almost shouting. "This can't work unless you promise to do exactly as we say and only what we say, understand?"

"Okay, okay. How'd you talk Mom into letting me do this?"

He looked at her, then closed his eyes to shut out her question.

"You didn't tell her?"

He shook his head.

"Oh, boy," she said.

"Take a very good look at your father, because the next time you see me, I'll have a rope around my neck."

"We won't tell her!"

"Yes, we will. But that's my problem, not yours. Now, I want you to go and put your makeup on exactly as you did last night. I'll call school and tell them—"

"Tell them I can't come," she called from down the hall, "because I have to go be a prostitute!"

"For Christ's sake, am I really doing this?" he asked, muttering to himself as he dialed the phone.


Three taxis pulled up, one right after another in front of the apartment building. Vinnie Jenkins was in the first one. He waved to Wood and Donnie to get in, and introduced them to Tom Cummins, who was holding a tape machine on his lap. Wood sat up front with another one of the linebackers he remembered from the pimp bar. "Hi. I'm Johnny Cremmers," he said shaking hands.

"Think of all the people cursing that they can't find a cab this morning," Wood said.

"In this town it helps to know the right people," Jenkins said.

Their banter reminded Wood of the days in Nam. Of the conversations in the back of the jeep on the way to the front.

Donnie was dressed in blue jeans, platform sandals and a low-cut, blue T-shirt with the words, "I love the Big Apple," written in white letters around a large, bright red apple. Wood smiled to himself when he realized she was also wearing a bra stuffed with something; Kleenex, he guessed. Once having made the decision to put the plan in operation, and having convinced himself she'd be in no danger, he knew he had to ignore the sharp pangs he felt when he saw her in the makeup again. As for the morality of the plan, he'd have to face that later. He wouldn't let himself off easy, either. For now he just concentrated on making it work.

Jenkins was showing her the tiny transistor microphone. "Let's see where we can hide it on her."

"Here," she said, taking it and slipping it inside her bra, burying it in the Kleenex.

"Okay, run a test on her, Tom," he said to Detective Cummins.

"Ready," he answered.

"Okay, talk, Donnie."

"This is Detective Donnie Wood speaking—"

They laughed. Cummins reversed the tape and played it back.

"This is Detective Donnie Wood speaking—"

"Is that how I sound?"

"It's a bit muffled," Cummins said to Jenkins. "I don't know what we're picking up—"

"I know what you're picking up," Wood said and leaned over to the back seat to whisper in Donnie's ear. "Can you get the Kleenex out of the way?"

"Oh. Yes, wait." And, reaching in, she moved the mike a bit. "Now try it."

It was perfect. They ran her through the instructions again. She was to give no information other than what she was told to say; she could say she was fourteen, because he'd expect her to lie about her age, and "just let him do all the talking," Jenkins said. "That's what they do, anyway. The 'poppin' game,' it's called. They talk on, nonstop, and never let you get a word in edgewise, which is what we want. But most of all, Donnie, you don't get up from that table. No matter what, understand?"

"Yes, I know. My father already told me that."

"Good. You can make up a name, though. Got one?"

"Uh-huh. Peaches."

They were across town and getting near the coffee shop.

"Is Danahy there yet?" Wood asked.

"Danahy, Cohen, and Halsey should all be there by now. McGeary and Drafts, in the car behind us, will be sitting at the counter, the rest of us'll be in the kitchen."

"Your friend Danahy collected on every favor ever owed him in the whole Department today," Jenkins said.

"Looks like you've got a few friends yourself, Vinnie," Wood said.

"Yeah. And they've all got kids."

"The pimp won't make them as cops?" Wood asked.

"No way. Those two guys are from downtown. They decoy as drunks sleeping in doorways, junkies, bums—wait'll you see them."

"What's the third cab for?" Donnie asked.

"For you. Very soon you're going to get in it. The man driving it is Richie; he's going to take you to the coffee shop."

Wood gave her two dollars. "Tip him well."

"Where's he going to go after he drops me? He can't come in or it'll look funny."

"That's right," Jenkins said. "She even thinks like a detective.

He'll park the cab around the corner and come into the kitchen through the back."

They turned onto Eighth Avenue. "Are there any women lieutenants?" she asked.

"No, not yet."

"Good. I'll be the first then." They pulled over to the curb. "What's Angie Dickinson?" she asked.

"A movie star," Wood said as he opened the door for her.

He watched her get into the empty cab, saw the "off-duty" light go off as the flag was put down and they drove off.

"You okay?" Jenkins asked Wood. "Some terrific kid. She'll be fine."

"Yeah," Wood said through clenched teeth.

The cabs each stopped at different locations, and the men, including Wood, took separate routes to the back entrance of the coffee shop, while Richie drove around another twenty minutes to give the others time to set up.

The windows in the two kitchen doors had been replaced with a one-way glass, and a man was already stationed as a waiter by the time Wood arrived.

Danahy was issuing orders to the men in sharp tones; he greeted Wood with just a nod, then asked, "How is she?"

"All set," he answered.

Danahy showed Wood where Donnie would be sitting, in a booth directly in their line of vision.

"Did you talk to Gallagher?" Wood asked.

"No go. He should be at the DA's right about now, getting the court order. The good news is, he doesn't know we're here."

"Thanks."

"It's my ass too, Wood."

"I know."

"Okay," someone said quietly, "here she is."

Wood felt his spine stiffen, his hands were cold; damp. She looked small and ridiculous walking to the booth alone. And not a bit nervous.

"Good girl," Jenkins whispered. "Straight to the booth without looking around."

"What time is it?" Wood asked.

"Ten fifteen. Our boy usually comes out at ten thirty." It was Cohen. "He either comes here or to Al's on the next block. Either way, he has to pass here first. He'll be able to spot Donnie from the window."

"Won't he freak—she looks so much like Freddie?" one of the men asked.

"That was Wood's idea," Danahy said. "We're counting on him to freak and have to come in to have a closer look."

"You don't figure he'll freak and run?"

"He's too fucking arrogant."

"Besides," Gus said, "all honkies look alike to us anyway."

"Who's making the arrest?" Wood asked.

"Not me," Cohen said quickly.

"Gus and I will," Danahy said. "Unless there's a problem, then your linebackers'll get there first."

"Don't—say—that," Wood said.

Donnie's voice came over the transmitter. "Just coffee, please, with three sugars."

"Loud and clear," Cummins said.

"She's not allowed to drink coffee," Wood said under his breath.

"Target approaching." Jenkins said it quietly.

Wood noticed they'd moved their guns around to the front of their belts. He began to feel perspiration soaking through his shirt. They were motionless, energy contained, pulsating in the air around them. No one spoke.

Out on the street Pretty Joey had passed the window, glancing in briefly, then stopped. He was wearing a light blue suit with a matching hat. His silk shirt was of a paler blue, opened at the neck, sunlight bouncing off the gold chains and the large medallion.

He looked again through the window, this time shielding his eyes from the sun's reflection on the glass. He seemed to be deciding.

Donnie, if she noticed, didn't show it, at least from the back. Her head was bent over the coffee cup. Wood was thinking he'd feel better if he could see her face.

Pretty Joey opened the door and walked in, his eyes on Donnie. He frowned when he took off his sunglasses. Then automatically his eyes swept the room, not stopping on McGeary and Drafts sitting at the counter with their backs to him. They looked like workmen on a coffee break.

But the pimp was visibly troubled, and Wood was ready to

say a prayer of thanks that the son of a bitch was freaking after all. He went to the cigarette machine near the door and dropped the coins in slowly, pausing a moment to look at her again.

Jesus Christ, she must have smiled at him, Wood thought, as he watched the pimp's face suddenly relax. He took his cigarettes and headed straight for her table, removing his hat and bowing ceremoniously to her; presenting himself before the queen.

"Allow me, lovely lady, to pay homage to your beauty. Beauty, you know, is the greatest power there is, and I bow before it, humbly."

"Holy shit," Jenkins said.

"If there's one thing I can't stand, it's an uppity nigger," Halsey said.

"If I may but begin the day by drinking in a bit of your loveliness with my morning coffee, I would be most grateful."

"Okay," they heard Donnie say.

"*Okay?*" Halsey said. "What kind of an answer is that?"

The pimp snapped his fingers at the detective dressed as a waiter and ordered two coffees and an English muffin, then he turned his attention back to Donnie.

"My name's Tommy. What's yours?"

"Peaches."

"And cream. Are you here on holiday?"

"Yes," Donnie answered.

"First visit?"

She nodded.

"Where're you staying? Wait—let me guess. The royal suite at the Waldorf?"

She gave a little laugh. "No."

"The Plaza?"

She shook her head.

"I know. The Carlyle. I'm told certain types of royalty prefer the privacy there."

Wood felt she must be beginning to squirm. He wished the pimp would make his pitch so they could move in and get it over with.

"I give up. Where are you staying, little Highness?"

"I—don't know yet. I just got here."

He reached into his inside jacket pocket; the men in the kitchen tensed, ready to uncoil and spring out. Someone grabbed

Wood's shoulder to restrain him. The men at the counter looked up sharply, at the reflection in the mirror; they too were ready.

The pimp took out a tourist map and spread it on the table.

"Let's see," he said, moving across to her seat, sliding in easily next to her. Donnie edged over, pressing against the partition.

Wood made a rasping, unintelligible sound.

"Wait," Jenkins said, "here it comes now."

"What can we show you—? The Empire State Building, the Statue of Liberty, Chinatown—"

"I've been to Chinatown dozens of times—" She froze, knowing she'd made a mistake. Without thinking, her hand flew to her shirt as though to hide the mistake from the microphone. "I don't mean I've—been there—I—"

The pimp watched her, his eyes narrowing until they were only dark, glittering slits.

"Okay, let's go!" Wood said.

In an instant the pimp had it all put together. He reached inside her shirt, tearing it, and extracted the microphone, some Kleenex tumbling out with it. At the same time, in the other hand, was the knife. Only the men at the counter saw it; they wheeled around, guns drawn. The waiter moved forward, taking his gun out from under his apron, and the kitchen doors swung open.

The pimp was speaking into the mike. "I got a knife a half inch away from her belly. Feel it, baby? Tell them you feel it." He thrust the mike close to her lips.

She opened her mouth in a scream, but no sound came out. She nodded her head.

"*Say* it!" She felt the point of it.

"Yes," she whispered, as loudly as she could.

"Princess Peaches and I are going to leave now, gentlemen . . ."

Wood's eyes burned with tears. He watched, paralyzed, as his little girl stood up and without looking back, walked with the pimp, his arm around her shoulders holding her close, the knife in the other hand pressed against her bright blue shirt.

"Peaches and I are going out the door now—"

"My name is not Peaches," she said loudly. "It's Freddie! And if you couldn't kill me by pushing me out the window, how do you know you can with a knife?"

He hesitated, gawking at her, his eyes wild, and she quickly pushed his hand away and leaped to the side.

"Down on the floor, Donnie!" Wood yelled.

"Hold it, Joey! You've had it!" Jenkins shouted as he took aim.

The pimp threw himself at her, the knife aimed at her when Jenkins fired. Wood was shoved out of the way, knocking over a tray of coffee as he fell to the floor.

Pretty Joey went down with a scream of pain, less than three feet away from where Donnie lay facedown, her hands covering her head. His pale blue trousers were ripped at the legs; blood spread in widening circles over one knee and on the calf of the other leg. It started to trickle onto the floor.

Donnie looked up and stared as Jenkins, still holding the gun, pounced, rolling Pretty Joey over on his stomach. He yanked Pretty Joey's wrists behind his back and snapped on a pair of handcuffs. Donnie's face went white and mascara-stained tears streamed down her cheeks, streaking her makeup. She opened her mouth but could make no sound.

"Get an ambulance," someone shouted.

"Get those people out of here, and seal off the front door!"

Wood got up, sweeping away the trays and dishes that had fallen on him, and ran, soaked with steaming coffee, to Donnie. He knelt and gathered her into his arms. "Donnie, are you all right, honey? Oh, God."

She shuddered, sobbing, and buried her face in his chest. "He was really going to kill me, wasn't he, Daddy—he was really going to—with that knife—"

"God," Wood whispered again, holding onto her tightly.

"How is she?" It was Danahy. He bent down. His face was grim, but he spoke quietly. "Donnie, are you hurt? Do you want to lie down a minute?"

"No—I want to go home." She looked up into Wood's face. "Can we go home? I want to—see Mom—can we call Mom?"

Cohen brought out a cool washcloth and handed it to Wood. He pressed it gently to her cheek, and she wiped her face with it, rubbing her nose. Wood and Danahy got her to her feet and led her away, toward the back. Wood was fighting to control his own unsteadiness.

"Was he really going to kill me, Dad?" She was taking short little breaths, shuddering with each one. "He was, wasn't he?" Pretty Joey's groans sounded in her ears.

"Sergeant Danahy? Excuse me, we just got a message your wife is trying to reach you. She says it's urgent." Danahy frowned. "Halsey! Take Wood and Donnie home, then come back and pick me up." He turned to Donnie, taking her chin in his hand; he raised her face and looked at her. His great baby-blue eyes were reddened.

"You are the bravest little girl I have ever seen. You acted quickly and intelligently. I'm very proud of you, Donnie Wood."

"Thank you, Uncle Jack," she said, her mouth trembling. His eyes became suddenly moist. He kissed her on the cheek and hurried away.

As they got to the squad car, a uniformed officer came running up and stopped them. "Are you Homer Wood?" he asked.

"Yes."

"Someone just called from communications with a message for you. I hope I got it right—he said to tell you 'winter is gone.' That mean anything to you?"

Wood's head fell back against the seat. "You got it right. Thanks."


Barbara was taking dictation when the call came, interrupting Mr. Stewart's flow of thought. "It's for you, Mrs. Wood," he said, trying to conceal his irritation. "Please make it short."

"I'm sorry," she said as she took the phone. "Hello, what—? Didn't she go to school? Tell me what's wrong—I can't come home. Is she sick?"

Mr. Stewart was watching her. "He hung up," she said. "Something's wrong with my daughter—he wouldn't say what—" She looked at him, agonized. "I'm sorry."

"That's all right, Mrs. Wood," he said, not meaning it. "I'll see if one of the other girls is free."

"I'll come back as soon as I can."

He pressed the intercom button on his phone. "I hope it's nothing serious. Rhonda, can you come in here and take dictation?" he said into the phone. He turned to his law book then and didn't look up as Barbara left his office. She closed the door behind her quietly, then grabbed her bag from her desk, and ran for the elevator.

\* \* \*

Donnie was still in the same clothes. Her T-shirt had been torn where the microphone was jerked out, and it was smudged with dirt from the coffee-shop floor. The remainder of her makeup was smeared and tearstained.

She ran to the door when she heard the key in the lock and flew into her mother's arms. Wood waited behind her at a distance and watched helplessly as Donnie, crying and talking incoherently, hung onto her mother. Horrified, Barbara stared at Donnie's face and clothes, then at Wood.

"*Knife?* What man? Tell me what happened, Homer!"

"Barbara, I used Donnie as a decoy this morning, in a police stakeout. I had her pose as a prostitute to trap a pimp who was responsible for the murder of a little girl Donnie's age." His voice was flat, matter-of-fact. "She wasn't hurt, but she's badly shaken up. She saw the man get shot."

Her expression of uncomprehending shock changed to rage. Her eyes grew wild. Unfastening Donnie's arms from around her waist, she took a step toward him, tense, like an animal about to spring.

"*You did what.*" It was not a question, it was a war cry.

"Mommy, I wanted to! Dad told me all about it and I wanted to. Why're you mad at him?"

"Go to your room, Donnie. I want to talk to your father alone." Donnie ran to Barbara and stood in front of her, between them. "Boy, you're so dumb, Mom! You'd rather be mad at Dad instead of being glad I wasn't hurt. Uncle Jack said I was the bravest girl he ever saw, but you don't care about that." She was forcing herself not to cry, holding firmly onto her anger. "I only wanted you to come home because I could have been killed and I needed to see you. Now you want me to go to my room so you can yell your head off at Dad. Well, I won't! You have to yell at both of us."

As Wood looked at Donnie, a slow, trembling smile crept over his face and tears came to his eyes. She's grown up, he thought. She's the only one here who's got the thing straight. He turned then, to Barbara, his partner and coauthor of this miracle, to share the moment, the awakening, and found she was glaring at him with a scalding anger.

"Thank you, Homer. Last night I needed you to remind me why I divorced you. Today you have."

Donnie lowered her eyes and frowned, screwing up her face as she always did when she needed to figure something out.

"I'll leave you to say good-bye to Donnie," Barbara said.

Wood waited till she left the room, then walked to the door, his arm around Donnie. "You okay?" he asked her.

"Yes," she said. "How about you?" He squeezed her to him. Words stuck in his throat. He kissed her forehead.

"Hey," she said as he opened the door, "how'd you like the way I threw Freddie's name at him like that? It really unglued him, didn't it?"

"It sure did. What made you think to do that?"

"I don't know, I was wondering that myself. Does that ever happen to you?"

"Oh, yes, but seldom as on the nose as that. 'Bye, honey," he said, feeling teary again. He started down the hall.

"Let me know the next time you need me!" she called. "And don't worry about Mom; she'll be all right."


He called Shawna from a phone booth, adding a nickel every few minutes in order to tell her the whole story. He wanted to find out about Winter too, and told her he was on his way to Lieutenant Gallagher's office now, to really get his ass broken— by an expert.

"Where's his office?" she asked.

"Fifty-first and Third. Why?"

"I'll meet you there. It's my fault we lost Winter, so if your lieutenant likes to break asses, let him try to break mine."

After he hung up, he remembered he meant to ask her if McKinley was Irish or Scottish. Meant to ask her a dozen times, in fact. Now he'd have a chance to see for himself, he thought with a smile.

It was hot for late May, and his shirt and jacket were damp from perspiration and covered with coffee stains. He hadn't slept, hadn't eaten; he was in great shape to go and face the dragon.


Danahy, Halsey, and Jenkins were in Gallagher's office when he got there. Cohen and the rest of the linebackers apparently didn't have to answer to the lieutenant. Gallagher, in shirt-sleeves, was standing just inside the door. He spotted Wood coming down the hall.

"Here he comes. Where's the picture?" he asked Wood.

"What picture?"

"Of the girl, Wood. You've got one, haven't you?"

"Of Winter? No—"

Gallagher turned full face to him. "You mean all this time you've been chasing around behind my back trying to prove my CUPPI is a homicide and *hiding* the only witness to what you *believe* to be a murder—and you never even got a picture of her? What the hell kind of a news photographer are you!"

There was a deadly silence in the room. "Any way to get some coffee around here?" Wood asked.

Young Connelly appeared, seemingly out of nowhere, and offered to get some. "Okay, boss?" he asked. Wood and Danahy exchanged looks. Jenkins went to use the phone in the adjoining room.

Gallagher nodded and sat down, running his hands over his hair, in a familiar gesture of frustration. "Nice piece of work, Wood." He sighed. "You got me a collar and lost my only witness. How'd you manage that? What am I supposed to do with a pimp in a hospital with his kneecaps blown off—go down there and beat him with a rubber hose until I get a confession out of him?"

"Arrest him for assault with a deadly weapon in the meantime," Wood said.

"Fine. So we've got your suspect in the slammer, and your witness hiding away in some slum in New Jersey. Now you can go sell a story to *New York* magazine about how a journalist jeopardized his own kid's life to prove that Homicide hides its cases in a CUPPI file. Great. Maybe you'll be able to afford a new wardrobe. You look like you could use one."

"You know, Gallagher, I think I've taken all the shit I'm going to take from you," Wood said.

"I guess I'm in the right place." They all turned at the same time. Gallagher's mouth fell open as he looked up and saw Shawna in the doorway, strikingly beautiful in a pale pink summer suit and fresh white starched cotton shirt. Her hair was combed loose, thick and straight to her shoulders. She was wearing high-heeled shoes and the way she stood, tall and straight, chin raised and tilted slightly, she looked like a heroine out of a

Greek tragedy making her entrance. Wood mentally applauded her.

Gallagher stumbled to his feet, knocking the chair back and trying clumsily to catch it.

Barely able to hide his amusement, Wood introduced her, taking particular care to use the word "doctor" in front of her name. Shawna greeted Danahy first and asked after Jacky and Charlene. Then Wood introduced her to Jenkins, who came in to say he had to leave. When she shook hands with Gallagher, she met him head on, looking straight at him, destroying completely whatever composure he had left.

"May I sit down?" she asked. Three chairs were immediately offered her, simultaneously. She opened her briefcase and took out Winter's note, which she handed to the lieutenant. Next she took out her notebook. She explained that Wood had called her and asked for help with Winter. She explained that it was while the child was in her care that she disappeared. Finding the page in her notebook citing Winter's history, Shawna passed it across the desk to Gallagher. "This is why she ran away; she found this and read it."

Gallagher looked at it, glancing at Wood first.

"If you turn the page," she said, "you'll see the notes I made about the incident itself as she reported it, to Wood and me, plus the descriptions she gave of the other people."

"What other people?" Gallagher asked.

Wood answered: "A girl named Candy, who was supposed to be a model, and a man she called Mr. Blue. He was supposed to be the fashion editor of *Seventeen*."

He read: "Very tall; long, light blond hair worn in bangs, chipped tooth . . ."

"Connelly!" Gallagher called out.

"He went out for coffee, Lieutenant," Danahy said.

"Where the hell did he go for it, for Christ's sake?" Gallagher said. Then, "Excuse me, miss—I mean, Doctor. Danahy, call over to Midtown North, see if they have a pross—a prostitute on the books who fits that description. Now what've we got on the man?"

"Lieutenant, if my being here puts a restriction on your usual style of communication, perhaps I should go and let you get on with it."

"No, no—that's all right." He blushed when he saw she was

smiling, uncertain suddenly whether she was teasing or not. He looked quickly down at the book again. "She didn't describe the man?"

"Not to me. Did she to you, Wood?"

"White, middle-aged businessman, that's all," Wood said.

"That narrows it down some, we can rule out all the fat, black hippies we know."

Detective Connelly came in with the coffee. "Sorry it took so long, they were—" He stopped when he saw Shawna.

Gallagher motioned him in, impatiently. "It's all right, Connelly, she's unarmed. Put the coffee down, Connelly, and say hello to Dr. McKinley." Connelly took the containers out of the bag, then looked around the room, confused.

Shawna put out her hand. "Hi, I'm Dr. McKinley." She smiled at him. "What's your name?" He stared at her.

"He'll tell you as soon as it comes to him," Gallagher said and handed Wood and Danahy their coffee, passing his to Shawna. "Black okay?" he said.

"I really don't want any, thank you. Really."

"Connelly, call downtown to headquarters and see if the police artist is free to come up right away." To Shawna he said, "I'd like you and Wood to try to put together a composite for us, of Winter. Since we don't seem to have a photograph," he added, looking at Wood.

"I guess I wish now I hadn't been quite so overprotective of her. Wood wanted to get a picture, but she was so frightened of anyone finding out who she was. I'm afraid I just wanted to see her get well."

"Sure, of course," he said as the phone buzzed. He picked it up. "Lieutenant Gallagher." He paused. "Fine, show him in when he gets here. Who? Tell him I'll call him back." He put down the phone and excused himself, saying he had to talk to Danahy.

Wood was smiling. What a trickster she is, he thought. "McKinley is Scottish, isn't it?"

"Yes. Why?"

"I'd have guessed you were Irish."

"I am. Half."

He frowned, puzzled. "Which half? I thought your grandmother was an American Indian."

"That's right. My father's Irish."

"But—"

"My maiden name's O'Neill."

"Maiden name?"

"Yes. I was married to Richard McKinley. I kept the name after I was divorced."

"The heart surgeon?"

"Wood, stop looking at me like that. I'm not a convicted felon. I'm divorced, like everyone else."

But Wood was going through his files, putting it together. Shawna O'Neill, eighteen years old, one of the first co-eds at Yale, married Dr. Richard McKinley, fifty-six, and for a year or so they were photographed everywhere, here and in Europe, at parties, openings, discos. Then it was announced that Shawna was going to complete her education and go on to medical school. The press lost interest in her until they were divorced two years later, and that was only mentioned briefly.

"You were divorced five years ago?"

"Six."

He nodded. That's why she was so defensive that first night. For two years she was Richard McKinley's living proof of his virility and attractiveness, and probably felt that's all she was.

Danahy stuck his head in the door. "Wood, the lieutenant would like you and Shawna to come into another office."

They followed him out into the hall, through a large office with six or seven desks, detectives working at typewriters, telephones, file cabinets, charts, the guns in leather holsters the only reminder that this busy, efficient office functioned to solve murders.

"Looks like you do a fair amount of paperwork around here," Shawna said, accepting the men's appreciative glances with good grace.

"All in triplicate," Danahy said. "It's the part of the job the men complain about most."

They went into a smaller room. One large table, some more file cabinets, a few chairs, a darkened window, and a telephone. Shawna wondered what this room was for.

"That's a two-way mirror," Wood explained.

"Oh. A line-up room," Shawna said, and they laughed. Gallagher was sitting on the edge of the table, a folder in his hand. Halsey was going through some others.

"Dr. McKinley, this is Detective Halsey." They shook hands.

"He and Sergeant Danahy just ran the whole thing through for me, and I'd like to compare one or two facts with what you and Wood know. Do you have your notebook there?" She took it out. "The pimp squad sergeant—the little guy, what's his name?"

"Cohen," Halsey said.

"Yeah, Cohen. He saw Pretty Joey talking to Freddie and Winter a couple of days before, in the same coffee shop you guys used to set him up this morning, right?"

"Right," Danahy said. "It was his idea to use the same place."

"And the old whore—what's her name?" Gallagher asked.

"Big Alice. Jesus, it's bad enough these people all have six different names, they have to have adjectives to go with them? Okay, Big Alice told Cohen she saw Pretty Joey give the kids twenty bucks. Did Winter tell you that?"

"Yes, and that Big Alice chased them away afterward."

"Good. According to Winter's description, was there anything either of you can remember that stands out about Pretty Joey— Wood, maybe you better not answer, since you've seen him yourself."

Shawna thought a moment, then, consulting her notebook, she said, "He wore lots of gold chains and one of them had a medallion on it, his astrological sign." She turned the page. "It was a crab. He's a Cancer."

"He's a fucking plague—" Gallagher flinched, started to apologize to Shawna, then shrugged. They both laughed.

"Do you have a photograph of him there?" Shawna asked. "I know it doesn't mean anything, but I think I have a picture of him in my mind."

"Sure." Halsey handed it to her.

She looked at it. "Well, he's not as pretty as I thought, but there is something sort of elegant about him, isn't there?" She shuddered. "Hey, I have a good idea. Let's catch him and send him somewhere where they still have capital punishment. Utah, isn't it? Don't they still have a firing squad? I think I've just stopped being a liberal."

"We've already got him," Gallagher said. "Danahy, put a call in to Judge Gutstein." He began pacing, deep in thought. No one spoke until Danahy announced he had the judge on the line.

"Judge Gutstein? No, my name's Raymond. Yeah, that's right, I used to be in the First, and you ought to remember me. I was the guy who taught you how it really works—when you became

ADA." He laughed. "Now you got it, Eddie. Listen, on that bed-side arraignment you were called to, at St. Clare's Hospital? Kingsley, that's right. I'd like to ask you to keep the bail low and put off sentencing as long as possible. Looks like the game's going into extra innings, you know what I mean?" He paused and smiled. "Yeah, I'm still playing detective. Thanks, Judge Gutstein. I appreciate it."

Shawna looked confused. "You mean you're not going to send him to jail? You're going to let him go?"

"We'll send him when we're through with him. Meantime, where's he going? Is he going to hop into his private jet and fly off to the French Riviera? Dr. McKinley, the hardest thing my new detectives have to learn is not to rush a case. Every case has its own rhythm, its own timetable. You have to be patient and let it take you where it's going, take the time to see how the whole thing feels. Right in your gut, not in your head. My gut tells me now to sit back and let Pretty Joey hobble out of that hospital in his plaster casts and crutches and take us straight to his friend in the pinstripe suit. Let's catch the creep playing with little girls in pigtails and see where that takes us."

"My God," Shawna said. "I think I've just met a Metaphysical Cop."

The police artist arrived and Wood and Shawna sat in a room with him, explaining and describing Winter's features until he came up with something that was so good, they were incredu-lous. When he finished, Gallagher looked at the composite. "Satisfied?" he asked Wood and Shawna. They both agreed they were more than satisfied. Halsey was told to circulate copies all over the city and in New Jersey, near where she lived.

"Do you have to do that?" Wood asked. "She's not going back home."

Gallagher looked at him. "Hey, Wood, do I tell you what kind of film to use in your camera?"

"She didn't want her parents to find out," he said, knowing it was useless.

"A lot they care. They never even filed a missing persons on her. Can I see you in my office for a second—excuse us, will you, Doctor?"

Gallagher closed the door and turned to Wood. "I just wanted to tell you I think what you did this morning took a lot of guts. I'm never wrong about anyone, mind you, but I guess I must have missed something." They were standing there avoiding each other's eyes, looking anywhere but at each other, and for a flash of an instant Wood was fifteen years old again standing in his grandfather's parlor, being told he did the right thing that morning to stand up and raise his voice at the minister in church, when in his sermon the minister said that nonwhites were genetically inferior.

"Now for Christ's sake, will you go home and get out of those clothes. How do you expect to hang onto a girl like that looking the way you do?" He walked to the door, opened it, and called, "Connelly! Take my car and drive these people home. How the hell am I supposed to get any work done with all these civilians hanging around?"

They dropped Shawna at the hospital, then went to search for the Volvo. Wood knew he'd left it somewhere near Donnie's but couldn't remember exactly which street. Finally they found it; parked on Second Avenue at a meter.

"Uh-oh," Connelly said, "looks like you got a ticket. You're lucky you didn't get towed."

"Connelly, if I ever got towed, and they added up all my parking tickets, I could buy a new Cadillac for what it would cost me to buy that thing back."

When Wood got back to his apartment, he peeled off his clothes and took a long, very hot shower. Then, with a towel wrapped around his waist, he flopped down on his bed and slept immediately; a deep, dreamless sleep.

It was almost dark when he woke up. He had a peculiar feeling; something nagging at him, something he'd forgotten. He fumbled for the light and put on his glasses to see the time. Seven fifteen. As he stood up, his head began to pound and he realized he hadn't eaten all day. Still groggy, he went into the kitchen to make some scrambled eggs and coffee, trying all the while to figure out what it was he'd forgotten to do. A call he was supposed to make? Someone he was supposed to see? After he'd eaten, his head felt clearer, and he went to his desk to look through the mail. There, underneath a stack of envelopes, was the one addressed to Mr. and Mrs. Arthur Charles, c/o Coral Sands Hotel, Bermuda; inside, the photograph of Freddie, with the words "Do You Know Where Your Children Are?" pasted on the bottom.

That's it. He should have given this to Gallagher. The Forensic people might be able to do something with it. He was about to pick up the phone when something caught his eye. Down there on the street where he'd been absently staring, a teen-aged boy rode by on his bike. Sitting on the seat behind him, arms wrapped around his waist, was a little girl. He watched them until they disappeared down the street. The little girl was hugging him, her face resting against his back, and she was laughing. They had the same coloring; brother and sister.

He didn't need Forensics. He got out his phone book and searched for the number.

Mrs. Charles answered the phone. He identified himself as Detective Wood, who'd been to the house a few days ago, and asked to speak to Michael.

"That's odd," she said. "I was just about to call someone at your office. I was looking for the sergeant's card this minute."

"Why, Mrs. Charles? Has something happened?"

"I had a very strange phone call, just now, from a little girl who wouldn't leave her name, but insisted I tell her where my son is, because—" She stopped. "This is really strange."

"Go ahead, Mrs. Charles. What's strange?"

"Well, she practically *threatened* me. A child! She said I'd better tell her where Michael was because she had some pictures to sell him, and if she couldn't find him right away, she'd sell them to someone else. Well, at first I thought it was some silly girl who had a crush on him and was playing some sort of a joke, but then she said, 'tell him Freddie kept the negatives.' And that if he wanted them, he should come to the newsstand down the street from the hotel tomorrow night at eight o'clock and ask for Alice. She didn't say which hotel and she hung up before I could ask. I still think it was probably a cruel joke of some kind, but I thought I should tell the sergeant anyway—is he there?"

"He's away from his desk at the moment, but I'll be sure to tell him. Do you know where Michael is?"

"Yes. He's at the Princeton Club in New York. He's playing in a squash tournament tonight."

"What time?"

"Seven thirty or eight—I'm not sure. Why were you calling him?"

"I was returning his call. You didn't tell the girl where he was tonight, did you?"

"Certainly not. I don't understand—why would Michael be calling you?"

"I don't know. Thank you, Mrs. Charles. We'll be in touch." He hung up and called Cohen. He was told the sergeant was out in the field. "Is he on the beeper?" Wood asked.

"He is, if he remembers to turn it on. He's not so good with mechanics."

"Look, this is urgent. If you can't raise him, send someone to find him. Tell him Winter's with Big Alice and to go to the newsstand and meet me there. I'll try to get there about nine. Tell him to wait for me. Got that?"

"All except your name."

"I'm in great shape. Homer Wood."

"Wait a minute, someone was just looking for you. Detective Brown was asking if you'd been around tonight."

"Who's he?"

"She. Patti Brown."

"Oh. Is she there?"

"No, she's out in the field too. Want to leave a message?"

"Yes, the same one. Thanks."

He dressed quickly, his mind spinning crazily in all directions. Winter had it figured out before he did. If it were so, if Michael were in that room taking pictures that night—my God, he knows everything. Knew everything the day Wood talked to him in his room. Could he possibly be that cool? He'd have to be a monster. A fucking, dangerous monster. He wondered if maybe he should call Danahy, then decided there wasn't time, he might miss Michael. Or did he, like Winter, want the satisfaction of a face-to-face confrontation?

He ran down the stairs to his car, thinking. Okay, Winter, you get points for thinking faster than I did and more points for bravery. Just stay out of the way and keep yourself safe and I guarantee you a crack at him, if he's our boy.

He drove up Sixth Avenue at breakneck speed, knocking off four red lights in a row, and instead of parking illegally, he pulled into a garage on Forty-third, next to the Princeton Club; a gesture of gratitude for not getting nailed with a moving violation.

Since it had moved out of the old building in the Murray Hill section, the Princeton Club was about as Ivy League looking as a Howard Johnson's Motor Lodge. As he walked through the modern, characterless lobby, he remembered the high ceilings, the polished mahogany, and the faded antique rugs downtown and wondered what sort of progress this was called.

He rode the elevator up to the squash courts and found the spectator area. It was raised and partitioned by a large glass window, giving a good view of the courts. The benches were filled with spectators, mostly wives. Wood looked at the schedule posted on the wall and found M. Charles listed as a "B" player. A tall, bony woman in a Pucci dress told him the "B" players were just about to begin.

"Such an exciting game to watch, isn't it? My husband had the most enormous black and blue spot where he got hit with that ball. I don't know how he could sit, poor thing. Here they come!"

Wood saw Michael through the glass, stooping to get through the three-foot door, and running out onto the court, his movements swift and graceful; the consummate athlete, the American Dream in tennis whites, even to the sweat bands on his forehead and wrist.

Wood couldn't help wishing as he watched the small hard ball ricochet back and forth across the court that it would smash right into Michael's American Dream face. There were several rounds of applause as his team won, and the players waved to their audience. Drinks were served while they showered and dressed; Wood had a scotch to help quiet his rage.

The first one down from the showers was the man with the black and blue spot. He was greeted with a dry kiss from the bony lady and a dry martini to wash it down. Next came Michael, in khaki trousers, blue blazer, and button-down shirt; rosy cheeked, glowing with health, his blond hair curled just to his collar and still damp from the shower. He didn't see Wood right away. He took a Coke from the tray and joined his teammates, grabbing their shoulders jock style. When he did see him, he automatically smiled; then realizing who Wood was, he excused himself and walked over to him, his smile gone.

"Is this a coincidence?" he asked.

Wood shook his head. "Baseball and football are more my style."

"I see. Well, sorry, pal, I'm not in the mood to be interviewed."

"I just came to deliver a message that your mother got on the phone. A friend of your sister's has some pictures she's interested in selling—to you or to the police, she doesn't care which. The message she left with your mother was: 'Freddie kept the negatives.'"

Wood watched the rosy glow leave his cheeks. "I have a picture too. I was just on my way down to the lab with it. Amazing what those guys can do. Amazing." He took the picture of Freddie out of his pocket and showed it to Michael. "Your father gave me this. Great lens, that Nikkor four hundred millimeter. You can always tell when a picture's been taken by a telephoto lens by the foreshortening effect it has on the stuff in the foreground. Like that cab on the street—see how it looks like it's right up on the sidewalk next to her?"

Michael looked around the room nervously.

"Why don't we go somewhere and talk photography?" Wood said.

They went downstairs and found a quiet place in the corner of the library and sat in armchairs facing each other next to the window.

"I know all about the negatives. Tell me—one photographer to another—what do they pay you to take those pictures?"

"Sometimes fifty—sometimes a hundred. Depends." Michael kept his eyes fixed on the floor.

"On what?"

"How many we are." There was a defiance in the way he answered. "If they want movies and stills, they'll use three or four guys. If it's just stills they want, they'll only need one or two."

"How'd you get into this business? I mean, do you have an agent—or what?"

"*Look*—" Michael's handsome features were contorted with rage. He started to get up.

"*You* look, you miserable little shit. You're either going to sit right here and tell *me* who pays you and who your friends are, or I'll have the cops come in and drag your ass out of here. Right in front of your Ivy League friends." He leaned forward, his face inches from Michael's, and said slowly, biting each word, "Were you in the hotel room that night?"

"No! Jesus, no." Michael dropped his head in his hands. "Christ, is that what you thought?"

"When did you take the picture you mailed to Bermuda?"

"Two nights before. The night before finals began. Richie, a friend of mine, called and said we could make a hundred apiece if we wanted to come into town. Some big-shot rich guy was in town for a few days and—wanted pictures. We were on our way to his hotel—"

"The Rockmoor?"

"Yes. That's when I saw Frederica. I freaked. She was all made-up like—a whore! A little whore walking down the street laughing and carrying on with an older man and another little kid—a half-black girl, I think she was. Jesus. I went out of my mind. I don't know why, but I took the picture. I guess I was going to show it to her later and have it out with her. Anyway, I didn't go to the hotel with Richie. I told him I didn't feel well, and then I went to some bar and got drunk. The next day I sent the picture to my parents, to make them get the hell home."

"Why didn't you grab her off the street yourself?"

"Christ. I've asked myself that a million times." He looked at Wood in agony. "I was ashamed. I didn't want my friend to know."

"You mean your friend who takes pictures for pimps?"

"This was my own sister!"

Wood looked directly at Michael and asked without emotion, "Who taught your sister about sex, Michael?"

He gasped. "Oh, God. You son of a bitch." He fell back into the chair. Wood turned his head and looked out of the window. Michael began to cry, silently, his shoulders shaking, tears rolling from the corners of his eyes. "I didn't really—I never—"

Wood took out his handkerchief and tossed it to him. "Blow your nose, Michael. I need names, dates, descriptions—everything you've got. Right now your sister's case is in a folder marked 'CUPPI'—circumstances undetermined pending police investigation. And you know where they keep that folder? In the back of the filing cabinet, in the last drawer down. Maybe that's all right with you and your family, to have the whole mess forgotten as quickly as possible. But it's not all right with me. In fact it gives me a very big problem. You can help me or I can go pester Homicide to follow up on it."

"Of course I'll help you. Jesus, what do you think I am? Please, you've got to know I never hurt my sister. I loved her—I wouldn't do anything to hurt her."

Wood's voice softened. "Hey, listen, Michael. I can't help you with that." He shook his head. "I'm sorry, I can't handle that. So let's get off it, okay?"

They talked for another half an hour. Wood took it all down, the names of four of Michael's friends who had all been hired several times by pimps and sometimes prostitutes to take pictures. Michael didn't know Pretty Joey by any of his names, but he'd ask around.

The first time he did it was with Richie, who worked part-time as a fashion photographer's assistant. A model had invited him to a party and told him he could bring a friend, provided the friend had a camera; the host wanted lots of pictures.

"It was an incredible turn-on. Gorgeous models, some of them hookers, I guess; drugs, booze—the works. We had to leave the rolls of film that night, but sometimes they'd let us develop them ourselves and we'd keep some of the prints."

"They were the ones Freddie—Frederica found and blackmailed you with?" Wood asked.

He gave a short laugh. "She hit me for twenty bucks. I knew a couple of other guys who had cameras and told them about it, and from then on, whenever Richie heard about a party or a scene that someone wanted photographed, he'd let us all know. We did it for the kicks as well as for the money."

"All right. What we're going to do is contact your friends and find out what they know about a pimp called Pretty Joey. And we want to know who the rich guy from out of town was that Richie photographed at the Rockmoor. By the way, he must know it's the same hotel Freddie was killed in. Didn't he say anything to you afterward?"

Michael shook his head. "I haven't spoken to him. Or any of them since."

"Do you think you can get them to cooperate without bringing in the police?"

"Sure, now that I know how. First you scare the hell out of them; then you upset them a lot. The rest is all downhill."

"You got it. You're a fast study."

"What about Frederica's friend—the one who called my mother about some negatives? Was that the little black girl I'd seen her with?"

"Yes. She doesn't have any negatives though. She just wanted to find out if you were there that night." He wrote down two phone numbers, his and Sergeant Cohen's. "If she calls you, arrange to meet her, but call either of us immediately. This girl could be in trouble, and we want to find her before something happens to her."

They were walking to the door. Michael stopped. "Mr. Wood? I want to thank you—for giving me the"—he paused, blinking hard—"the opportunity to help."

Wood looked at him and understood. He felt his own throat tighten. "Yeah," he said quickly and left.

He found Mark Cohen in front of the newsstand, sitting on the hood of his car. He was wearing a seersucker jacket and eating an ice-cream cone. "Hi," he said, catching a chocolate drip before it fell on his lapel. "Hey, did you ever see *Mildred Pierce?*"

"The movie? No, why?"

"How old are you? You were probably too young anyway."

"I'm forty-two, how old are you?"

"Twenty-nine."

"How can I be too young—?"

"Oh, well, see—I watch old movies on TV all the time. I can tell you're not the type to watch TV. You probably don't even have one."

"That's right. I don't."

"I would've made a great detective. See, I don't think Ann Blyth killed that guy. Joan Crawford was the only one with a motive, do you know what I mean?"

"Mark—where's Alice? Have you seen her yet?"

He shook his head and jumped down off the car. "Nope. She wasn't here last night either. And the old man's not going to give up anything, if she told him not to. C'mon, we're supposed to meet Patti, she's got something." He threw the rest of his cone in a basket and wiped his hands with a paper napkin.

As they walked, Wood told him about his conversation with Michael and Winter's call to Mrs. Charles.

"So she wanted to find out if he was there that night?"

"She'd just been telling us about the dirty pictures Freddie found in her brother's drawer, then when she started to talk about that night—the boys in the room taking pictures—she decided he might have been one of them. Everyone's trying to do your job for you, Mark."

"Everyone wants a chance to say, 'Where were you on the night of January the ninth?' So do I. I've been a cop seven years and I never got a chance to say that. By the time I do, watch, I'll get it wrong. You don't think the brother was there?"

"No, I'm sure he wasn't. But he may know who was. I told him I'd call him in an hour and see if he's talked to any of his friends." He showed Cohen the list of names and addresses.

"Good," Cohen said. "Where're you from?"

"Madison, Wisconsin."

"Yeah? We were going to move out west after my father died. My mother has some relatives who live in Wyoming—but my mother decided against it. I think she was worried about all the *shiksas* out there, that I might marry one of them."

"She's right, the place if full of them. You're not married then?"

"Are you kidding? Where would I find a Jewish girl who'd marry a cop?"

"I see the problem." They were on Fifty-third near Sixth.

"Here we are," Cohen said.

Wood looked around. "Where?"

"In here, upstairs. Patti's getting her hair done."

"At nine o'clock at night?"

"This is an all-night beauty parlor—the hookers all come here." They walked up a flight of stairs and into a noisy, brightly lit room the size of a factory. Dozens of women sat around in various stages of undress or in short, cotton kimonos; their hair wrapped in tin foil or plastic, or rolled up in wire curlers and hairnets. Some sat under dryers, their feet propped up on stools, pieces of Kleenex stuck in between their freshly painted toes.

They found Patti lying on her back on a chair, with her head in a sink, while a tall, muscular woman stood over her, scrubbing her hair. They peered down at her.

"Hi," Cohen said.

She squinted up at them. "Hi—ow! Inga, that's too hot!"

"Good for the scalp. Now I give you cold, to close the pores."

"Yikes! Enough, let me up, I want to see. Look fellas, I'm a redhead." The chair was put up and wheeled around to face the mirror. "Inga, this is Mark and—what's your first name?" she asked Wood.

"Homer, but Wood is fine."

"That's cute—Homer. Quick, Inga, bring me a blow dryer so we can see how it looks dry. They were wrong, blondes do not have more fun, how could they, with dark roots showing all the time? Brunettes are sultry. What are redheads?"

"Dizzy," Cohen offered.

"Fiery," Wood suggested.

"I like fiery better." She aimed the dryer at her overturned head, her face completely covered, and went on talking over the sound of the dryer, into her hair.

Cohen turned to Wood. "Do you believe it?"

"I don't think so," Wood said.

A slim young man in a sleeveless T-shirt and gold earrings slid by, stopping when he saw what Patti was doing to her hair, and scolded her. "Don't hold the dryer so close, Patti, you're going to burn your hair!" He took it from her, and holding it further away, he began to run his fingers through the length of her hair, like a comb. He looked up at the men. "Are you cops, too?"

"Just me," Cohen said.

"Ooh, and is that a suspect you've got with you?"

"Bobby, will you cut it out? He thinks acting like a fag's good for business. He's really a closet macho-man."

Her hair, when it was dry, was a rich auburn. She turned to them. "Well, isn't that a far-out color?"

"Very," Wood said.

"I'm going to go get dressed now. You two walk over to the far end of the room. See that glass case over by the window? It's full of junk jewelry. Go look at it, so June can see you. Then go downstairs and wait for me outside. I'll just be a minute."

"We didn't bring a car," Cohen said. "We walked."

"That's okay, we'll wait for the Posse van."

June came down first, and walked by them, ignoring them. Patti came down a minute later, wearing a black silk dress and jewelry. June was dressed up too. Wood wondered why. "C'mon," she said, "we'll follow her till we see the van. Nice night."

"Look," Cohen said, "she stopped a guy. She doesn't know we don't have a car."

"That's not a john, it's a pimp. Name's Sam, don't you know him?" Patti said. "He's usually on the East Side. Let's take him."

She waited until June got out of the way, then broke away from Cohen and Wood, and started walking slowly, aimlessly down the street.

"What the hell is she doing, with no backup! Jesus."

"Looks like you're it, Sergeant," Wood said, trying to cover his nervousness.

The guy was big; six two, and heavy. He was wearing a bad hairpiece and had a deep tan. Wood thought he saw a gold cross around his neck, under a checked shirt open at the collar. He wore no jacket. "He can't have a gun," Wood said.

"The hell he can't. They wear them strapped to their ankles. Oh, shit, there she goes."

He'd stopped her. She stood, one hand on her hip, thrust to the side, the other hand resting on her bag. She reached into it for a cigarette, which he lit for her with a gold lighter.

"She turned on her tape then. She doesn't smoke."

"Uh, Mark? If we don't have a car, how do we take him in?"

"We—walk—him—in."

Wood did some quick arithmetic. The precinct was one block north, but three long, dark blocks west. He looked up and down the street, not a radio car in sight. The sergeant stood about five foot seven and maybe weighed a hundred and fifty pounds. Patti, feisty as she was, was sub-fly weight. That left Wood, the biggest of the three, but with no gun.

Sam had her by the arm now and was walking toward a bright blue Olds parked down the street. "Rule number one for decoys: never get into a *car!* What's she doing?" Cohen wailed. "Stay here, I've got to go get her." He started to run, reaching in back for his gun. Terrified, Wood ran after him, with no idea what he'd do when he got there.

A taxicab suddenly turned into the street headed the wrong way and screeched to a stop an inch away from the Olds. Wood wanted to cheer when he saw his favorite linebackers burst out of the cab and surround the pimp.

Patti looked at Cohen with his gun drawn. "What're you doing with that thing?"

"Goddamnit, what do you mean, pulling a stunt like that with no backup? I could've gotten us all killed!"

Jenkins was unstrapping the gun from the pimp's ankle, while Drafts cuffed him, none too gently, and shoved him in the cab.

"I just wanted to try out my new red hair. Didn't you know I was hooked up to Vinnie tonight?"

"Hey, Wood," Jenkins called, "the lieutenant let you come back out and play with us again?"

"How was I supposed to know you were hooked up to Vinnie!

What am I, chopped liver? What're you doing, hooked up to him, anyway?"

"Well, if you'll stop *kvetching* a moment and listen, I'll tell you!"

"I'm not *kvetching,* I'm *nudzhing!* There's a difference, you know."

Jenkins told Drafts to run the pimp over to the precinct and come back. As soon as the cab drove off, June came back. "I saw the van, it's on the way."

"Good," Patti said. "Mark, we got a lead on Candy. She hangs out with a rough crowd, so I called Vinnie to stay close. June was going to take us into the club over on Fifty-second Street, near Lex, where she hangs out. Here's the van; let's get in and talk inside where she won't be seen."

A white van pulled over to the curb, and a young cop in jeans, a work shirt, and sneakers got out and opened the door for them. He wore his hair long, just over his collar, and had a beard. Even so, he looked no more than eighteen or nineteen. "Hop aboard, folks! 'Cause next on our first-class guided tour of Fun City," he said as they climbed in, "we'll show you our famous massage parlors, porno bookstores, the latest in head shops, and if we have time, we can even take in a skin flick on Forty-second Street, Fun City's street of dreams you've all heard so much about." He waited until they'd all climbed in, then he slid the door closed and turned around and said, in a loud stage whisper, "Then we can sneak away to Studio Fifty-four and stay up all night and boogie," snapping his fingers to the rock music playing on the radio.

His name was Sonny, a graduate of Columbia, with an M.A. in sociology. Shortly after making detective second grade, he was assigned, because of his expertise, to that unit of the Department in charge of controlling prostitution, commonly known as the Pussy Posse. Wood naïvely thought that was a euphemism used only privately, among the inner circle of that unit. He soon found out that that's what it was called by everyone; reporters, the Department brass, as well as the hookers themselves. It was tacitly understood, in the Posse, that Sonny wouldn't make an arrest. Instead he was singularly responsible for more girls leaving the street and finding jobs during the two years he was on the Posse than ever before.

He and his partner, Wimpie, a more traditional cop despite his name, made several sweeps a night, bringing in any girl seen soliciting, but concentrating on new girls in the hope of changing their minds. The job of the Posse was to try to keep the lid on prostitution in the city, so that it didn't become any more of a mecca for whores and runaways than it already was.

June was explaining how to get into the club. She could take Patti and Cohen in as her guests and leave Wood and Jenkins's names at the door. She was pretty sure Enrico would remember her, but either way they had a better chance of getting in with just one man. The club had no name; only regulars were admitted inside, unless a name was left with Enrico at the door.

It became fashionable the day a well-known member of the French Olympic ski team removed her cashmere turtleneck sweater and threw it in her opponent's face after having lost two thousand dollars to him. She was said to have shouted in a heavy accent, "Now I have lost even my shirt, you peeg!" and walked through the club bare-breasted. She would have made it out onto the street were it not for two bouncers who forced her into a tuxedo jacket and put her in a cab.

"Hey, it doesn't sound like my kind of place," Cohen said. "Why don't you take Wood in with you and Vinnie, and I'll wait out in the bar. The bar's public, isn't it?"

"Oh, Mark, that's silly," Patti said. "You're dressed as well as Wood."

"Yeah, but he's taller."

Sonny said, "I'm going to let you beautiful people fight it out among yourselves; we got to get back to the guys. Shall I tell them where you are?" he asked Jenkins.

"Yeah, would you? And tell them to wait out front here. I'm wearing the Nagra and the word tonight is 'popcorn.'"

Sonny and Wimpie both laughed. "You Anti-Crime cowboys are too much!" Sonny jerked his head in Wood's direction. "Tell him what a Nagra is and how much it costs. He's cool, isn't he?"

"Sure. A Nagra is a body recorder. You can pick one up for about sixteen hundred bucks."

"Wow!" Patti said. "It must be small. Can I see it?"

Jenkins, Sonny, and Wimpie burst into laughter. "What's so funny?" she asked.

"C'mon, get out of here, you guys. Thanks for the ride." He was still laughing as they got out of the van.

"That's not fair," Patti said. "Do you know?" she asked Mark.

"I have an idea," he said.

"You know, you guys give me a real pain, with all your jock secrets—oh! Is that where?" She looked in the direction of Jenkins's crotch. "Far out."

They went into the outer bar and sat down at a small table to outline the game plan. It was dark, and they were the only people in the bar. The bartender seemed content to ignore them, for which they were thankful. Once they got inside, they'd have to order something, but they didn't want to drink any more than necessary.

"June," Jenkins said, "the important thing is to get Candy out of here alone. How can we best do that?"

"She's more likely to be attracted to you, Vinnie—no offense, Wood, I think you're adorable, but I think she goes for the California type. Also, you'd know how to come on with her."

"Nobody's apologizing to me, I notice," Cohen mumbled to himself.

"The trouble is," Patti said, "if you say there're some rough characters in there, someone might recognize Vinnie."

Vinnie shook his head. "Absolutely. Cohen and I both ought to stay out here. Wood, you're on. Just do like the ladies tell you; you'll be great."

"Okay," Patti got up. "Let's go."

"Wait a minute!" Wood said. "You didn't tell me what to do."

June looked at him. "You got to be told how to pick up a girl?"

"He's from Wisconsin," Cohen said.

"Oh," June said, "well, do whatever it is they do out there to get a girl. Drag her by the hair, or tie a rope around her neck—you know, whatever works. I'll introduce you, you do the rest."

Wood got up uncertainly. "Do I proposition her—or what? I mean—do I offer her money?"

Patti put her arm through his. "Homer, you're cute enough to get it for free. C'mon, loosen up!"

June went to the door and rang the bell. Patti tugged at Wood's arm and led him away from the table. He heard Vinnie and Mark laughing as the little speakeasy-type door opened and a man's face looked out.

June smiled and said hello to Enrico, calling him by name, and the door was opened to them.

They were let into an anteroom first: red carpeted, mirrors

facing each other on opposite walls, a crystal chandelier hanging overhead, and doors leading to the men's and ladies' rooms.

Past that was a pair of tall mahogany doors, brass fitted, which the man called Enrico opened for them. Suddenly they were in a huge room packed with people. They huddled around backgammon tables, they stood three deep at a horseshoe bar in the middle of the room and at a smaller bar in the far corner.

"Are you kidding?" Wood said. "They're all thin and blond—they probably all have a chipped tooth."

"Stay close," June said. "We'll just move around. Do you play backgammon?"

"Yes, but I didn't bring two thousand dollars with me."

"How well?"

"Well enough to beat my twelve-year-old daughter—sometimes."

"See that table over there, underneath the fancy mirror?"

Wood looked at the couple playing backgammon. The girl's white-blond hair hung almost to the board, bangs to her eyes, skinny brown cigarette in her hand, it was unmistakable.

"Let's go watch the game. Just sort of comment, Wood, on what a good move that was, that sort of thing." June was leading the way.

He looked at Patti. She said to him, "Wood, remember, the idea is to get her out of here."

June stopped short of the table, to let Wood go first. He walked slowly by, to get a look at his competition, then paused, as though he just decided to watch. The man was older, well into his sixties. He wasn't paying close attention to the game. A waiter came by. The man handed him his glass for a refill, then asked whose turn it was.

Wood walked around behind him to get a better look at Candy. She reacted immediately, watching, appraising Wood as she shook the dice in the leather cup. Wood made an attempt at something he hoped looked like a sexy smile as she tossed the dice. "Fuck," she said, obviously not pleased with the roll.

She made her moves rapidly. Her partner was more deliberate —or drunk, and her impatience began to show. When one of his dice spilled onto the floor, she shot daggers at him with her eyes, then looked up at Wood, showing him her exasperation and inviting him to be a co-conspirator. He smiled back, spontaneously, and beckoned to her to end the game. As she opened her mouth to speak to the man, he saw the chipped tooth and tensed for just a moment, until he caught a glimpse of Patti watching him from a distance. She winked reassuringly. He could have sworn he saw her lift up her shoulder bag and say "popcorn" into it.

Candy picked up her small silver bag and said to the man, "Excuse me, darling. I have to pee." The man nodded and finished his drink.

She brushed by Wood; a giant. She had to be nearly six feet tall. He caught her perfume as she said, "God, I need a drink," and walked quickly to the bar. Wood hurried to keep up with her. He reached the bar just as she was saying to him, "Vodka on the rocks," and waited, none too patiently while he tried to get the bartender's attention. Clearly this lady was used to men more assertive than Wood when it came to getting her service. He snapped his fingers and made a sound ridiculously close to a bark and it worked. He ordered a scotch for himself. She finished her drink before he had a second sip and said, "I've got to split."

He fumbled frantically for his money, found nothing smaller than a five, slapped it on the bar, and rushed to find her. She was halfway out the door, her white-blond head impossible to miss, floating inches above the rest. She stopped suddenly, just as he caught up with her. "There's someone I ought to see first—" The disappointment on Wood's face was so genuine that she laughed and said, "Screw it, right?"

Taxis were lined up in front, waiting. She headed straight for the first one.

"Wait!"

She turned to him. "What?"

"Could we walk—just a little? All that smoke in there—"

"Sure, okay." She walked fast, or seemed to, because her legs were so long, and they were almost to the end of the block. Wood began to worry they hadn't seen him come out.

A taxi pulled up beside them and stopped. Jenkins jumped out and stood in front of her, badge open in his hand.

"Yes?" she asked, indifferently.

"I'm arresting you for soliciting. Get in the car."

She gave a short, sarcastic laugh. "Go shove it, mister. I wasn't soliciting." She turned to Wood. "Was I?"

Jenkins didn't give Wood time to answer. He put his hand on her bare arm, and Wood could see the skin whiten from the pressure. "Then I'm arresting you for thinking about it," he said without expression and herded her into the cab instantly, without looking at Wood, and they were gone.

Wood looked around, wondering where the others were, then heard a horn blow twice.

"Come on, what're you waiting for, a limousine?" Cohen and Patti were in the back of a cab, a real one. "Get in," Cohen said.

Cohen gave the driver the address of the precinct. "Now what was all that about—you don't know how to pick up a girl? We barely had time to call the lieutenant to tell him to expect her."

"Just my natural charm, I guess. Where's June?"

"She must have decided to stay," Patti said.

"I don't understand about her," Wood started to say.

Cohen interrupted, "As soon as we get back to the office, we should get Michael on the phone and feed Gallagher any information we get from him."

"Was Jenkins really going to arrest her?"

"Arrest her? What for?"

Michael had waited at the Princeton Club for Wood's call. He sounded excited. Richie had gone to the Rockmoor the night Michael begged off and a pimp called Pretty Joey—

Wood motioned to Cohen to pick up an extension.

"—was there. The other guy, the one I told you about? The big shot? He hauled off and slapped the pimp in the face, for bringing him 'used, old merchandise.' The girl he was talking about was probably all of seventeen, Richie said."

"What else, Michael? What did he know about the man?"

"Nothing. The guy was very secretive. The only thing he heard was the pimp call the guy Danny. Anyway Richie grabbed the girl and beat it the hell out of there. Mr. Wood? He said he was glad I called—he felt terrible about Frederica, but he didn't think I'd want to hear from him. So you can call him, he'll tell you anything he can."

"That's good. I'm glad to hear that."

"I called the other three guys and struck out. See, we all had finals that week, so no one came into town. They never heard of Pretty Joey or the other guy, and they were a little scared to talk about the whole thing. So if you call them—"

"Gotcha, Michael. Don't worry. You have our numbers, right? Stay in touch. And thanks."

Cohen called Gallagher. Candy had just come in and he was letting her cool her heels in the interview room while he put together the parts of the puzzle he already had. Then he'd see what was missing. He'd use the name Danny on her, at the right time. He told Cohen to go ahead and call the boy, Richie, and see if he could get a description of Danny.

"Right away, Lieutenant."

"No hurry, Sergeant. Candy and I—we have all the time in the world."

Richie was straight with Cohen. He ran down the story from the beginning, giving him the names of the models he knew were involved. He'd heard of Candy, that she'd tried to become a top model and hadn't quite made it. Drugs, he heard. But she was right up there as a call girl. The real problem was Danny. Richie explained that as a photographer's assistant, he had a pretty good eye, but this man was simply impossible to describe. There was nothing about him that was in any way distinctive. The world's most forgettable face. He swore he didn't think he'd be able to recognize him if he saw him again.

Cohen phoned that last bit of information in to Gallagher, then he put the receiver down, with finality, and turned to them. "Okay, everybody, all together now—"

He jumped up onto the desk and sat, his arms extended, leading them in song:

"Now run along home
and hop into bed.
Say your prayers
and cover your head.

"What's the matter, you didn't go to camp? What kind of a childhood did you have?"

Wood and Patti were both struggling hard to keep a straight face, looking just beyond Cohen, to the door.

"Then it goes:

Just one more thing
I say unto you.
You dream of me
and I'll dream of you—"

He turned around then, to see what they were looking at. "Oh, good evening, Captain. Just trying to entertain the press . . ."

Wood stopped to make a phone call before he left. He let the phone ring several times and was about to give up when she answered.

"Shawna? I'm sorry. I woke you, didn't I?"

"I'm glad you did. I was worried about you. Any news?"

"Some. Listen, I know this is crazy, it's late and you must be exhausted, and you're probably all tucked in for the night—"

"Are you about to invite me down for a sleep-over date?"

"With pickup and delivery service, door-to-door. Breakfast included; you can even bring down your laundry."

"I'll pack my toothbrush and meet you downstairs. Fifteen minutes?"

"Make it ten and I'll buzz you."

He'd never seen her in blue jeans before. She looked long and lanky in her close-fitting suede vest, fringed to her hips. Under it, she wore a tailored shirt with the sleeves rolled up.

"Hi, cowboy," he said, opening the door for her. She sat close to him.

He kissed her at every red light, without going through a single one.

Jenkins took Candy only as far as the desk sergeant with instructions that she be taken to Lieutenant Gallagher's office; then he left. She was put in an outer office and told to wait. By the time the lieutenant called her in, her rage had reached its peak.

"If I'm under arrest, you damn well better read me my rights and give me that phone."

Gallagher looked puzzled. "Arrest? What for? You didn't kill anybody, did you?"

"No, but I'm about to. That gorilla who picked me up tried to hit me with a phony soliciting charge—"

"Soliciting? That's odd. Then he brought you to the wrong place. We don't book prostitutes here; this is a homicide office. You sure you didn't kill anybody?"

"Look, I know a goddamn setup when I see one. You've kept

me sitting out there for twenty-five minutes. Now what the hell is this all about? If you want to question me about something, I want my lawyer here. Otherwise I'm leaving."

He looked at her and shrugged, shaking his head regretfully. "I wish I had something to question you about. I never get to question a beautiful woman. They brought a girl in here last week, a model—in connection with the Gregory killing—you know, the dress manufacturer who was stabbed in his apartment? But lieutenants never do the Q's and A's, except in the movies. We're just the administrators; it's the detectives who get to have all the fun. I got a look at her though. Gorgeous girl.

"I did get to go to the scene of the crime, and, Jesus, what an apartment. That man knew how to live—triplex overlooking the East River, everything covered in this chocolate-brown velvet. Walls, sofas, everything. See, I was the duty officer, it was on a Saturday. Lieutenants take turns working Saturdays, and it was night—what a view. He had mirrors all over the place, so the lights from the bridge were reflected all over the apartment."

"Wait a minute, you lost me. What turned you on, the apartment or the model?"

"Well—"

"Because what I don't understand is, if you're the boss and you feel like getting your jollies by 'grilling'—is that what you call it?—a pretty lady, who's to say you can't?"

"The reason is whoever does the 'grilling' has to go to court and testify. We've got twenty-five detectives here, but only one lieutenant. They can't spare a lieutenant to go down and sit in court for three weeks, right?"

"Okay, now I got it. It's a quiet night, no one around, so you thought you'd send an undercover cop out to bring you a consolation prize tonight. A little blow job under the desk, Lieutenant?" She shook her head. "Uh-uh. Sorry, you can't afford me. Not on a cop's pay." She got up. "But listen, if I ever need a favor someday, maybe we could work something out. In the meantime, in return for a car and driver back to Enrico's, I'll be glad to keep your dirty little secret just between us." She gathered up her bag. "I'm not in the mood for any more cab rides tonight, so get me a car."

Gallagher stood, too. "Okay, but Danny's going to be awfully miffed that you turned down a homicide lieutenant, especially with Pretty Joey lying there in St. Clare's with a couple of sore knees that my sergeant gave him today. You should hear him complain."

Candy stood, frozen, staring at him.

"He's yelling his head off. Danny could at least send him a private nurse—the service is lousy over there. Sometimes he has to wait an hour for a bedpan, and he can't get a painkiller when he needs one. But worst of all, he's screaming that his top bitch, Candy, hasn't even come to see him. I don't blame him, that's not nice, Candy."

She snapped open her bag and took out a long, brown cigarette, holding it for him to light. Gallagher waited a moment, watching the tremor in her hand. She put it down on the desk and said, "Is there a ladies' room I could use?" The bangs on her forehead were getting damp, she wiped them away.

"Men's room all right? There's no one here."

"As long as it has a lock."

He showed her the way, standing there as she locked the door, and listened. He heard her bag snap open, then the toilet flush three times in a row. A moment later he heard the bag snap shut again, and he moved out of the way, toward the filing cabinet. He took a folder out and put on his glasses, not looking up when the door opened and she came out.

"Your toilet doesn't work too well," she commented.

"We're waiting for a plumber. Would you like some coffee? I was just about to call for some."

"Okay. Black, no sugar."

"Me, too, that's how I drink it. My wife won't let me use sugar, and my daughter keeps telling me the substitutes give you cancer. I don't care. As long as they don't take away my two bourbons before dinner, I can live without sugar."

They were back in his office. Candy sat in the same chair, on the other side of his desk. He came up next to her chair and reached across the desk to pick up the phone. He ordered the coffee, and was about to replace the phone when he noticed she was waiting for a light again. He looked in his pockets for a match, at the same time trying to reach across the desk, and stumbled, losing his balance for an instant, and knocked her bag off her lap and onto the floor.

"God, I'm sorry," he said, kneeling quickly to pick up the contents that had scattered on the floor.

"It's all right, I'll get it!" she said. But there was no way she could; he was in the way, already gathering them up and putting them back in the bag.

"*Please,*" she said and tried to push him out of the way.

He stood up and handed it back to her, holding on to a small leather case, examining it curiously. "Interesting. Lizard?"

"Crocodile." She reached out to take it from him.

"What is it, a cosmetic kit of some kind?"

"It's my diaphragm case, if you must know. Now will you please give it back to me."

"A crocodile diaphragm case? Boy, what will they think of next? How does it open? Like this?"

"You can't open that without a search warrant!" she blurted out.

He laughed, looking at her. "Can't I? Watch me." Then, turning it around in his hand, he opened it slowly. Inside, in neatly fitted compartments, were: a gold razor blade; a mirror, about an inch and a half square; a gold straw; and a glass vial with a miniature spoon, also gold, attached to its top. The vial was filled with a fine, white powder.

"He flaked me. The cop in the taxi flaked me!"

"Candy, with this? I'm afraid this neat little piece of equipment is out of our budget. And look at that! Your name's engraved on the razor. Beautiful. Feel better now after the little snort you had in the bathroom? Good, now we can talk. Oh,"—he struck a match—"your light. Sorry."

She took a deep drag on her cigarette, blowing the smoke across the desk at him. "You threatening me with a bust? A little coke bust doesn't scare me. I can pay the fine."

"Coke? Who said anything about coke?"

She looked at him; the pupils of her eyes were dilated and her cheeks were flushed. He opened the vial and turned it upside down, holding his finger tip over the top, and tasted it.

"You know, there's nothing that'll turn a guy off a broad quicker than heroin. Even a pimp. Bad news, nothing but trouble. And Danny, he'd get rid of you so fast, you wouldn't know what hit you. Coke is one thing, but heroin—that's dirty." He made a gesture of finality with his hands. He paused, looking at her. "Take off your shoes and stockings."

"No!"

"Oh, that's right, you like search warrants." He picked up the phone again. "Get Judge Gutstein at home for me."

"Never mind," she cut in. "Hang up." She kicked off her shoes, stood up, and with her back to him, she reached under her dress and pulled off her pantyhose.

Gallagher put on his glasses and walked around the desk, bending to look at her feet. He lifted first one, then the other. The needle marks were between her toes.

She moved her bare foot slowly in his hand as she spoke, making her voice as soft and seductive as she could, trying to sound slightly amused at the same time. "You know, that—deal—we were talking about before? I think we may have found a bargaining point."

"I told you—my wife doesn't let me have sugar." He dropped her foot unceremoniously, letting it bounce on the floor. "No, we're going to talk about Danny."

The coffee came, and Gallagher apologized for the lack of cups, complaining about the paper-clip mentality of the department again. He held up the crocodile case. "Here's our bargain: if I like your story enough, neither Danny nor Pretty Joey will find out about this—unless you let them nibble your toes, that is."

"Will they know I talked to you?"

"No."

One of the Gallagherisms his men liked to quote was: "The only tape recorder I can trust never to break down is the one inside my head"—to which the men would answer among themselves, "Sure, and it's the only one he knows how to work." The lieutenant turned it on now and listened.

She didn't know his last name. It was true that he was a publisher of one of the hard-core porno magazines. She didn't know which one though. Danny had a run-in with the DA a long time ago, and his identity was a strictly guarded secret now.

She worked for Pretty Joey as a recruiter, or talent scout, as he preferred to call it, on a flat fee basis: fifty dollars for every girl she helped convince to work for him. Candy had two pitches; the girls who hadn't ever turned a trick were promised successful modeling careers; those who had, fame and fortune as call girls in the big city.

Since so many of the girls arrived in town with instructions to contact Pretty Joey, Candy assumed there was some sort of network operating in cities all over the country, and her hunch was Danny had a lot to do with it.

Gallagher asked her if she was one of Danny's girls, and she laughed at the idea. "*Sixteen's* too old for Danny," she said. "Pubic hair turns him off, I guess."

The movies he had shot were to be made into video cassettes and sold by direct mail through his magazine. Pretty Joey told her that it was going to be a million-dollar operation one day. They planned to sell the cassettes to whore houses, massage parlors, private clubs, as well as retail outlets.

"If he's so worried about his identity, how come he's in the movies? I heard he's the leading man," Gallagher said.

"Those are just used to get backing to make the ones he'll sell. And no one's allowed to photograph him from the front anyway."

Candy was as much at a loss to describe Danny as Richie was. He tested her truthfulness by making her run him through the night Freddie died, step by step, right up until the moment Freddie bolted, running away from her to look for Winter. (He still refused to say murdered.) By the time Candy got to the hotel, there was already a crowd around the spot where she fell, and Pretty Joey and Danny had split. She didn't know what happened to Winter, but Candy laid low for a few days and didn't try to contact either of the men. The next thing she heard was Pretty Joey'd been shot and was in the hospital under police guard.

It all matched.

"Okay," Gallagher said, "stop by tomorrow about ten A.M. I'll need you for fifteen minutes, then I'll give you back your little traveling case. You have enough at home to last you the night?"

"That's rotten!"

"Could be a lot worse. No big deal—I just need you to make a fast phone call."

It was twelve thirty when he let her go, after getting names and descriptions of some of the girls she'd "recruited," but that was useless. They were all made-up names, and with the thousands of runaways drifting around the city, go find one thirteen-year-old girl with light brown hair and a pony tail.

He told her to find her own transportation. Let her walk, maybe she could still turn the evening into a profit.

He felt like washing his hands after she left. He went into the bathroom and let the water run hot. Well, the city politicians wanted to get prostitution off the streets and close down the porno film houses. Looks like they're going to get what they wanted. Danny ought to be presented with the key to the city.

When he got back to his desk, he called Sergeant Danahy and Detective Halsey, waking them both up, and told them to get in early tomorrow. Then he called Manhattan North and got Sergeant Cohen's home number. His mother answered and refused to wake him, no matter who was calling, but promised to give him the message in the morning—with his three-minute eggs.

"Mrs. Cohen, I wish I had a mother like you."

"Lieutenant Whoever-you-are, if you had a mother like me, you'd be home in bed, too, instead of calling up people in the middle of the night."

"You're absolutely right, Mrs. Cohen. Thank you for reminding me."

"You're welcome and good night."

"Good night, Mrs. Cohen."

He sat there, looking at the phone, running his hands over his hair, thinking, what am I doing in the middle of this? All his thirty years in the Department the one thing he did his best to stay away from was anything to do with prostitution and narcotics. Hated all of it. Mindless, filthy people. He tore open a package of Di-Gel and chewed two. Murder was something he could deal with. He could walk out of an autopsy room and go eat a cheeseburger; this girl leaves his office, and he has to scrub his hands and chew Di-Gels.

The criminal mind was something else; he could understand it and stay outside of it. He remembered what his first lieutenant told him when he came into Homicide, a hotshot kid of twenty-seven ready to rid the world of injustice, protect the innocent, and all that. This is a business, he said, just like any other. They kill people; we catch them; it's that simple. Remember that and you'll stay sane and sober. Listen to their motives but not their stories, or it'll drive you crazy. Nobody kills anybody without a reason, except maniacs, and they've got stories too. Learn to hear the difference between a story and a motive and you'll be all right. Lieutenant J. E. Mahoney was one old cop who died quietly and peacefully at the age of eighty-two in his sleep, with his wife holding his hand. He knew something.

Mrs. Cohen's admonitions notwithstanding, he made a few more phone calls and by two thirty in the morning there was a large package on his desk. He spent another hour and a half going through the pictures and photographs; a half an hour reading the dossier, and said out loud, "Okay, Homer Wood, you wanted to take the word CUPPI and spell Homicide out of it, you're going to do some work."

Shawna opened her eyes and saw the sunlight starting to creep in between the slats of the shutters, forming a pattern, geometric, like a grill, on Wood's sleeping face.

She moved closer to him, fitting herself into the hollow of his shoulder and along the length of his body so that even their legs touched.

Still partly asleep he moved his arm under her head and pulled her closer, resting his lips against her brow.

She thought about their lovemaking last night, how just before he came, he had grabbed her shoulders and pushed himself inside her roughly and said in a voice that was hoarse and choked, "Jesus Christ, it's a fucking battlefield."

She knew it was true. It hadn't been like this with anyone since Richard. And then only until she gave up the fight and became what she used to refer to as some appendage of his.

"Good evening, Dr. So-and-so, have you met my lovely appendage? Yes, isn't she beautiful?"

And, "How do you do, General. I'm the decoration Dr. McKinley wears on his arm when he goes to parties. No, I'm the new one; the other one wore out and got sent to a duplex on Park Avenue to live on alimony."

The fight was ended and then the sex became polite. Richard won the fight and lost the girl; the girl left to become a woman. Yet here she was falling in love and declaring World War III all over again, but now this time it was against someone who was on her side.

It's a good thing I'm only in charge of other people's problems; I'd sure hate to have to figure out my own.

"Shawna?" he murmured.

"Hmmm?"

"I have a good idea. Why don't we go out and find some bad guys to beat up?"

"Just what I was thinking." She kissed him.

\* \* \*

While they were cooking breakfast, Danahy called to tell him that Gallagher had some negatives and prints that he wanted Wood to look at. He was sending them down with Connelly now.

"When you've looked at them, bring them into the office."

"What are they?" Wood asked.

"Gallagher just wants you to look at them. The same way you looked at the Fornetti picture, okay?"

When Connelly got there, Wood asked him if he'd mind driving Shawna home. He didn't mind at all, in fact he nearly fell down a flight of stairs telling her how much he didn't mind.

"Sit up front with him, Shawna. That way at least his head will be pointed in the right direction."

He took the package into the kitchen and put the dishes away, changing the kitchen into a darkroom.

Gallagher had sent four sets of pictures, of four different men, and some negatives. I get it, Wood said to himself, I'm supposed to figure out which one is Danny. If I get it right, they'll let me play in the big kid's game; if I don't, I have to stay on my own side of the fence and watch.

It was easy. He looked for the one that was hardest to describe, bland, clean-shaven, baby-face in a business suit. He put the others aside and decided to start with the negatives. He put a record on and got to work. By the time he'd printed the second set of negatives, he needed a drink. It was ten o'clock in the morning. He filled the bottom of the glass with straight scotch and gagged on it. He wished he had the nerve to finish the whole bottle. He didn't know how Gallagher had gotten hold of them, but they all turned out to be pictures of Winter, taken while she was being raped.

He tore his eyes away from Winter's tortured face and concentrated on the man's back, looking for a birthmark or disfiguration of any kind. The son of a bitch had the skin of a baby. He hung them up to dry and turned his attention to the other pictures. One of them had been cut out of a newspaper. It was of three men standing in front of a courthouse with a couple of newsmen standing around, but the story and caption had been carefully snipped off. Wood wondered if Gallagher had done that. The others were photographs: one taken on a beach; Florida, perhaps, or the Bahamas, in which one of the three men in the newspaper photo, the baby-faced one, was lying on a towel sunbathing, his hands folded up behind his head, his face turned toward the camera. It was a color snapshot, taken with an Instamatic probably, and like most amateurs the person who'd taken it had framed it in such a way that there was a palm tree growing out of the top of his head.

The next was an eight-by-ten black and white, taken in a nightclub by one of those club photographers. Three couples sitting around a table, glassy-eyed, silly, drunken smiles on their faces. It was easy to pick him out here. Two of the men had real faces, the other had a pair of eyes, one nose, two ears and a mouth. Everyman. What does Gallagher want me to do—turn the picture of Winter being raped inside out and put this man's face on the naked man's back?

He got out his magnifying glass and studied the man's back in the rape pictures, taking particular care to avoid looking at Winter again, and tried to find some characteristic somewhere that would match him up with the man in the other three pictures. Nowhere in any of the rape pictures did any part of his face show. Wood looked at the hair. It was full, rough textured, wavy, and curled at the neck.

He moved the magnifying glass to look at the hair on the other three pictures and struck out. The baby-faced man in these pictures had straight, fine-textured hair, neatly cut. Totally different hair types. He put down the glass, got up and walked around, stretching out his back muscles. After a moment he went back and picked up the beach picture and looked at it again.

There was something off. Like one of those puzzles on backs of cereal boxes that Donnie used to sit at breakfast figuring out. "What's wrong with this picture?" it would say across the top, and there'd be a car with three wheels or a house with no doors . . . or a man with no hair on his chest. He grabbed the magnifying glass. Or under his arms. What does the creep do—shave his armpits? Wait a minute, there was no hair on his arms and legs either. He checked the other pictures quickly. Baby-faced, he thought when he first looked at them, because, for one thing, the man was so clean-shaven in all of them, there was no hint of a growth or shadow on his face. He was hairless. Caused, possibly, by a childhood disease, like scarlet fever, so that he had to be wearing a wig—and false eyebrows.

Wood decided to enlarge the beach picture. Make a negative and blow up the face, just the upper half, and see. He worked fast, anxious to find out for certain. A wig and false eyebrows, okay. But who's going to take the trouble to put on false eye-lashes to wear to the beach—even Danny Boy couldn't be *that* vain. The sun was shining right on him, it ought to be easy to see.

There it was. He was squinting, unable to protect his eyes from the glare without the natural protection of eyelashes. Now he enlarged a series of the rape pictures, six of them, and spread them out on the counter. Different wig or different man? It was difficult to tell; the pictures were shadowy, and enlarging them didn't do much for the sharpness. Danny, with his obsession about concealing his identity, would have more than one wig. Several, probably, which is what threw Wood off in the first place. He wished the pictures were good enough to see if there were hair on the arms and legs. The last two enlargements showed Winter struggling. Her hand was pushed against his ear, trying to shove him away. The pictures were identical, shot one right after the other. He held them up side by side, comparing the two for several minutes, then he went to find a ruler.

It was only a difference of a quarter of an inch, but it was enough. During the course of the struggle Winter had managed to move the wig so that the part, measured from the ear, was a quarter of an inch closer to the middle, making the whole wig tilt slightly at an angle. He smiled. Okay, Danny Boy, gotcha now.

He called Shawna and had her paged at the hospital. "Hey, Doc—got a question for you. What causes baldness?"

"Loss of hair."

"Yeah, yeah. What disease?"

"Scarlet fever, or it could be congenital or toxic in origin. They could all produce alopecia."

"Alopecia?"

"That's what the condition is called."

"Far out. Thanks, kid, see ya around—by the way, I love you." He hung up and packed up all the pictures, with the negatives, and tore uptown to Gallagher's office. The street was lined with squad cars, so he pulled into the garage underneath the building and left his car in an empty space marked "Captain."

He ran up the stairs, and as he turned the corner into the hall leading to the lieutenant's office, he began to whistle "Danny Boy."

Cohen, Danahy, and Halsey all heard him. They all turned at once and watched Wood as he strode into the office, going straight to Gallagher's desk, and dropped the package right in front of him.

"Alopecia," he said.

"Raymond," Gallagher corrected. "Name's Raymond."

"Not you, *Danny*."

"Wood, go out and come in again. What the fuck are you talking about?"

He turned around and addressed the group. "That's the name for what Danny Boy's got—or in this case hasn't got. Hair. He's bald, not just on his head. Everywhere." He took out the pictures and spread them out on the floor, showing them with the magnifying glass and the ruler what he meant. When he finished, he sat back on his heels and said, "Well?"

They sat thinking. Wood stood up. "What the hell's the matter with you guys?"

They didn't answer right away. Finally it was Gallagher who spoke. "Interesting," he said.

Wood stared at them incredulously. "I don't believe you guys!"

Gallagher went on, not hearing him. "Candy made a remark last night—about Danny not liking girls with pubic hair."

"There!" Wood said. "Now we know why."

Halsey answered Gallagher. "Of course there's got to be a few other men in this city walking around without any hair on their bodies. It's not all that uncommon."

"Yeah," Wood said, "but how many of them are publishers of porno magazines? You've got a make on this guy, don't you? Look up his medical records." They still weren't listening to him. "They're not going to let me play after all," he muttered.

"I like it," Gallagher said thoughtfully. "What about you, Jack?"

"I like it," Danahy said. "I don't know if it's enough, but I like it."

"You, Cohen?"

"Me, I love it."

Gallagher stood up. "Okay, then, let's move. Wood, you got your camera with you?"

"Whew! Gee, thanks, Lieutenant. Yeah, I've got my camera; it's in the car."

"You left it in the car? That's not too smart."

"Where I parked it, it is."

"Cohen," Gallagher said, "get your best decoy and have her here on the double. Looking good; no overalls. Jack, call the Legal Bureau and tell them you're coming down for a search warrant. What's the best recording equipment the Department has? Transmitting, not cassette."

"Aid's the newest. We can probably get one from Narcotics."

"Get on it. And, oh, have someone call down to court and find out who's sitting today. If it's Gutstein, we're in good shape."

"Lieutenant?" It was Connelly at the door. "The girl's here."

"Good." Gallagher started out. "What's your decoy's name, Cohen?"

"June Shea."

Wood stared at him. "You're going to use a *prostitute* for this?"

Cohen smiled, amused, and winked at Wood. "FBI," he said. "Investigating interstate prostitution rings." He picked up the phone and waited for an outside line.

"You guys are really cute, you know that?" Wood said. Danahy and Gallagher were both out of the room. "You're all so busy running around playing detective, looking over your shoulder to make sure no one's behind you, you can't tell the good guys from the bad guys anymore. I'm on your side, remember?"

Cohen talked into the telephone, giving a message for June. When he hung up, he said to Wood, "Nothing personal. Patti didn't know either. She thought June was a hooker too—helping us because she needed a favor. You've been around cops long enough to know, Wood, they don't trust anyone. Even each other. Comes with the shield and the parking permit. Haven't you noticed—a cop won't even talk on the phone? Start to say something confidential, they'll cut you right off and say it'll wait till they see you. Haven't you noticed that?"

"I don't know, it just seems out of character for you—the little I know of you, it's hard for me to put that together."

He nodded. "Yeah, well, scratch a cop and you know what you'll find underneath? A cop. Ask ninety-nine guys out of a hundred, from a foot patrolman on up, why he became a cop, and you know the answer you'll get? They heard about the test so they went and took it. *They* don't want to know their reasons."

"You, Mark?"

He laughed. "I'm short and funny looking—I thought it might make me tall and handsome."

Gallagher had Candy make the phone call to Dan Stoll's office, publisher of *Lollipop* magazine, to make an appointment for a friend of hers, June Shea, who was looking for a job like Candy's. June, she said, had been to the hospital last night to see Pretty Joey, and he thought June would be terrific. He was doing fine, she added; he'd be out in a day or two. The appointment was for two thirty.

*Lollipop* magazine was located on lower Broadway, near Canal Street, five minutes from One Police Plaza, where Danahy would be waiting in the office of the Legal Bureau. From there it was only a short walk to the judge's chambers.

Cohen, Halsey, and Wood got to the building on Broadway forty-five minutes early with the transmitter to look for an office on the same floor where they could set it up and listen. They saw a door down the hall marked "Certified Public Accountant."

"Let's just hope it isn't a bookie joint we're walking into—like the last time we did this," Halsey said.

"Do you think they'll let us in?" Wood asked.

"Sure," Cohen said. "If you can't dazzle them with your beauty, baffle them with your bullshit, I always say."

Danahy, in the meantime, had to do his own kind of dazzling down at the Legal Bureau, with promises of evidence that would warm the heart of the DA if they'd stand ready to draw up an order for a search. Gutstein, they found out, was sitting that day and would be on hand to sign it.

June arrived at two thirty. They heard her ask for Mr. Stoll and give her name. A woman's voice answered, asking June to have a seat, and she'd tell him she was here. The sound was clear; there was very little background noise. They heard her get a pack of cigarettes out of her bag and the snap of a lighter. Perfect.

"Through that door, miss, second office on your left."

"Thank you." They listened to the sound of her footsteps. When they stopped, they assumed it was because she had gotten to his office and the floor was carpeted.

"Hello, Miss Shea. Come in and sit down, I'll be right with

you. Yes, but I have someone in my office now, can I reach you later on? Good. Thank you." There was a sound of a receiver being put down. His voice was coming through fine.

"Well, Miss Shea, what can I do for you?" Smooth as silk, Danny was.

"I'm looking for a job, and since I've had experience as a booking agent, Candy thought you might be able to use me. I worked for the Tower Modeling Agency—I have a letter of recommendation with me—" The paper rustled against the mike in her bag as she took it out.

There was a pause. "Uh-huh, very nice. What other sort of work have you done?"

"I majored in Film at UCLA, but it isn't an easy business for a woman to break into. That's my real dream. To direct films. In the meantime—"

"You have to pay the rent, right?"

She laughed. "Right. I share a loft with my girlfriend, and guess what? She's getting married. I hate to give up the space. I've put a lot of money into a darkroom—"

Cohen and Wood exchanged smiles. "Nice," Cohen said.

"That's some kinda smart lady," Halsey said.

June went on. "I was even hoping to buy a Movieola someday, so I can do my own editing. I love to walk around the city on a weekend and shoot movies—just whatever happens to interest me. But that's beside the point. For the time being I'm happy to book models. You do have a modeling agency, don't you?"

"Oh, yes. The magazine's the smallest of my businesses. I have agents all over the country finding me fresh faces. You'd be amazed how many kids are dying to come to New York to make a try for the big time."

"You must have a lot of applicants, I've never seen so many filing cabinets."

Cohen nodded. "Good, he keeps them in his office."

"I noticed some in the next office too. Are they all yours?"

"You're very observant."

"A filmmaker has to be. I had a professor once who used to play a game in class. He'd send a student out of the room and then he'd rearrange everything; desks, chairs, books. Then he'd call the student back in and give him twenty seconds to look around and then go back out and write it all down. It was good training. Helps to develop an eye for detail."

"That's fascinating." Danny sounded like his interest was fading.

"See, I can close my eyes right now and tell you a lot of little details in this room. At least I hope I still can. I haven't been practicing. Shall I try?"

He laughed, a small offhand sort of laugh. "Sure, go ahead."

"Okay," she said. "A bunch of keys on the desk—seven or eight big ones, and about three small ones, probably for the filing cabinets. A tape recorder on the table behind your chair. About a dozen stamped manila envelopes, eight-by-ten size, for photographs. A little girl's pink cardigan sweater over on the couch. Three pairs of sun glasses—"

"Jesus Christ," Halsey said. "Where'd you find that girl?"

"You're marvelous!" Danny suddenly sounded alive again. "I didn't see that sweater. The little girl who was in here this morning looking for a job modeling must have left it."

"Oh, are you looking for models now? Because I know of two adorable girls, very photogenic. Great personalities."

"How old are they?"

"They're sisters; one's eleven, the other's twelve and a half. Do you ever use black models?"

"Yes, I just signed one today. A little mulatto girl. She must have been the one who left her sweater—but I won't be able to use her for a while. The little devil got herself in trouble with police. Stealing, I think."

Wood was ready to jump out of his skin. "Cohen, let's go!"

"Cool it, Wood," Halsey said. "He hasn't said one goddamn thing that's going to get us a warrant yet."

June said, "I'm afraid these two might be a problem too. You know what they asked me yesterday? If they could meet Pretty Joey. Can you imagine! At that age?"

There was a long silence in which the three men stood watching the tape wind slowly around the reel, waiting.

"Have they already had sexual experiences, do you suppose?"

"If they haven't, they soon will, the way they act."

There was another silence. Then, "What is your fee, June?" His voice sounded less silky now; huskier.

June didn't hesitate a second. "For these two? A hundred apiece. And a hundred for me if you want pictures."

The men held their breaths, frozen, watching each other.

"How soon?" Danny asked.

"Tonight soon enough?"

"My secretary goes home at four. The shades on these windows are black-out shades, and the sofa opens up into a bed." He was almost whispering.

"If you sign them, what would our deal be?"

"We could discuss that later. Let me see them first."

"Why don't we discuss it now?"

He sighed. "If I sign them and give them a place to live, you get ten percent of everything they bring in."

"And if I find you more?"

"Ten percent under thirteen, five percent under sixteen. I can't use girls any older."

"Mr. Stoll, nice to have met you. Looks like I may get my Movieola after all. See you at four."

"We got it." Halsey grabbed the tape. "Mark, call Danahy down at Legal and tell him I'm on the way. I'll be back as fast as I can. Get your camera ready, Wood."

The bust went down like a dream. Halsey said it was one of the top ten, all time, great busts. The shades were drawn shut when they got there, and the sofa had been pulled open into a bed. The only lights in the room were from the two spotlights hung from the ceiling and directed at the bed. Danny had changed into a white silk robe.

The detectives, four of them, from Vice and Morals, smashed open the filing cabinets and found, along with several hundred photographs of young girls, huge boxes full of Quaaludes and amyl nitrite. Each photograph was attached to a sheet of paper giving the girl's statistics: age, height, weight, and a brief summary of her problems; home and school. It also stated whether or not she'd had any sexual experiences. Their estimated time and place of arrival in New York was given as well as who they were to contact. Almost all of them had one of Pretty Joey's names listed as the contact. The recruiter's name appeared at the bottom.

Wood shot three rolls of film and got a hell of a story. Danny was charged with promoting prostitution, disseminating material to minors, and when they found Winter, and she identified him, he'd be charged with forcible rape, a class-B felony that could send him away for twenty-five years. But Danny was calm. He sat at his desk watching as the men ransacked his offices; detached and only mildly interested, as if it were a television movie. Halsey said he was stoned out of his head on Quaaludes.

The sweater was Winter's, Wood was certain it was. But Danny just looked at them with soft, mellow eyes, refusing to answer a single question without his lawyer. They put the sweater in a plastic bag to send to the lab. Everything else was hauled out in cartons and loaded onto a truck parked outside, while Danny changed back into his business suit, smoothed down his hairpiece, and went agreeably along to the precinct to be booked.

For the next three days Wood walked all over the neighborhood around Eighth Avenue in the Forties and Fifties looking for Winter. Often Shawna went with him, as often as she could, chasing after every small-headed, black-haired child they saw, hoping when they caught up with her and saw her face, it would be Winter's. They stopped in every coffee shop they passed and asked the waitresses to look at the drawing the police artist made. They'd all seen it before; the cops had already canvassed the area more than once, and by now the waitresses and countermen were beginning to feel hassled.

Wood and Shawna stopped kids on the street to ask them if they recognized the girl in the drawing. Most of the time the kids reacted hostilely: some of the time they just laughed and walked by.

Big Alice swore Winter hadn't come looking for her, no matter what message she left with Freddie's mother. Wood felt she was telling the truth. Her relationship with the police was too important to her to mess around with anything that hot. She'd heard that Pretty Joey was out of the hospital and wasn't bragging anymore about what he could do to a bitch who gave him trouble. He was keeping a very low profile. The assault charge was upgraded and now included an additional one of promoting prostitution.

And the lab found nothing on the sweater to prove it was Winter's. But the worst shock of all came when Danahy and Halsey got Winter's parents' name from the principal (a fairly good candidate for a creep himself) and went to see them. They didn't want to let them in the house. As far as they were concerned, "the little nigger whore was already in hell getting the punishment she deserved." Danahy had to remind Halsey that they were only supposed to solve homicides, not commit them.

Shawna spent those nights with Wood, in his apartment. Automatically, without discussing it, she went with him and they crawled into each other's arms, hiding, for those hours, from what they'd come to think of as the dark side of the moon.

On the third morning, a Saturday, while Shawna was still asleep, Michael called. Wood filled him in on the arrests.

"But what about the investigation?" Michael wanted to know.

"I don't know what more there is to investigate, Michael. There was no witness, no one saw it happen."

"What about those other people—guys taking pictures?"

"The police haven't turned them up yet. But even if they did, all they'd be able to do is place Pretty Joey in the living room with your sister at the time it happened. That we already know. Everyone else was in the bedroom, with Winter, where they couldn't possibly see anything."

"Has she been found?"

"No."

"So you mean they're just going to chalk it up as an unsolved homicide?"

"No, they're going to chalk it up as what it is. A CUPPI. It never was a homicide."

"God. That pimp and the other guy must be laughing their heads off." Michael's voice was strained; it cracked as he spoke. "How can I help? I feel guilty and shitty—and I don't know what to do."

"Hey, two little kids, for whatever their reasons—all of their reasons, decided to split. If you want to include yourself as one of the reasons, you can. I don't know quite who that helps, but the point is, one of them's dead; the other one still has a chance. And she's the only one who can nail Danny for forcible rape. You know your law, that's the heaviest charge they've got him on, but only if there's a complainant. So if you want to do something, go out and find her."

The phone call left him feeling even more depressed. He put on some coffee, then went into the bedroom to look at Shawna. She was curled around his pillow, holding it to her breast as she might a baby. He tried to picture her with one; he could, easily. He wondered if she'd ever wanted to have one. The war she was waging when he met her seemed to have deescalated. That was not to say, however, that she stopped believing there was a war to be fought. It might simply be that she'd decided to take a furlough and could, at any moment, head back to camp and take up arms again.

He went to the bed and eased himself down beside her, sliding the pillow out from her embrace, offering himself instead. Her arms closed around him and she nestled close, murmuring something he couldn't understand.

"Hmm?" he whispered.

"Guess what?" she said dreamily, her eyes still closed.

"What, love?"

"I don't want to be away from you now." She opened her eyes and looked at him, and slowly raised herself up on one elbow to study him closely, as though to make certain she really meant it. "I don't want to be away from you," she repeated, putting her head back on the pillow.

"Nor I you," he said quietly, looking into her eyes. He kissed her gently.

"I'm not sure I'm going to like it here though," she said.

"We can live anywhere you want."

"I don't mean here, geographically. I love your funny apartment. I mean here, in love. It's so—vulnerable."

He nodded. "Yeah, it's pretty vulnerable here, in love."

"We'll have to be awfully kind to each other, won't we, because it can really hurt." She looked at him. "Aren't you scared?"

He shook his head. "Big boys don't cry." Then he took her in his arms, pressing his body to her, and kissed her.

"What's that noise?" she asked, listening.

"Shit. The coffee." He jumped up. "One thing you're going to have to learn is—don't distract me when I'm in the kitchen."

She followed him in, wearing his robe. "Wood, what about Donnie?"

He cleaned up the boiled-over mess and started over, making a fresh pot of coffee. Shawna cut the grapefruit in half and began sectioning it. "We should find out how she feels about us," she said. "You've been pretty much her private property since the divorce, haven't you?"

"It's time she and I started letting each other grow up," he said. "Hey, you look pretty cute in my robe, let's forget the coffee. Why am I all dressed? It's Saturday, why don't we take the day off?" He put his arm around her and walked her back to the bedroom. He was almost undressed, ready to get back into bed, when the downstairs buzzer rang.

"Christ!" He stood a moment. "Maybe they'll go away." The buzzer rang several times, insistently.

"They're not going away," she said.

He went to the intercom. "Who is it?"

The voice was muffled. He hit the speaker with his fist. "Who?"

"Detective Connelly, Mr. Wood. Lieutenant wants to see you."

"I don't believe it," he muttered, hesitating. Then he called, "Okay, be down in a minute." He was furious. "Goddamn it, who does he think he is. I don't work for him—what the hell right does he have," he cursed, climbing into his pants.

Shawna jumped up and started to dress. "I'm going with you. Maybe it's about Winter. You know, I found this really good place—in Connecticut—for kids. I know the people who run it." She was dressed, combing her hair. "They said they might be able to take her."

Wood was ready. "Let me go down first and see if Connelly knows what it's about. I'll be right back."

Connelly was standing next to the car with a strange grin on his face.

"What's going on?" Wood asked, and stopped when he saw Donnie sitting in the back of the car.

"Hi, Dad."

He was stunned. "What're you doing back there?"

"I told her she could ride in front," Connelly said.

"Shut up, Connelly. Donnie, what is this?"

"I don't know. The lieutenant called and said he needed to see me. Mom didn't want me to go, so Uncle Jack got on the phone and she hung up on him. Then the lieutenant called back and talked to Mom and finally she said okay. Maybe it's another stakeout. I brought my makeup, in case."

Wood looked at Connelly, who was still smiling. Suddenly Wood got it. "Wait here one second, I just have to get something." He ran back up. "Shawna, let's go—" He took his camera from the shelf and checked it for film.

"Hi," Donnie said when she saw Shawna. Then she frowned

slightly, screwing her face up. "I didn't know you lived around here. I thought you lived uptown."

"I do," Shawna answered as she climbed into the back next to Donnie, "but I spent the night down here. Wood, why don't you ride up front?"

A curious smile began to break on Donnie's face. She looked at Shawna appreciatively; in a new way.

"That's a nice dress," Shawna said to her.

"You don't think the sleeves are a little funny?" Donnie asked as she fiddled with the overly large cuffs.

"Look," Shawna said, "why don't we roll them up?" She reached over and showed her. "Like this."

Donnie rolled up the other sleeve to match the one Shawna turned up and looked at them, pleased. "That's neat," she said. "Thanks."

"Why're we going to Gallagher's office?" Shawna asked.

"I think the Lieutenant has some questions to ask me—about the other day," Donnie answered, sitting up straight in her seat. "You probably heard about it."

Wood turned around and looked at the two of them.

"Not all," Shawna said.

"Well, see," Donnie began, and described in detail the stakeout, complete with sound effects and dialogue, not finishing the story until the car pulled up to the entrance of the Seventeenth Precinct.


Lieutenant Gallagher put on his jacket when he saw them coming down the hall. He greeted Shawna with an un-Gallagher-like smile that was almost boyish. Then he looked at Donnie. "How do you do?"

"Fine, thank you, sir. Are you going to ask me questions?"

"Why, do you want to call your lawyer?"

She laughed and turned to her father. "Could you get him to say that thing to me?" she whispered loudly.

Gallagher heard her. "You mean—you have the right to remain silent and refuse to answer questions—"

"Anything you say may be used against you—" She stopped. "What comes next?"

"If you know the rest, you're watching too much television," Gallagher said. "Danahy! Halsey!"

They came in, hugging Donnie when they saw her, and shook hands with Shawna. Then they took their places.

Gallagher took Donnie by the shoulders and put her in front of the men. Wood walked around behind the lieutenant and got his camera ready, as Gallagher handed her a package wrapped in blue with a bright red ribbon tied on it.

She looked at it. "For me?" Then she looked over at her father, puzzled. She opened it as they watched. It had been framed in red. The fancy black lettering stood out. She stared at it. "What's this mean?"

Wood began shooting away as Gallagher, in his most official tones, said, "This is a Certificate of Commendation, awarded to Donna Wood in recognition of her valuable assistance rendered to the members of the Police Department and to the City of New York."

Donnie smiled, a huge, beaming smile. "It's signed by"—she read the name—"'Thomas Brennan, Police Commissioner.'" She looked up at Gallagher. "Thank you!" she said. "*Thanks,*" and was just about to reach up to kiss him, when he took her hand in a handshake, for the camera.

Then he leaned down and kissed her on the cheek, and said, "We usually call these 'atta-boys.' I guess we call this one an 'atta-girl!'"

Suddenly they were crowded around her shaking her hand. She blushed happily as she thanked them, saying, "Oh, boy," and "Wow!" and finally, the inevitable, "This is really far out!"

They went to Red's for lunch; Wood, Shawna, Donnie, Danahy, and Halsey, where Red had a table set, with flowers carefully arranged. A few minutes after they sat down, Mark Cohen came in, then Vinnie Jenkins. Red joined them, telling old cop stories that held Donnie fascinated, and she begged him to tell her more, loving the sound of his gravelly voice.

"Is this a cop hangout?" she asked Red, noticing that several other uniformed policemen had come in while they were eating. "Because I want to have my birthday party here, okay, Red?"

"I'll bake the cake myself."

"And I'll tell everyone about how I was in a shoot-out with a pimp."

When Wood and Shawna were alone with Donnie, after the men all left, Wood asked Donnie straight out how she'd feel about Shawna moving into his apartment.

Donnie looked at both of them. "You mean live together?"
Wood nodded and smiled.

Donnie's face broke into a grin. "Gee, Dad, I don't think that's
the sort of thing they do back in Madison, Wisconsin."

Wood laughed. "You don't know how long Donnie's waited to
toss that one back at me," he said to Shawna.

"How would you feel about it, Donnie?" Shawna asked.

"I think it would be neat." She screwed up her face then,
thinking. "I think it's neat that you asked me too," she added.


One week later Wood went to an address on Park Avenue. He
went there on a tip he'd gotten from Big Alice and then checked
out with June. The elevator stopped on the ninth floor. It was a
small, elegant old building, and there was no other apartment on
that floor. He rang. A receptionist answered the door; an attractive woman in her early thirties, dressed for an office, even to
the glasses, which she pushed back on her head to see at a distance.

"I have an appointment," he said through the three-inch opening. "My name's Collins, Andrew Collins."

She nodded and unchained the door. The foyer was carpeted
in deep burgundy-red. In the center was an antique desk, highly
polished and decorated with brass accessories, and over in the
corner was a tall, healthy-looking Ficus tree with a red ribbon
tied around it. A row of telephones, three of them, all with buttons, sat on a long, low table, out of sight. There were no chairs
other than the one behind the desk. "I'm sorry," she said. "We
haven't gotten all our furniture yet."

He glanced up at the chandelier. It was a simple, brass fixture
with tiny pink silk shades that added to the rosy glow of the
room.

"Mr. Harris, who recommended me, suggested a young
mulatto—"

"Yes. He told me. Follow me, please—what would you like to
drink?"

"Nothing—right now. Thanks."

He followed her down a hall, carpeted in the same color, and
stopped at the first door. She turned to him. "That will be a hundred dollars. One hour, drinks are on the house, ring when you
want one." He handed her the money, which she took and said,

"Wait here." Then she went into what looked like a more conventional office, and put the money away.

She took him to a door at the end of the hall, knocked twice, and left him.

He opened the door. The whole room was done in pink, except the ceiling, which was mirrored. She was sitting on the edge of the bed. Her back was to him and she was naked to the waist, head bent over, doing something. A chest of drawers, painted pink with gilt handles, was the only furniture in the room beside the bed. On it were glasses and an ice bucket.

"Hello, Winter."

She swung around and stared at him, and for a moment he thought she might cry. He started to go to her. Instantly she turned her back to him again and said, "Wait a minute, I'm rolling a joint."

He froze. "Oh, God, Winter, stop that and talk to me."

She cut him off. "My name's not Winter, it's Summer. And my orders are to make you undress, so I know you're not a cop."

"Come on now, get dressed. I'm taking you out of here. Do you have any idea how crazy we've been looking for you? Who made you do this—how did they force you? Winter, Danny can be sent to jail for twenty-five years for what he did to you, don't you know that?"

She stood up and faced him. She was wearing nothing but white silk bikini panties trimmed with lace and a fine, gold chain around her neck. "What Danny did to me?" She looked at him with her chin raised, her hands on her hips, holding an unlit joint. "You mean like give me beautiful clothes and money to ride around in taxicabs wherever I want to go? And show me how to wear my hair—look." She ran to the dresser and took out some hairpins and, putting them in her mouth, she rolled her hair into a neat bun in back, securing it with the pins. Then she turned to him and struck a pose. "Well, aren't you going to tell me I'm pretty?"

Wood's eyes were hot with tears. "Winter! This isn't what you want. You can still be a model, like you and Freddie planned."

"And I will in a few years. But first I have to have clothes! Nobody's going to hire me if I look like some orphan." Her eyes went blank. "I'm doing exactly what Freddie wanted—for both of us—to be rich and have men want us. And to be able to tell our shitty parents to go fuck themselves!"

She lit up the joint and went to the bed, stretching herself out fully, catlike, in a pose that had been recently mastered and that was intended to be sexy.

Wood felt his heart splinter into a million ragged pieces as he watched the absurd caricature she was showing him. He turned his head.

She took a deep drag and looked at him a long time. Her eyes wavered for just a second; then, flaming with renewed defiance, she said to him in a voice icy and dead, "You have thirty-five minutes left, mister. So why don't you unzip your pants and let's see what you've got there."

**POLICE DEPARTMENT**
NEW YORK, N.Y. 10038

FROM:   COMMANDING OFFICER, THIRD HOMICIDE ZONE

TO:     CHIEF MEDICAL EXAMINER'S OFFICE, NEW YORK COUNTY

SUBJECT: INVESTIGATION INTO THE DEATH OF FREDERICA CHARLES, FEMALE, WHITE, TWELVE YEARS. M.E. #6195, DOCTOR. IRWIN AUSLANDER.

    1.      On May 13, 1977, at 2120 hours this command was notified that an unknown female white was found lying on the sidewalk in front of the Rockmoor Hotel, 220 W. 48th Street. Subject was pronounced dead at the scene by Attendant Rodriguez of St. Clares Hospital. A complaint was filed at the Mid-Town North Precinct by Police Officer Vincent Mulshine, shield #5525 of the Mid-Town North Precinct.

    2.      On May 14, 1977, Dr. Irwin Auslander of the Chief Medical Examiner's Office performed a post mortem examination and listed the cause of death as: Multiple fractures and internal injuries including depressed fracture of skull, legs, and arms. Contusions of brain. Intermeningeal hemorrhage. Lacerations of lung, liver, aorta, heart, and spleen. Fall from height: Circumstances undetermined pending police investigation.

    3.      On May 16, 1977, this case was assigned to Detective Augustus Halsey, shield #222 of the Third Homicide Zone, under Manhattan Detective Area Log #3306, CUPPI #112. This investigation disclosed that the subject apparently exited from a fully opened window of room #1406 of the Rockmoor Hotel, which would be in the direct line of the fall. The subject, when falling, struck the side of the hotel marquee, breaking the neon lights, then fell through the canvas awning which fronted the hotel cocktail lounge. The body landed approximately six feet from the building line.

4.      Interviews of hotel occupants disclosed that at no
time during the evening of May 13th did they hear any commotion
or disturbance of any kind coming from the room on the fourteenth
floor.

5.      Examination of the windowsill which had an accumulation
of dirt and soot was undisturbed, indicating the absence of
a struggle. Examination of the room also indicated that there
had not been a disturbance.

6.      Interview of the night clerk, Joseph Pergola, disclosed
that at about 2130 hours on the night of the occurrence he heard
a noise and looked outside and saw some police officers. He went
out and observed a body of a female lying on the sidewalk. He
remained there for about three minutes, then went back inside to
his desk. When questioned as to why he didn't immediately attempt
to ascertain the identity of the female, he stated that he did
not want to get involved.

7.      Further investigation disclosed that room #1406
which the deceased had exited from was rented to a Mr. John
Blue. No identification papers or cards confirmed this, but
Joseph Pergola, the night clerk, stated Mr. Blue had been a
guest in the hotel previously. He also stated that he had not
observed any female accompanying Mr. Blue that night and that
Mr. Blue had left the premises at least half an hour before the
incident occurred.

8.      Investigation relative to the background of Frederica
Charles disclosed that she had been exhibiting signs of depression
due to a sudden decline in her school work and subsequent truancy.
Personal interviews with the subject's parents, Mr. and Mrs.
Arthur Charles, disclosed that Frederica had become involved with
a friend or friends outside her normal circle of acquaintances,
and stated they believed that to be the cause of change in her
behavior. Miss Harriet Andrews, her sixth-grade teacher, observed
the change in the deceased as "so sudden it seemed to happen
overnight."

Mr. Archibald Wallace, the principal of the school, who also holds a degree in Psychology, stated that Frederica was a very depressed, impulsive girl who would act out her depressions. It was his opinion that Frederica Charles could have been capable of taking her own life while in a state of depression.

9.      Due to the fact that this investigation has not produced any evidence to the contrary, and that nothing of a criminal nature that could be substantiated was found to indicate that the deceased was the victim of a crime, the assigned has concluded that the subject either fell or jumped to her death.

10.      Case carried under UF61# 44791 Mid-Town North Precinct #6195, Third Homicide Zone CUPPI #112, Detective Augustus Halsey, shield #222 assigned.

                              Raymond J. Gallagher.
                              Lieutenant


                         1st ENDORSEMENT
From C.O.M.S.H. to C.O.M.D.A. Contents reviewed by the undersigned re: death of one Frederica Charles. Recommend approval as to determination that the deceased either jumped or fell.

                              Bernard M. Dougherty
                              Deputy Inspector